THE DEFECTION OF
A.J. LEWINTER

THE DEFECTION OF A.J. LEWINTER

A NOVEL OF DUPLICITY

ROBERT LITTELL

THE OVERLOOK PRESS
WOODSTOCK & NEW YORK

This edition first published in the United Slates in 2002 by
The Overlook Press, Peter Mayer Publishers, Inc.
Woodstock & New York

WOODSTOCK:
One Overlook Drive
Woodstock, NY 12498
www.overlookpress.com
[for individual orders, bulk and special sales, contact our Woodstock office]

NEW YORK:
141 Wooster Street
New York, NY 10012

∞ The paper used in this book meets the requirements for paper
permanence as described in the ANSI Z39.48-1992 standard.

Cataloging-in-Publication Data is available from the Library of Congress.

Littell, Robert.
The defection of A.J. Lewinter /
Robert Littell.
p. cm.
to come

Manufactured in the United States of America
ISBN 1-58567-347-1
10 9 8 7 6 5 4 3 2 1

For my mother and father

CONTENTS

PART I
THE OPENING

1

THERE WAS a curtain of silence between the end of the play and the first ripple of applause. Distracted by the silence, Chapin let his attention drift from the balding American in the aisle seat.

It was his first lapse of the day.

Chapin was a fat man and he envied grace and poise the way a cripple admires athletic agility. He sat on the hard wooden chair breathing heavily, a massive form in the midst of the diminutive Japanese, and watched with almost sensual pleasure as the masked actors of the Kanze Noh Company glided soundlessly across the *hashigakari* bridge to the wings. Without understanding all its subtleties, Chapin was drawn to the Noh drama. He had never admitted that to anyone, for he recognized it as a strange obsession—especially for someone in his line of work. He wondered vaguely what had brought the American to the theater.

The American!

When Chapin glanced back at the aisle seat it was empty and his man was sprinting up the carpet toward the exit. Still caught up in the mood of the Noh, Chapin was reluctant to break the cobweb threads of imagination that bound him to the stage. Wearily, he pulled his bulky body over the legs of four Japanese and headed up the now jammed aisle toward the lobby. For a man of his size and age, he moved rapidly. But by the time he reached the front steps of the theater, the American had disappeared into the river of people flowing through the streets of downtown Tokyo.

Chapin stood on the steps and threaded his fingers through his thinning hair. It was his first "fadeout" in years and his professional pride was bruised. Control would be furious. As he turned to search for a telephone, something caught his eye: the familiar profile of a man, framed in a window of a taxi pulling away from the curb.

Chapin squeezed into another taxi and told the driver: *"Ano kuruma o otékure."* In Japanese, Chapin thought, the phrase didn't sound quite as ridiculous as it did in English.

The two taxis, 100 yards apart, swung past Toronomon and the black wrought-iron gates of the American Embassy and struggled up a steep hill, caught in a jagged mob of cars and buses and trucks noisily converging on Roppongi. The early evening breeze blew through the open window against Chapin's face, and with it came the reddish dust from a torn-up stretch of road where a new subway line was being built. Chapin saw that his driver was enjoying the chase; with his forehead almost touching the steering wheel, he cut in front of a dump truck and put the car onto the rough bedding of the trolley tracks near the crest of the hill. Using only his left, white-gloved hand, he spun the wheel full left and broke into the small intersection of Roppongi Crossing. By now he was directly behind the other taxi. Chapin leaned forward and tapped the driver on the shoulder. *"Kimi Wa, beteran no untenshu da né*—That's nice driving."

At the far end of the crossing workmen wearing thick ocher-colored waistbands and bandannas on their foreheads strained against a stalled dump truck. Drivers leaned on their horns as the traffic piled up. In the taxi ahead of Chapin, the impatient passenger stepped out, paid the driver, and edged between the two cabs toward the curb. As his face came into full view, Chapin realized that he had been following an American—but the wrong one.

Chapin paid his driver and hurried to the telephone booth in front of the Kinokuniya Supermarket. Before dialing, he unwrapped a piece of dietary chewing gum, popped it into his mouth, and rolled the tin foil into a ball, which he toyed with throughout the conversation.

The number rang twice. A man's voice said in Japanese: "Four-nine-nine-six-five-two-nine."

Chapin read off his own number in English and hung up. Fifteen seconds later the phone rang.

"Hey, George, this is me," Chapin said, wheezing nervously.

"Where the hell've you and Honeybucket been?" George said.

"In Marunouchi," Chapin answered. He tried to make the rest sound like an afterthought. "Everything's fine. Our friend just treated me to five and a half hours of Noh. Now we're in Roppongi. Honeybucket's across the street in an antique shop. I'll stick with him through dinner and tuck him in at the hotel."

2

LEWINTER HAD LIVED through the moment a hundred times in his imagination, but it had never occurred to him that the guard wouldn't speak English. He looked across the glass-topped table at the obstinate, Slavic face and had to fight back the frustration and fear welling up inside him.

"Listen," Lewinter said again, this time more patiently, more respectfully, "I've got to speak to the *ambassador.*" And he repeated the word three times, as if the mere repetition would make the guard understand. "I'm an American-ski," he added.

The two Japanese cleaning ladies scrubbing the marble floor of the embassy lobby looked up, curious. The guard, new to his job and still unsure of himself, hesitated. Finally, with a shrug, he picked up the telephone and summoned the duty officer.

Watching him dial, Lewinter felt some of the tension drain away. At last he was getting somewhere. For the first time, he took in the surroundings: the Japanese women, by now hard at work; the uniformed guard concentrating on a Russian newspaper; the small portrait of Lenin in a too elaborate gilt frame; the cracks in the marble floor; the chandelier with its dusty black electric wire coiling up to the flaking ceiling. It was not what he had expected. Not at all.

Tiptoeing over the still-wet marble, the duty officer, a small, brooding Armenian with thick eyebrows, came over and planted himself directly in front of Lewinter.

"Yes," the Armenian said, smiling and pointing at his watch, "since fifteen minutes, we are completed for the day."

"I must speak to your ambassador," Lewinter said, wondering how much English the Armenian understood. "I want to go to the Soviet Union."

"It is misfortunate," the Armenian said, "but the visa department completes at five. Re-try tomorrow after nine."

"You don't understand me," Lewinter said. "I'm an American. I want to go to the Soviet Union permanently—to live there."

"Permanently?" the Armenian repeated, and searched for the meaning of the word. He found it, and understood it. He thought of a friend of his who once passed up an opportunity to buy some documents in Istanbul—and wound up franking stamps in Tbilisi. With a jerk of his head, the Armenian motioned to the American to follow him down the hall.

Left alone in a large, mildewy room jammed with overstuffed furniture, Lewinter settled into an easy chair with a broken spring and waited. In the last half-hour he had taken the most crucial step of his life, and yet the whole thing seemed ludicrous. He had planned the defection for months with his usual relish for detail—the trip to Japan, the pills, the shampoo, the X rays, the last-minute postcard to Maureen, even the book to read on the plane to Moscow. But somehow he had ended up on the set of a Hitchcock film—in a shabby embassy, in an antique room, in the midst of people who did not speak his language. He could almost see himself sitting there looking faintly uncomfortable, faintly ridiculous, staring at the high ceiling, crossing and uncrossing his legs, and wondering if he was being watched by someone other than himself.

Lewinter emerged from his thoughts and realized that he had been listening to the sound of men's voices. The door opened. The man who entered looked as if he had strolled off an American college campus. He had everything except the pipe between his teeth; thin and stoop-shouldered, he wore a bow tie, a beige button-down shirt, an open Harris tweed sports jacket with suede elbow patches, rumpled slacks, and a pair of loafers. His kinky hair was long and bunched at the sides and back; that and his high forehead made him look like an intellectual. His eyes were khaki-colored and there was something about them that projected the man's ironic cast of mind.

He smiled warmly and pulled up a chair next to Lewinter. "What high school did you go to?" he said in perfect English.

"What do you mean what high school did I go to?" Lewinter said, edging back his chair. He had a reflex suspicion of people who tried to strike up instant friendships. "First you keep me waiting half an hour, then you walk in with a question like that. Do you have the vaguest idea why I'm here?"

"Look, calm down," the Russian said. "It's only been twenty minutes. They had to get me back to the embassy. Anyhow, my question about the high school has a point. You can tell a lot about an American from the high school he went to. Take me, for instance. I went to Horace Mann. All the guys there were upper middle-class bourgeoisie—not exactly the kind of person you expect to see in a Soviet embassy after closing hours asking for political asylum. You see," he said, tapping his forehead and laughing, "I *do* know why you're here—and I'm always thinking. Watch out!"

Lewinter couldn't help but warm to the Russian. "What were you doing at Horace Mann?" he asked.

"My father, good Communist that he was, worked his way up the Soviet Foreign Service to Riverdale," he said. "He was attached to the UN Secretariat for six years. What high school *did* you go to?"

"Bronx High School of Science," Lewinter said, surprised to find that he wanted to answer the question.

"Aha!" the Russian said, slapping Lewinter's knee. He pointed a finger at him in mock accusation. "Petit bourgeois, intellectual, I.Q. of at least one thirty-five, not very good at sports, didn't have sexual intercourse until you were in college—if then. I'd say you were Jewish, except you don't look Jewish. How did I do?"

"Fine except for the sexual intercourse part," Lewinter lied. He turned serious: "We could argue the merits of Bronx Science over Horace Mann all night—*but I haven't got all night*. I've figured out my chances very carefully. Either I get out of Japan on your eight o'clock plane or I'm probably not going to get out at all." He pulled out his pocket watch and clicked it open. "I've got two and a quarter hours left. I've got to speak to your ambassador."

"I suspect that my ambassador is the last person you want to see," the Russian said. A smile spread across his face. "He's great at cutting ribbons, but he passes on his serious problems to me. If you're a serious problem"—and here he put the palms of his hands flat against his chest—"I'm your man."

Lewinter believed him.

The Russian took a small green notebook from his breast pocket and uncapped a felt-tipped pen. "Now that I've broken down your defenses with my spontaneous charm, it's time, for the real Yefgeny Mikhailovich Pogodin—that's my name—it's time for me to reveal myself. Sitting before you is a man who is one-quarter Marxist, one-quarter humanist, and one-half bureaucrat." His pen hovered over the notebook. "Your name?"

Lewinter felt as if he was in the hands of a painless dentist. "A. J. Lewinter. Initial A, initial J, capital L, small W."

"What does the A stand for?" Pogodin asked.

"Augustus. The J's for Jerome. But I only use the initials."

"Well, Mr. initial A initial J Lewinter, age?"

"Thirty-nine."

"Address?"

"Cambridge, Massachusetts."

Pogodin looked up. "What do you do in Cambridge?"

"I'm an associate professor at M.I.T. and a specialist in ceramic engineering. For the last four years I've been working on ceramic nose cones for the MIRV Program."

The Russian jotted down Lewinter's answer in his notebook, then lingered over the page, rereading what he had written. Without looking up he asked: "What brought you to Japan, Mr. Lewinter?"

"The ecological symposium at Waseda University. I delivered a paper there yesterday. When I'm not working on nose cones, I'm a bug on ecology. A couple of years ago I developed a scheme for a national solid-waste-disposal system. Its potentials are fantastic. It involves collecting solid waste in regional centers for processing and recycling. Would you believe, with our problems in America, I couldn't get a rise out of Washington—even though I proved on paper that the entire system would amortize itself in thirty-five years." Lewinter paused. "Am I going too fast for you?"

But Pogodin had stopped writing.

"Why do you want to go to the Soviet Union?"

"How can I even begin to answer that question?" Lewinter said. "I could tell you about the deterioration of the American dream—the pollution, the crime, the political corruption, the isolation of intellectuals, the drugs, the repression of dissent. But there's another reason. I'm part of that famous military-industrial complex. I've lived inside it. I know what I'm talking about. My country is in the process of constructing a first-strike nuclear arsenal. And as sure as we're sitting here some general in Washington is going to suggest we use it. I want to give you parity so that they won't be tempted. I want to give you MIRV."

It suddenly occurred to Pogodin that he was dealing with an insane man. In Pogodin's world, intelligence operations were long, tedious affairs in which hundreds of people labored over scraps of information, constructing a single piece of a jigsaw puzzle that might—perhaps—fit into some larger picture. Strangers didn't walk in off the street and offer you the pot of gold at the end of the rainbow. And yet . . .

"Let me tell you what's going through my mind," Pogodin said. Having interrogated hundreds of people, he had long ago discovered that candor was a powerful weapon—more so because it was the last thing in the world people in Lewinter's position expected. "If you have what you say you have, it would be an important break for us. And you would naturally find us very grateful. But people don't walk in off the street with this grade of information. So I am obliged to consider the other pos-sibilities. You may honestly believe that you have this informa-tion; but you may believe it because other people want you to believe it. Knowingly or unknowingly, you could be a plant, someone sent to make us swallow false information. Or you could be a class-A nut. There are other permutations, but they're too complex to go into. So I put it to you: If you were in my shoes, what would you do?"

"If I were in your shoes," Lewinter said, playing the game, "I wouldn't pass up the possibility that I'm at least as important as I say I am—and maybe more so."

"Yes, you could," Pogodin said. "You don't know the rules of this game."

"What are they?"

"At this point in our relationship, you have to provide us with a token of your sincerity," Pogodin said. "Defection"—the Russian stressed the word—"is a delicate matter. You have to give us something to chew on."

The invitation dangled before Lewinter. He considered his laminated I.D. card, his M.I.T. faculty card, his passport. But he knew that none of these would get him on the eight o'clock plane to Moscow.

"Look," he said, "I could give you the formula for the trajectory of one of the decoys in a MIRV. You can cable it to Moscow. Surely there must be someone there who can vouch for its value."

Without a flicker of expression, Pogodin offered the green notebook to Lewinter.

"Do you need a pen?" he asked politely.

"No, thank you, I have my own," Lewinter said, and he began to write in a precise hand.

3

"**N**OW, WAIT, here comes the important part," Diamond said, and the tall, carved wooden doors of the Soviet Embassy opened. "That's their K.G.B. station chief, Mickey Pogodin, in the back. The guy on the right is one of his Armenians. Lewinter's the dumpy guy on the left. As soon as they pass the gate, the camera will zoom in on him. Now, right there, Mr. Lawson, would you freeze it right there."

The face of A. J. Lewinter, grainy and slightly over-exposed, filled the small screen at the end of the room. It was a curiously ambiguous portrait: his eyes had been caught, narrowed, darting apprehensively to the side; but his mouth, half open, relaxed in a confident smile.

"O.K., Mr. Lawson, could I ask you to let it run to the end?" Diamond said.

The camera zoomed out, lost its focus, then regained it. A passing bus blocked the scene for a moment. Lewinter was about to get into the back seat of a waiting limousine when he turned abruptly to Pogodin and began gesturing toward the embassy.

"Looks like the bastard's having second thoughts," someone said.

Diamond didn't bother to answer, and the flat figures on the screen went through their silent motions. Pogodin said something to the Armenian, who sprinted back into the embassy and returned with a small plastic flight bag. The three men got into the back of the car and it drove off camera. The screen went white as the end of the film flapped on the reel. The lights came on and the four men around the table squinted self-consciously.

"Do we have any idea what was in the bag?" Steve Ferri asked.

"That's the million-dollar question," Diamond said.

"How come Tokyo Control . . ."

Diamond cut off Ferri with a wave of his hand. "Mr. Lawson, I wonder if I could trouble you to rewind that later. And thank you very much."

The door clicked closed behind the projectionist.

Sitting at the head of the table, his back to the vertical Venetian blinds, Diamond took stock of the situation. The men around him should have been familiar faces; he had, after all, worked alongside them for years. But this was the first time he had *presided* over them. And the new perspective (Diamond was occupying the deputy assistant secretary's seat) made all the difference. That much was clear from a glance at Bob Billings and Steve Ferri—both of whom confronted Diamond with faces he couldn't quite place. They were too hard, too distant, too elaborately casual. The only one who seemed completely familiar was Gordon Rogers, a pink-cheeked smile—his flag of insecurity—playing across his soft features. Diamond could handle Rogers. But Billings and Ferri, Billings with his hard profile and Ferri with his hard eyes, yes, Billings and Ferri would be another matter.

There were no ground rules for the terrain Diamond was about to cross, and so he stepped off evasively. "Well, gentlemen," he said, "it's really hit the fan this time."

Steve Ferri walked over to the window and opened the blinds. Bars of sunlight slanted across the carpet. "Isn't that judgment premature?" he asked. Ferri had spent twelve years as an officer in the army, where he had acquired a flat, vaguely Southern accent. When he spoke, his thin lips and jaw hardly moved; he seemed to talk through clenched teeth, a physical trait that gave his words a sense of blunt authority. "If the chief were here, I suspect he'd want us to move cautiously on this one."

"Not everybody has your feel for the deputy assistant secretary, Steve," Diamond said. "The fact is that he's over in Bethesda with endocarditis and I'm here in the catbird seat." He avoided Ferri's eyes. "Look," he said, "there isn't a man in this room who isn't in trouble. We're in charge of security for the MIRV program and we've screwed up."

Diamond settled deeper into the unfamiliar chair and stretched his legs. He cut a casually elegant figure; a man in his mid forties, slouching gracefully, sleeves rolled above his elbows, a thick shock of brown hair falling across his forehead. He looked as if he could cope. But he wondered if he could. Everything seemed to be happening at once. First there had been that incredible scene ten days ago in his office with the deputy assistant secretary gasping for air on the carpet. And then, less than a week later, the job. And now the defection. On top of all this there was Sarah, the one problem he could have avoided—but chose not to.

And yet he hadn't felt this elated—there was no other word for it—since his days at the Agency. Somehow the problems nourished him, feeding his ego, energizing his ambition. The old equations that had constituted his life were suddenly obliterated, and the new ones seemed infinitely more inviting. If he handled the defection smoothly, Diamond had little doubt that the job of Deputy Assistant Secretary of Defense for Security Policy would be permanently his. The girl was another story, a love story, and he hadn't had a love story in his life since he'd gotten married.

"I still think you're exaggerating," Ferri said, and looked at Billings to see if he would back him up. But Billings remained silent; if he was going to tangle with Diamond, he, not Ferri, would pick the moment.

"Exaggerating?" Diamond said. He was careful to keep his voice, if not his words, polite. "Christ, from the very beginning this whole affair has been one big fuck-up." He flipped open a manila folder and began to rummage through a sheaf of onionskin papers. "Here's a report from the Investigative and Personnel Branch—that's your bailiwick, Steve. Three weeks before Lewinter applied for permission to attend a symposium in Japan, your people reported that Lewinter bought"— Diamond ran his finger across the page—" bought five hundred Chlor-Trimeton hay-fever pills and a dozen plastic bottles of Head and Shoulders dandruff shampoo. According to this report, we also knew that he had gone to his dentist—a Doctor Donald Fishkin in Boston—and retrieved his dental records. In some corner of this huge security network of ours an alarm bell should have gone off. But what happens? Lewinter applies for permission to go to Japan—and someone named Stefano Ferri, the director of the Investigative and Personnel Branch, signs the chit." And Diamond flattened the wrinkled paper on the table.

"What's so unusual about someone buying hay-fever pills in bulk?" Ferri said aggressively, but his voice was just off pitch. "And Head and Shoulders—really, come on, Leo. As for the dental records, we checked that out two days after it occurred. And it so happens that Lewinter had a fight with your Doctor Fishkin and was asking around for another dentist."

"Have you ever heard of anybody buying five hundred pills?" Diamond asked. "Not unless he doesn't expect to be able to get more. It's my hunch that if you opened Lewinter's flight bag, you'd find the pills, the shampoo, and Doctor Fishkin's X rays."

"I don't know, Leo, it seems to me you're reading too much into this," Gordon Rogers said. "In view of what happened, I grant you we should have done more than put a routine surveillance on him in Tokyo. But if we lock up everybody in the MIRV program who buys pills in bulk, well, we're going to have our hands full." Rogers, a slightly effeminate man with thick, soft lips, cleared his throat, satisfied that he had made what he thought was a good point.

"I hope that the secretary of defense can find it in his heart to be as charitable as you," Diamond said. "But don't count on it. When I left his office late last night, he was waiting for a phone call from the President. I want to tell you something, the air conditioner was on full blast—but the secretary of defense was sweating bullets. And if we had any sense, we'd be doing the same. Next to the Single Integrated Operations Plan and the National Strategic Target List, we're dealing with the most crucial element of national security that exists."

"I'm sweating, all right," Rogers said, and he plucked a soft white handkerchief with his initials on it from a pocket and began patting his brow. "When in heaven's name are we going to get a smaller conference room or a larger air conditioner? My Lord, you don't see the strategic planning people down the hall putting up with this sort of thing."

"What about the office space reorganization?" Ferri chimed in. "With the chief laid up, we're likely to get shafted when they start giving out the square footage. You've got to keep at them. It's the squeaky wheel that gets the oil. Maybe I ought to send you a copy of the memo I worked up for the chief. Jesus, I've got filing cabinets in the janitor's closet and three assistants falling over each other in a six-by-six cubbyhole that was meant to hold a water cooler."

Diamond felt as if he were straining against a rudder, trying to hold a sailboat on course in a stiff wind. "I'm as anxious about getting what's coming to us as the next man," he said, "but can't we put that on a back burner for the moment?" Without waiting for an answer, Diamond walked over to a cabinet near the door. "Listen to this," he said, and snapped on a tape recorder.

"Hey, George, this is me," said a voice that seemed to come from the end of a tunnel.

"Where the hell've you and Honeybucket been?"

"In Marunouchi," the voice answered. *"Everything's fine. Our friend just treated me to five and a half hours of Noh. Now we're in Roppongi. Honeybucket's across the street in an antique shop. I'll stick with him through dinner and tuck him in at the hotel."*

Diamond switched off the tape recorder.

"Jesus," Rogers said. "That god damn Chapin. What an idiot."

"It's not only Chapin," Diamond said. "It's Tokyo Control—they violated every rule in the book. Chapin loses Lewinter, then he wastes three and a half hours waiting for him to show up at the hotel before he reports the fadeout. It turns out Control had movies of Lewinter going in and out of the Soviet

Embassy, but they didn't develop the film until forty-eight hours after he left the country. According to your own regulations, Gordon, those films are supposed to be turned in and developed three times a day, at the end of each shift. If I'm wrong, stop me."

Rogers nodded lamely.

"Then there was the simple, elementary business of the code traffic," Diamond went on. "Forty minutes after Lewinter stepped through the doors of that embassy, there was an unusual burst of after-hours code traffic to Moscow. Obviously something was up. Where the hell was Control?"

"The Russians had after-hours code traffic on twelve nights last month," Rogers said. Diamond waited for him to say something else, but Rogers stopped there.

"O.K., forget Chapin, forget the films, forget the traffic," Diamond said. He picked up another report. "One hour and forty-five minutes after Lewinter entered the embassy—a full hour before the plane with Lewinter and Pogodin on board took off for Moscow—Control had its hands on a report from a local agent. She was a Japanese charwoman who worked in the Soviet Embassy. She told them that an American had come in after closing hours, that the duty officer had hustled him into a room, that there was a flurry of excited phone calls from the main switchboard. The charwoman only spoke Russian; she didn't understand English. She reported—now get this—she actually told Control she overheard snatches of an argument between Pogodin and Stanchev, their ambassador. The ambassador apparently lost the argument and stormed out, and right after that all the Japanese local hire were sent home early. This wasn't even a jigsaw puzzle anymore. This was like one of those kids' cutouts."

Rogers was reduced to silence. He sat with his head resting between his hands, staring down at the table.

Robert Billings, a thin, aristocratic bureaucrat who prided himself on his ability to split hairs, refused to be ruffled. "I must say, Leo, it seems to me you're going out of your way to put the pieces together so that the picture reflects badly on us. I read that report—all those reports went through my hands. The charwoman didn't say she saw an American; she said she saw a man whom she *thought* was an American. She didn't say she heard Pogodin and Stanchev arguing; she said she overheard an argument in a hail after which the ambassador hurried out. Not stormed out."

Billings spoke offhandedly, the casual defender of the faith, the cool champion of his colleagues against Leo Diamond. As director of the Security Plans and Programs branch of the department, he ranked immediately under Diamond; as the senior member in length of service, he was acknowledged by everyone to be unsurpassed in technical expertise. Brilliant, devoted, totally committed to the department, he probably would have long ago been appointed chief if it had not been for his professorial, prissy personality.

"I'll grant you that a leakproof security net might have caught him before he defected, but a really leakproof security net is out of character in this country," Billings went on. "But you've missed the point"—Billings said this very quietly, letting the words carry their own weight—"yes, I'm quite certain you've missed the point. The quintessential question right now is not how he was allowed to defect, but rather what he took with him—other than hay-fever pills and hair tonic, of course. In a word, how much can he help our friends on the other side and how much can he hurt us? And I submit the answer, based on the available evidence, is: not very much at all."

Leo Diamond doodled with a pencil, drawing various sized *S*'s on the yellow pad. "And what is the available evidence, as you see it, Bob?" he said, his eyes on the pad. Billings' "you've missed the point" hung in the air between them.

"Why the only evidence I have is the evidence we all have," Billings said, still nonchalant. "Who, after all, is A. J. Lewinter? His security record"—Billings tossed a rolled-up computer print-out onto the table as if he were placing it in evidence—"is fairly nondescript. Age thirty-nine. I.Q. one forty-five. Graduated with honors from an Eastern ceramic school that nobody ever heard of named Alfred University. A fairly proficient specialist in the field of ceramics. Married. Two children. Divorced. Came to work four years ago on the MIRV program designing ceramic nose cones. Salary seventeen five. At the time he was given a security check. No debts. Heterosexual. No known perversions. Slightly left of center politically, but who up there at M.I.T. isn't? At any rate, he wasn't an activist. About the only extraordinary thing in his file is his passion for ecology—hardly a cause for alarm. Seven months ago he took up with a research assistant who seemed like another version of his wife. She was checked out. No debts. No known perversions. Slightly to the left politically." Billings—the only man at the table other than Diamond who stood a chance of getting the top slot in the department—was very much in control of the conversation. "Mickey Pogodin may be in for a surprise when they start to debrief our Lewinter," he continued, supremely confident. "Why are we worried? A specialist in ceramic nose cones defects and we go off the deep end? The Soviets are every bit as good as we are, perhaps better, in the field of ceramic nose cones. They could probably teach Lewinter a thing or two. It's all so bland it's hard to see why our Soviet friends even took him."

Diamond finished blacking-in a particularly thick *S* and looked up, his lips pressed tightly together. Gordon Rogers wrote in a looseleaf notebook. Steve Ferri and Robert Billings stared at Diamond. The only sound in the room was the whirr of the air conditioner.

Diamond broke the silence. "I haven't missed the point, Bob—but you have." The challenge had been accepted. "The single most important piece of evidence is not that security record, which tells you next to nothing about Lewinter—about the real, living, breathing, flesh-and-blood Lewinter. The single most important piece of evidence—and the only one we should concern ourselves with at this point—is the fact that the Soviets took him. They allowed him to defect. They risked a diplomatic incident in Japan. They risked getting involved in the whole business of plants and misinformation. And they took him. That's where the truth begins—the fact that they took him. They're not stupid. Lewinter would have had to prove he was worth taking before they flew him off to Moscow."

Diamond started in on another *S* and gave it up. "What do you think was in that late-hour code traffic between the embassy and Moscow?" he said. "We've got every damn reason to be worried about our bland Mr. Lewinter. *Because they took him.*"

4

"I'M NOT A MATERIALIST," Sarah said. "I just like things."

"I gathered as much," Diamond said. He looked around the room. Practically every flat surface was cluttered with Sarah's "things"—sea shells, painted egg shells, rocks, ivory combs, French licorice tins, Japanese *kokeshi* dolls, paperweights, antique pocket watches, secondhand buttons. "I could never live in a place like this. Funny, I admire people who can, but for me it's too distracting. It's too . . . *bouillabaisse.*"

Sarah sat cross-legged on the bed, naked, angular, boyishly ripe—a fresh-cut flower on a strong stem. She studied Leo, propped up against a pile of brightly colored pillows, the toes of his right foot jutting from beneath the sheet. Sarah had had her share of love affairs, but she rarely brought the men home.

Those that she did, she put to a private test—measuring them by their reaction to her collections. She wanted Leo to like them because she liked Leo. But she was put off by his ambivalence. She leaned across the bed, her long brown hair brushing his chest, and plucked a small mahogany box from the night table.

"What do you think of this?" she asked. "I picked it up in the Paris flea market on my last junket."

"What is it?" Diamond said, instinctively noncommittal. He opened the lid. Inside, embedded in worn purple felt, were six bulb-shaped brass objects and a steel thermometer.

"I haven't the faintest idea," Sarah said, laughing at the private joke. "Can't you like something without knowing what it is?"

"I liked *you*." Diamond was playing games again—and that annoyed him. He had thought that with Sarah he could let down his guard. He had never entirely trusted anyone in his adult life and it was painful to begin now. Yet he wanted to try. He picked up one of the brass bulbs and turned it in his fingers, straining to make out the etched inscription. "It's really quite nice. Really. But what is it? When you bought it, you must have known what you were buying."

"But that's just the point, Leo," she said. "This is part of my I-don't-know collection. I've got lots more." And she slid off the bed, rummaged around a low shelf and began to pile boxes and odd-shaped objects on his lap. "For this particular collection, I only buy things when the man who sells them doesn't know what they are."

"There's a guy in the department who could trace these things for you," Diamond said. "He'd not only tell you what they are, but who made them and when."

"Thank you, but no thank you," Sarah said. "That would spoil everything. If I knew what they were, I wouldn't love them—or keep them."

Diamond basked in the casual intimacy of the moment. It had always been a special time for him, that period after the love making was over. The few love affairs in his life, including the one with his wife, had soured not when the sex act became commonplace, but when the sense of intimacy that should have followed was missing.

Sarah sat down on the bed facing him. She brushed the hair back from her eyes with fingers covered in antique rings and smiled that tentative half-smile of hers that had first caught Diamond's eye. "How was it?" she asked sheepishly.

"You're not supposed to ask that question," Diamond said. "I am. It was great—you were great." He didn't sound very convincing.

"It'll get better," Sarah said, "it always does. I mean, after we've gotten to know each other, we'll do other things . . ." She let the thought trail off.

For a while neither of them said anything. "We were talking about things," Sarah said finally.

"Things?" Diamond said.

"Yes, things. Materialism versus things. Remember?"

"Oh, I remember. You're not materialistic, but you like

things. Only a woman could make that kind of delicate distinction. You don't collect things, Sarah, you collect collections. How long does it take you to dust them all?"

"You're not supposed to ask that kind of question," she said playfully. "What do you know about dusting? I have a black lady who comes in once a week. She picks up my things one by one and dusts them. The really fragile stuff—like those little Czech figures made out of dough—those things she doesn't even touch; she blows the dust off them."

"Sarah, you're a little girl in a doll house," Diamond said, moving to kiss her.

She ducked her head. "Don't talk down to me, Leo. I'm not a simple-minded college girl. You haven't understood a thing. I'm *not* materialistic. There is a distinction. Materialism has to do with economics and capitalism and Marx. But my things are roots—like trees sending down roots. When you walk into an apartment, you see all the roots, the things that make it familiar . . . the things that make it uniquely yours."

"You'd find familiar things in any apartment you've been to more than once," Diamond said.

"It's not the same," Sarah argued. "These are special things, special roots. Everyone has them. I've never heard of anyone who wasn't attached to things, who could simply up and leave them."

Diamond picked up one of the I-don't-know boxes and began to examine it. "I have," he said. "I know someone who left everything behind—everything but a jar of hay-fever pills and half a case of dandruff shampoo."

Diamond welcomed the change in subject and the chance to impress Sarah. "I've got a defector on my hands," he began to explain, his tone purposely undramatic. "It hasn't hit the papers yet, so I can't say too much. But a few days ago, this guy—a scientist—skipped to the Russians. I have a gut feeling that he took some enormously important secrets with him."

Sarah was genuinely intrigued—and amused. "A defector . . . a scientist . . . real Russians . . . I adore secrets, Leo.

What are you going to do about it?"

"Well, the first part of the drill is to find out precisely what he took with him. We re-create this fellow's life, from the day he was born to the day he got on the plane for Moscow. We put it together, piece by piece—why he defected, what he had access to, how much information he could give them."

"How?"

Diamond slid off the bed and began pacing the room. He was conscious of being naked and thought that he would forget about it as he talked. But he didn't. "We've got something called a C.P.P.—that's for Comprehensive Personality Profile. The whole thing runs to about eighty thousand dollars and takes ten days. Essentially, it's a two-phase operation . . ."

By now Sarah was less interested in what he was saying than in how he was saying it. For this was a Leo Diamond she had never seen before. He spoke with icy detachment, as if human beings were not involved.

". . . only used half a dozen times. Actually, it's pretty straightforward. We put one crew in the field and they pick up all the pieces of his life like a vacuum cleaner. Then we assemble a team of experts in New York. There's a psychologist, a physicist, a nuts-and-bolts cop, maybe one or two others. They'll take the raw information supplied by the field crew and—"

The phone rang. Diamond and Sarah looked at each other—and laughed at the surprise they saw in each other's faces. She picked up the receiver.

"Hello," said Sarah. "No, no, sorry, there's no one here by that name. That's all right." She hung up. "Somebody wanted a Madame Defarge. They must have been putting me on; imagine going through life with a name like that."

The phone rang again. "Let me take it," Diamond said. He wasn't smiling. He listened for a few moments without saying a word, his left hand covering the mouthpiece. Then he said coldly: "You're a god damn son of a bitch, Harry. A real prick. This isn't my idea of a joke . . . No, there isn't anything to it . . . As far as we know, the guy had nothing . . . That's just part of the drill . . . Negative, negative, you can't put one of your people in the group . . . Be my guest, go to the assistant secretary, but it'll be over my dead body . . . Fuck you, too." Diamond slammed down the receiver—and exploded in laughter.

Caught up in Diamond's mood, Sarah jumped up on the bed and started laughing with him. "Well, are you going to tell me or aren't you?"

"Listen, this kind of thing doesn't happen all the time—at least I hope to God it doesn't," Diamond said. "That was an old friend of mine over at the Agency. The call was his perverse idea of a joke—sort of like twisting a knife in my back, letting me know that he knew where I was. It was his way of boasting."

"But you lied to him about the defector."

"Yes and no. We have to keep it in the family until we find out what it's all about—and the Agency is definitely not part of *my* family."

"Aren't you supposed not to tell me secrets," Sarah said. "I mean, I could be . . . anybody."

"You could—but you're not; you've been cleared."

"Cleared?"

Diamond's intuition warned him he had made a mistake by telling her. But he plunged ahead. "After we went swimming that time at Virginia Beach, I slipped your name in with a batch of job applicants over at the Defense Department. The background checks came through last week."

"You bastard," she said. Then: "Can I see it?"

Diamond laughed. "I've already destroyed it, but I'll tell you what I remember. I know more about you than any man you've gone out with: your parents' divorce; your college record—you majored in French; your brother's fiasco at Colgate; the abortion; the fight over the TV residuals last year. I know about the men in your life too. Your first real love was a very sweet guy back in college named Edward Something-or-Other . . ."

"Eddie Harmon," Sarah said. "Ohmigod, I haven't thought of him in years."

"What do you think he's doing now?" Diamond said.

"Do you know that too?"

"He's a customer's man on Wall Street."

"Ohmigod. Eddie Harmon on Wall Street! I still have some of his short stories."

"If I remember correctly, you've had roughly two or three affairs a year since Harmon. Only two of them were really serious. Kenneth Sorensen and that guy last year."

"Peter."

"Sorensen's done very well for himself. He invented a Communist version of Monopoly in which the object is to lose money. The first person to go broke wins. He made a bundle on it and moved to the south of France. As for Peter . . ."

"I know all about that," Sarah said glumly.

Neither of them spoke for a few minutes. Then Sarah said: "Let me see if I understand this. You had me cleared by your security men. That means you must have been pretty confident you'd get me into bed." She cocked her head as if she were putting two and two together and getting four. "That sort of takes the spontaneity out of this, doesn't it?" And she gestured to the rumpled sheets and the clothes scattered around the floor.

"Not really," Diamond said. "Listen, it's part of the reality of life in Washington. Thousands of people who work for the government, from the President on down, have affairs. We've got to keep track of the girls. It's an obvious precaution."

"I've heard of men taking precautions before screwing," Sarah said, "but this takes the cake."

"That's probably how Harry knew I was here," Diamond said, pursuing his own train of thought.

"Why did he call you Madame Defarge?"

"My code name during the war," Diamond said. "It sounds pretty corny now, but whenever London wanted to send me instructions they had the BBC broadcast a message to Madame Defarge. The ironic part is that I got into the whole business purely by accident. They were processing millions of men. When my turn came, someone wrote UKR under my birthplace instead of UK."

"I don't understand."

"UKR is short for Ukraine. UK is the United Kingdom— my parents were living in London when I was born. Anyway, army intelligence took one look at the UKR and grabbed me for a possible drop into Russia. When they found out that I had some French, they dropped me into the Alpes Maritimes instead. To set up an escape route for allied pilots who were shot down. I lasted a grand total of fourteen weeks. I was betrayed by a chicken-shit pilot. Maybe he was a German plant; I never did find out. Anyhow, I had to use the route myself, and I barely made it. We were crossing the Pyrenees into Spain with two British pilots when the Vichy border guards picked up our trail. Their dogs tracked us to a barn. I had all the men urinate out the window. That made the dogs piss and they lost our scent. We went out the back door and the dogs went on their merry way. Just one of the tricks of the trade."

"That's a fabulous story," Sarah said, and she burst out

laughing. Gradually, her laughter faded. "Did you ever kill anyone? That's kind of naïve, I know, but did you, kill anybody, I mean?"

"Not during the war." Diamond's tone changed. "After the war, after college, I joined the Agency and ran agents in Eastern Europe. It's not an episode I like to remember. During the Hungarian business in fifty-six, someone—the guy on the phone just now, as a matter of fact—came up with this scheme—Jesus . . ." Diamond shook his head as if he were trying to rid himself of a bad dream.

"You don't have to tell me."

"No. I want to. The idea seemed bright at the time. If it had worked, I'd probably still be at the Agency. Anyhow, he thought there was a chance we could promote the same kind of thing in Czechoslovakia that was going on in Hungary. But first it was important to lull the Russians into a sense of security. To do that we purposely betrayed the Cernú network; we gave them twenty-seven of our own, agents. We put ourselves in the place of the Russians and decided that they wouldn't be expecting much trouble in Prague after that. But not the Russians. They executed them, twenty-six men and one woman. And nothing ever came of it—except I was squeezed out of the Agency when I couldn't prove I had verbal authorization for the operation."

"Can I get you something to eat?" Sarah said after a while. "I have some cold *ratatouille* in the fridge."

"No," Diamond said. "I'm not very hungry."

"What time do you have to go home?" Sarah asked.

"About midnight."

"Tell me what she's like, your wife?"

"No, I don't think I want to do that."

"How come you don't have children?" Sarah asked.

"Ah, well, I guess we never wanted any. Neither of us ever turned to the other and said: 'Let's have a child.' We never discussed it. It just seemed natural not to have children."

"Are you sorry now?"

"No, not really. Children are a pain in the ass."

"Leo, can I ask you a question? What would you have done if the security people who checked up on me told you I was a security risk?"

"I would have taken you to bed—but I wouldn't have talked to you. All right?"

"Right as rain," Sarah said. She tried not to laugh—and failed.

5

"IT MADE MY DAY," Dukess said over the roar of the engine.

The young man beside him pointed at the pedal and mouthed the words: *I can't hear you. Push the pedal.*

Dukess nodded vigorously and depressed the pedal. His voice, tinny and nasal, came over the headset. "It made my day."

Fred Van Avery smiled appreciatively. "I'd have given anything to have been on the extension," he said. "Hey, Harry, did he ask how you knew where he was?"

"I'll give him that much," Harry Dukess said. "He's still enough of a pro not to ask. But, boy, was he pissed."

High over the Virginia countryside, the helicopter hit an air pocket and the two men behind the pilot reached down between their knees and gripped the seat. The pilot's voice came over the intercom: "Sorry about that. You still back there? That's Andrews Field coming up to starboard now."

"How long you think it'll take you in Bangkok, Harry?" Van Avery asked.

"I should be able to pick up the pieces and be back in two weeks," Dukess said. "With any luck, this will be just another fuck-up nobody ever heard of."

From long experience, Van Avery knew this was no off-the-cuff estimate. Dukess dressed casually, even sloppily. In the office he wandered aimlessly around, his arms weighted down at his sides, as if he had just misplaced his best friend or his cigarette lighter. But behind this façade of good-natured befuddlement was a man who calculated the odds with precision—and always knew the score. If Dukess said he'd be back in two weeks, he'd be back in two weeks.

The helicopter settled onto the Central Intelligence Agency's pad at Andrews Air Force Base. At the edge of the pad, a sergeant stood by the open door of a black air force limousine.

"Listen," Dukess said, "try to line up an academic type for the China trip. And if you think of it, see if you can get to one of those creeps on the C.P.P. Diamond must be on to something or else he wouldn't have gone to a C.P.P. But don't get carried away. You ever hear about the Cernú business—this guy's got a history of going off half-cocked."

"Were you in on the Cernú thing?" Van Avery asked.

"Yeah, you could say I was in on it. Diamond got the bright idea he could fake the Russians out by giving them a network. When the whole thing turned sour, he tried to claim the idea originated with me." Dukess' voice had taken on a bitter undertone. "It's the oldest trick in the book—grabbing credit for the ones that work, ducking behind nonexistent verbal orders for the ones that don't. A departmental investigation tagged him because he had nothing in writing and only a fool would go out on a limb without something on paper. There was some suspicion he was shooting off his mouth to his mistress at the time, but they didn't bother to pin that down. They kicked him out of the department—not for breaking security regulations with his girlfriend, not for the fuck-up, but for trying to blame me for the fuck-up."

By now Dukess was engrossed in the story, telling it more to himself than Van Avery. "I'll never forgive him for what he did to Viktor."

"Who was Viktor?" Van Avery was engraving the details of the Cernú affair in his memory. It would make a great story when the younger staffers at the Agency got together for a nightcap.

"It's a name everyone's forgotten. Viktor was Viktor Lenart. He was half Czech, half French. He did some work for us in France in forty-four and later he and Diamond and I bummed around Europe a bit. He and Diamond were very close. I guess we all were. When Diamond ran agents in Eastern Europe, he recruited Viktor. Viktor was the head of the network that Diamond gave to the Ruskies."

"What happened to Viktor What's-His-Name?"

"He tried to run but they hunted him down and stood him against a wall and drilled little holes through him. If you're ever up against Diamond, Fred, watch out for him. He has no such thing as friends. He uses everybody. He used Viktor. He tried to use me; there are still some people around who think he was telling the truth about Cernú, and that hasn't helped my career any. He's a manipulator, a puppeteer."

The pilot was looking back, politely waiting for Dukess to be on his way.

"Have I covered everything, Fred?" Dukess said, businesslike again.

"Just about. There hasn't been a peep out of the Russians about this Lewinter thing yet. But when they trot him out, who's going to handle it?"

"That's all been arranged already. Interpol has a straight missing-persons alarm out on the defectee, and the Boston police are working up some background material—child-molesting charges or homosexuality, I don't know which they'll use this time. When the Russians break the story, play dumb and let the newspapers dig the dirt out for themselves. If we keep our hands off, the public will write off A. J. Lewinter as a pervert and say good riddance."

Clutching a worn canvas Valpac, Dukess climbed out of the helicopter.

"And, Fred," he yelled back through the door, "if you do get to one of those guys on the C.P.P., for Chrissakes, remember the budget. Try not to go over twenty-five hundred this time."

6

EVEN IN THE SHADE of the tree, it was oppressively hot. Yefgeny Mikhailovich Pogodin yanked at the end of his bow tie and opened his collar. Across the road in the distance, he could make out a line of women working their way across a field, bending and straightening and filling their sacks with something—Pogodin was too much of a city boy to know what. Below him, on the side of the road, a mechanic squatted next to the broken down KGB pool car, dipping a small part from the engine into a coffee can filled with benzine.

"Mechanic, have you found the trouble?" Pogodin called down.

"It looks like the fuel pump," the mechanic said without looking up.

"How much longer?"

The mechanic plunked the part into the can and turned around to look up at Pogodin. "Don't rush me. You're lucky to get anybody out here at all."

"Damn it," Pogodin said in English, and turning to the man next to him he repeated the epithet in Russian. "You'd think the KGB could keep its cars in working condition. Ah, well, Zaitsev, it shouldn't be too long now. Finish the story."

Stoyan Alexandrovich Zaitsev was not a pleasant man to look at. His profile was the opposite of chiseled; from some angles, the features actually looked as if they were eroding. Not that there was anything repulsive about his face. Rather, there were a lot of little things wrong with it: small bloodshot eyes; enormous nostrils with strands of hair coming out of them; a mouthful of crowded, slightly discolored teeth. He let out a roar of laughter at what he was about to say.

"And so picture this: Furtseva hiked her skirts and climbed up onto the stage of the Bolshoi and screeched"—here Zaitsev pinched his flaring nostrils with his fingers and launched into a falsetto imitation—"'Look at all those nipples! I'm the Minister of Culture and I tell you it's decadent. Either get new costumes or the premiere is canceled.'" Zaitsev rose to his knees and flung out his arms. "The ballet master was magnificent. He looked Furtseva straight in her doctrinaire eyes and bellowed: 'The costumes are integral to the spirit of this ballet. If they go, I go.'"

"Who won? Furtseva?"

"You think so," Zaitsev said gleefully, settling back against the trunk of the tree. "Well, I went opening night and there was our new liberalism bouncing up and down on the stage—nipples, nipples, nipples, nipples, nipples, nipples, nipples, everywhere you looked, nipples. And our socialism survived."

The two men whooped in delight.

"Zaitsev, my friend, you're still in great form," Pogodin said. "Things have gone well for you, eh?"

"No complaints from me. I live a beautiful life. I'm a Grand Master now, which entitles me to a comfortable stipend. I get up at ten every morning, have a leisurely cup of tea and then it's work, if you can call it that, for four hours. I teach some advanced students—I have one who is very promising. I play in three or four tournaments a year—and always win. Last year I wrote another book—this one called *The Aggressive Pawn*. Actually, in places it's quite brilliant. My work is published in France, and they let me collect part of the royalties. I supervise the translations and get more money for that. The hard currency brings me everything I need. You saw my apartment when you picked me up: the West German stereo, the suits from Italy, the latest books from France. Even with a face like this, I get all the women I want." And Zaitsev motioned with his head toward their companion, a thick-set blonde with skin that gathered in places like shirred fabric. She was dangling her feet in a nearby stream and blowing her nose in an embroidered handkerchief.

"I'd heard you'd turned into something of a Don Juan," Pogodin said. "And does it satisfy you, this flitting from one girl to another like a butterfly?"

"Ah, my dear naïve, old-fashioned, tight-assed Yefgeny Mikhailovich!" Zaitsev cried. "I always knew you were bourgeois at heart. Does it satisfy? Better ask, do I enjoy emptying my bowels. Better ask, do I take pleasure from a bottle of good Polish vodka. You get my point?"

"And what of the political atmosphere in which you live this wonderful life of yours?" Pogodin asked.

"Aha! I knew you'd come to it, you always do. Sometimes, when things get to me"—Zaitsev turned to make certain that the girl was still out of earshot and continued in a lower voice—"sometimes, I send the girls home, I turn off the Nazi stereo, I switch to Russian vodka, and I write essays. Oh, God, you should read what I write."

"Where is this Pushkin?"

"It's where everything good that's being written in Russia is. It's in my desk drawer. Oh, *they* know about it, but as long as it stays in the drawer . . ."

The two men regarded each other in somber silence.

Behind them, the surprisingly musical voice of the girl drifted up from the stream. "Zaitsev, darling, do you miss me?" she called, and sneezed again into her handkerchief.

Under his breath, Zaitsev muttered, "What a cow," and smiled and blew her a kiss. He turned back to Pogodin. "One can never talk seriously with women around—especially when they suffer from hay fever. And you, what of you? What brings you back to Russia?"

"To sit under a pear tree between Moscow and Obninsk and listen to you talk."

"Seriously."

"Seriously, I can't tell you."

"Bullshit, you can't tell me!" Zaitsev exclaimed. "Since when? Beguiling candor is your weapon; you use it to disarm people and then conquer them. So disarm me." And he threw up his arms in mock surrender.

"Do you know what's going through my head?" Pogodin began.

But Zaitsev interrupted. "There you go again. They should make you the commissar of candor."

Pogodin acted hurt. "With you, Zaitsev, it's different. My candor is not a weapon but a testimonial to our friendship." And to prove the point, Pogodin began to talk about the man who had preoccupied him for the last two weeks—A. J. Lewinter.

". . . I'm not a scientist and I can't vouch for the quality of his information. But I tell you this. I spent fourteen hours on the plane with the American and if he's someone other than who he says he is, he's the best-rehearsed actor you've ever seen."

Zaitsev nodded thoughtfully. "If this works out," he said, "it could give your career quite a boost, couldn't it?"

"It could, yes."

"Is that clouding your judgment?" Zaitsev asked.

"Probably." And they laughed together.

"If you were writing for the desk drawer, what would you say?"

"It's too complex for the desk drawer," Pogodin said. "Our technical people debriefing Lewinter in Obninsk are impressed.

He's been spewing out formulas. There's no doubt that these formulas are trajectories. And there's no doubt that the trajectories are for warheads and decoys. But until the Americans shoot at us, we have no way of knowing if these are the trajectories they actually use in their MIRVs."

"So you'll never know for sure if the information is genuine?" Zaitsev said.

"That's it," Pogodin said. "We can't verify this information. All we can do is check out the man. And the people in Moscow don't like the look of him. They think it's too easy—too pat. If they had paid for the information, it would be a different story. But he came free."

"And you, do you believe him?"

Pogodin thought for a moment. "I believe that . . . that *he* believes he has genuine information."

"As usual, my frank friend, you haven't answered the question. Never mind, I let you off the hook. But tell me, what's the American like?"

"He's not a man you'd want to drink with," Pogodin said, "but he's interesting. He's full of emotional contradictions. That's what makes him so believable. One minute he's arrogant, the next he's full of self-doubts. One minute he's filing his nails, the next he's biting them. He spent half the trip back to Moscow lecturing me on ecology . . ."

"On what?" Zaitsev asked.

"On ecology. He was lecturing me on ecology. The rest of the time he kept asking me whether our people would regard him as a hero or a traitor. When he spoke of his homeland, he used slogans; he didn't appear to be able to define specific political issues in any depth. He presented himself as a lady's man, flirting with the stewardess every time she walked by. After we arrived in Moscow, I arranged for him to have one of our girls, and she told me later that he didn't perform. I'll tell you something even odder. He didn't bring any clothes with him, he didn't bring any money with him—not even a toothbrush. But he lugged along a six-month supply of allergy pills and a satchel of dandruff shampoo. Oh, and some dental X rays too. The funny part is I took everything away from him the minute he boarded the plane; you never know what's in those things."

Zaitsev stood up and stretched. "Fascinating, fascinating. I'd like to meet him someday. Tell me, is he running away from something—or to something?"

"I'm not quite certain, but I have the impression that he is a man who has only regret for everything that has happened to him in his life."

"I never realized that your job was so mental," Zaitsev said. The words came out with their usual satiric cast, but he meant it as a compliment.

"So you finally understand," Pogodin said. And he too stood up. "Actually, you and I do pretty much the same kind of thing. My profession is not espionage—it's gamesmanship. I'm your aggressive pawn. I try to figure out what the Americans are doing. They try to figure out what we're doing. Then I try

to figure out what they think we're doing. And they try to figure out what I think *they* think we're doing. And so it goes, ad
infinitum."

"It does sound a bit like chess—except your end games are
usually more painful than mine," Zaitsev said.

Below them on the road, the repairman wiped his hands on
an oily rag. *"Gospodin,"* he called up—using the pre-revolu-
tionary form of address for "citizen" instead of the more acceptable *comrade*—"climb into the driver's seat and depress the gas
pedal. I think we can start her up now."

Pogodin and Zaitsev slid down the embankment and dusted
themselves off. A moment later they had the car engine purring,
and Zaitsev honked the horn for the girl. "When you drop us at
the dacha, can you stop for tea?" he asked.

"No, I don't think so," Pogodin said. "I'm supposed to be
in Obninsk by three, and I'm already late."

"Then come to us on your way back to Moscow—
we always have a houseful of friends, an endless supply of
vodka, a generous supply of women, exactly the thing for a
bachelor like you. Someone's even promised to give me some
hashish."

"I'll try," Pogodin said. "They won't be through for ten
days at least. There's a real fight brewing between Moscow and
Obninsk on this one. I've seen these things before—they have
a way of dragging on."

"Let it drag on without you and come to us sooner,"
Zaitsev said.

"I can't afford to," Pogodin said. "I have too big a stake in this one."

The girl came sliding down the embankment, revealing a fleshy thigh and a length of garter belt. Zaitsev and Pogodin watched her descent with open delight.

PART II
THE RESPONSE

1

Comprehensive Personality Profile 327

Subject:	Lewinter, A. J.
Director:	Billings, Robert
Staff:	Kaplan, Dr. Jerome S.Farnsworth,
	Frederick F. Schindler, Prof. Erich T.

Enclosures: Transcripts of field interviews conducted:
12, 13 August

Edited transcript of conversation between Agent N. Wilson and
Maureen Sinclair, a research assistant in China area studies at
Harvard. 12 August. Subject, divorced female aged 33, has

known Lewinter for approximately eight months and has cohabited with him for approximately two months, up to the time he left for the ecological conference in Japan.

WILSON: I appreciate your seeing me on such short notice.

SINCLAIR: Yes, of course, not at all. Please sit anywhere. Is that a tape recorder? Here, let me, I'll move those. Oh, my God, what will you think, I mean seeing the place like this. I'm not usually this messy. I promise you. But the lady who cleans for me is out sick. German measles. God, I hope she's not pregnant again.

WILSON: Please don't apologize. Compared to my place, yours is immaculate.

SINCLAIR: Oh, dear, you're one of those polite ones, aren't you? You know what the Chinese say, don't you? They say, "Politeness is the most acceptable hypocrisy." The original—you don't by any chance know some Mandarin, do you? No, I don't suppose you do—the original is particularly charming because the character for hypocrisy can also be translated—

WILSON: I don't mean to sound impatient, Miss Sinclair, but I wonder—

SINCLAIR: Oh, my, you people are running around like chickens without heads over this. I told the other man who was here that the poor dear is simply using this opportunity to see a bit of Japan.

WILSON: The other man? What other man?

SINCLAIR: Well, I've read about this kind of thing. The left hand not knowing what the right is doing, and all that. But to see it in the flesh, well . . .

WILSON: What man was that, Miss Sinclair? It's important.

SINCLAIR: Well, let me think a moment. Ah, yes, day before yesterday. He was here the day before yesterday. Short man in his late forties, very pleasant. Well, not that pleasant. He asked a few questions, said something about Augustus having gone AWOL in Japan. Took Augustus' papers with him too.

WILSON: He took documents with him!

SINCLAIR: Yes, that's right, a carton full of them. It was a Maxwell House Coffee carton, if that's any help to you. Is there anything wrong? I mean, he was from your department, wasn't he?

WILSON: I'm positive he was, Miss Sinclair. I think we may have gotten our assignments crossed, that's all. Did he leave a name, a card, anything like that?

SINCLAIR: No, nothing. Come to think of it, he never really introduced himself. Why are all you people worried about Augustus? I told your colleague, Augustus is sightseeing, that's all. I wouldn't be surprised if he walked through the door this very minute.

WILSON: How can you be so sure he's sightseeing? The ecology conference ended more than a week ago, you know.

SINCLAIR: Augustus wrote me a postcard. I still have that if you'd like to see it. You'll probably want to take that with you too.

Wilson insert: The postcard is dated 3 August. On one side is an aerial view of Tokyo. The handwriting has been positively iden-

tified by Agent G. Moorer as Lewinter's. The message says:

> Darling Maureen, my paper received enthusiastically at the conference—not much time to take in local color yet but spending afternoon at Noh and plan to stay on a few days for sightseeing if can exchange air ticket without losing money. If anyone from the shop asks after me tell them I've defected to the Russians. Think of you constantly.

The rest is indented and looks like a poem:

> Measure me by my ability to penetrate
> But pay attention:
> The tongue is a great exaggerator, making
> > mountains out of molehills,
> > caverns out of cavities
> Whatever you do
> Don't settle for the dentist's drill,
> which word of mouth has it
> Lubricates as it does the work of men.

The postcard is signed with the initials A and J. End insert.

SINCLAIR: He's only kidding, you know. I mean the part about him defecting. You don't take that seriously, do you? Oh my good gracious, I'll bet you do.

WILSON: This poem, can you tell me something about it, Miss Sinclair?

SINCLAIR: Like what, for instance?

WILSON: To start with, why is it in the postcard? It's sort of odd—surprising—the way he just threw it in like that.

SINCLAIR: It surprised me too, to tell you the truth. I had no idea he remembered it. Augustus and I met eight months ago, in the reading room of the university library, as a matter of fact. But you probably know all that already. When we met, I was reading a back copy of the *Kenyon Review.* That's a literary journal. There were some examples of modern Chinese poetry—perfectly horrid little things about Chairman Mao. The translations were atrocious. But that's another story. Anyhow, Augustus leaned across, out of the blue—it really was very out of character, when you come to know him—he leaned across and asked me what I was reading. I'd finished the Chinese poetry and was reading this poem, the one in the postcard. I forget who wrote it. Augustus took the magazine and read it once. He laughed; I remember he laughed. Well, that was all there was to it. I'd no idea he would ever remember it. What a sweet dear, putting it in the postcard like that.

WILSON: Maybe he copied it down that night in the library? Or later?

SINCLAIR: If he had done that he could never have kept it a secret. No, he either suddenly remembered it—A.J. has an extraordinary memory, you know—or he came across a copy of the poem in Tokyo and sent it to me—the way someone would send flowers.

WILSON: I see. Can you tell me, Miss Sinclair, before he left for Japan, did he give you any reason to think he was distressed, unhappy, chafing at the bit? I'm sorry to pry, but like I say, it is important.

SINCLAIR: Oh my good heavens, no. Augustus is very happy here. I suppose it's no secret that we, er, how should I put it, we share this apartment. Things are going well for Augustus. We're going to be married, you know, in September. Three weeks from today, as a matter of fact.

WILSON: And his work?

SINCLAIR: I suppose it's going well. I really don't know. Augustus never talks about his work. But I can tell you he isn't depressed or anything like that. He is very excited about his solid-waste-disposal project. Do you know about his solid-waste-disposal project? It's really very revolutionary. He saw a congressman or senator or something of that sort recently about it, and came back terribly excited. He said the senator or congressman or whoever it was planned to introduce a bill allocating funds to create a federal solid-waste-disposal corporation along the lines Augustus suggested. It would really be quite a triumph for Augustus. Have you heard anything about such a bill?

WILSON: I'm afraid I don't follow those things, Miss Sinclair. Then there was nothing troubling Mr. Lewinter, you think?

SINCLAIR: Only what troubles us all, Mr. Wilson—money. Augustus is behind on his alimony payments. Not much behind, mind you, but enough to worry him. His wife—his ex-wife—is a, pardon the expression, bitch. Augustus used to go there every Sunday to see his children, but *she* turned them against him. I can just imagine the stories she told, the lies she made up.

Anyhow, Augustus is worried she will make trouble about the alimony, the wife that is, though Lord knows she doesn't need it. She gets a very generous allowance from her father.

WILSON: Why was he behind on alimony? He makes a good salary and he couldn't have many expenses.

SINCLAIR: Ah, money, Mr. Wilson. Augustus and money. Maybe he has holes in his pockets. Who knows why? Somehow he never has enough money. Which of us does? I think he is just a bad money manager. He is still paying off some debts—the automobile, a cottage on the Cape. The alimony takes a chunk out of his check, a big chunk. To tell you the truth, a week or so before he left for Japan, Augustus swallowed his pride and went to one of those finance companies, the ones that consolidate your debts. You've heard of it—something-or-other debt, in Boston.

WILSON: You mean Consol-O-Debt?

SINCLAIR: Yes, that's the one. Consol-O-Debt. Do you know what the Chinese say about money. Mr. Wilson? They say money gives a man wings that can take him everywhere—except heaven. Now the Chinese word for "heaven" . . .

Edited transcript of conversation between Agent D. Matthews and Rupert Brooke Lewinter. 12 August. Subject, aged 45, a research chemist with Norton Pharmaceuticals, Inc., is the only brother of Lewinter.

LEWINTER: I'm terribly sorry, I forgot your name?

MATTHEWS: Matthews.

LEWINTER: Yes, of course, Matthews. When you mentioned on the telephone where you were from, I thought it best we have some privacy. I hope you didn't have too much trouble finding this place.

MATTHEWS: Your directions were excellent.

LEWINTER: It's about Jerry, isn't it? I knew that crowd at M.I.T. would get him into hot water. If I told him once, I told him a thousand times, Jerry, I told him, stay away from those professional anti-Americans. I don't know what kind of work Jerry does, but I knew it wouldn't sit well with you fellows when word got around who he was hanging out with. I'm right, huh, aren't I? Jerry's in hot water?

MATTHEWS: If it's all the same to you, Mr. Lewinter, let's take things one step at a time. Can you tell me something about your brother's background? Did he, for instance, have a happy childhood?

LEWINTER: Quite Frankly, Mr. Matthews, Jerry—

MATTHEWS: Excuse me for interrupting, Mr. Lewinter, but everyone else seems to call him by his initials. Why do you call him Jerry?

LEWINTER: Jerry is the name the family uses. In Bronx High School of Science, he was Augustus. He started out college as A. Jerome, but switched to initials in his senior year. But we always called him Jerry. Just plain Jerry. I don't think he likes it very much, but it's hard to break one's childhood habits, isn't it?

MATTHEWS: I see. You were going to say something about his childhood when I interrupted.

LEWINTER: Yes, his childhood. Frankly, Mr. Matthews, Jerry was coddled, and I don't think it's done him any service. He grew up on a diet of instant gratification. If he set eyes on a toy boat or plane or train, he was playing with it the next day. I suppose one would say he was happy in the sense that he was never frustrated, but I'm not sure he could be described as happy in a larger sense. That is to say, everything came too easily, and therefore nothing meant very much to him. Am I making sense in all this?

MATTHEWS: Yes, I think so. Go on.

LEWINTER: Interestingly enough, my parents—my father was an inventor of sorts—my parents didn't make that mistake with me. Jerry and I are really something of a case history in child raising. I was the older brother, of course. When my parents had me, they were quite preoccupied with making ends meet. As a result, I learned at an early age to put up with the frustrations that one finds in life as a matter of course. Just before Jerry was born, my father struck it rich in a modest way—he invented a home garbage grinder, a pedal affair that would pulverize household waste, everything except tin cans. Ever hear of it— the Lewinter Disposerizer? Sold in the Sears, Roebuck catalogue. One can still occasionally find Lewinter Disposerizers on farms. At any rate, my parents were determined to give Jerry every advantage. That was the phrase they used, *every advantage.* What they actually gave him, it seems to me, was every disadvantage—in the sense that they didn't prepare him for the setbacks and frustrations in later life.

MATTHEWS: Very interesting. So you trace a lot of his problems to his childhood, then.

LEWINTER: Don't misunderstand me, Mr. Matthews. Jerry was an eager, bright boy. He had a phenomenal memory. They actually had him to doctors when he was very young to see if he had a photographic memory, it was that good. I remember once when my father had lost his wallet, Jerry rattled off the number of every card in it. And another time, he recited every word of a fourth-grade reader the day after he got the book. It was quite a stunt.

MATTHEWS: Did he?

LEWINTER: Did he what, Mr. Matthews?

MATTHEWS: Did he have a photographic memory according to the doctors?

LEWINTER: He did—and he didn't. I know that sounds strange. For some reason, he turned it off when he saw the doctors and turned it on again when he wanted to impress somebody at home. I myself am convinced that he had it, yes—that is, until the accident.

MATTHEWS: The accident?

LEWINTER: Yes. He was about eight, I think. Eight or nine. He fell off a garage roof and landed on his head. He was unconscious for almost two days—it was really touch and go. He recovered, of course. But he never did those memory tricks again. I'm convinced he lost his extraordinary memory capacity in that fall, absolutely convinced. No telling what he might have become if he had retained it, is there? I mean, he was quite intelligent to begin with. That, and a photographic memory, well . . .

MATTHEWS: Tell me about his wife, that is, his former wife.

LEWINTER: She was a good mother, a good wife, a handsome woman in her own way, and very ambitious for Jerry. She made demands on him, which is something our parents never did. If he amounted to anything, it was because Susan pushed him.

MATTHEWS: Apparently he didn't share your view. Why did he leave her?

LEWINTER: Your guess is as good as mine. He didn't know a good thing when he saw it.

MATTHEWS: I understand he's planning to marry again. Do you know the girl?

LEWINTER: That's news to me. I knew he was pretty thick with her, but he never mentioned a word about marriage. So Jerry's planning to marry again, eh? Interesting. I never met her, so I can't tell you anything about her. Yes, I do know one thing. She encouraged him to take his solid-waste-disposal scheme— I used to tell him it was just a colossal Lewinter Disposerizer— to some congressman.

MATTHEWS: What about the group at M.I.T. you mentioned before?

LEWINTER: There's not much to tell. I've met one or two of them—they're a noisy bunch, professional look-for-the-worst-in-everything types, if you get my meaning. I told Jerry that, given his line of work—mind you, I have no idea exactly what he does, except that it is very secret—given his line of work, those were not the kind of people with whom he should be hanging around.

MATTHEWS: He didn't take your advice, I gather?

LEWINTER: Jerry never took my advice.

MATTHEWS: What is his attitude toward the Soviet Union?

LEWINTER: Now you do have me frightened. Why are you asking a question like that?

MATTHEWS: Absolutely routine, Mr. Lewinter. I'm asking it because it's on my list of questions.

LEWINTER: In his own way, Jerry is very idealistic, and I suspect he thinks the Russians are too. Oh, don't get me wrong, Jerry is no fellow traveler. Nothing of the sort. If he thinks much about Russia at all, it is probably with the vague notion that they might be interested in his waste-disposal scheme. Jerry is very frustrated about that project, you know. He just can't seem to interest anybody in it, no matter how much he tries. It means a lot to him, getting someone to accept his waste-disposal scheme.

Unedited transcript of conversation between Agent R. Grotten and Susan Bidgood Lewinter. 13 August. Subject, aged 37, a housewife, is the divorced wife of Lewinter.

LEWINTER: I was expecting a Mr. Bodkin. When they called, they said a Mr. Bodkin was coming. I wasn't expecting you.

GROTTEN: Bodkin's wife had a baby late last night. They asked me to fill in for him.

LEWINTER: Boy or girl? Was it a boy or girl?

GROTTEN: I really don't know. Nobody said.

LEWINTER: In this day and age, boys are so much easier to handle, don't you think so, Mr. Grotten? Do you have any children?

GROTTEN: Why, yes, as a matter of fact, I do.

LEWINTER: Boys or girls?

GROTTEN: Eh, why, actually, one of each. Eh, Mrs. Lewinter–

LEWINTER: Excuse me for interrupting, Mr. Grotten, but I use Miss. Since the divorce. Miss Lewinter.

GROTTEN: Yes, of course. Now, eh, Miss Lewinter, I'd like to ask you a few questions about your former husband, if I may.

LEWINTER: Does this have anything to do with alimony? I filed a complaint with the court last week—August is three months behind in his payments—and they said they would send a court officer around.

GROTTEN: Actually, I'm—

LEWINTER: Not that it's critical. The money, I mean. Luckily, I have some income of my own to fall back on. But it's the principle of the thing. The divorce settlement stipulated he was to provide a hundred and twenty-five dollars a week. That's not unreasonable, is it? In this day and age, a hundred and twenty-five dollars doesn't go very far when you're trying to hold a household together and raise two small children, does it?

GROTTEN: We're not from the courts, Miss Lewinter. I thought they made that clear to you when they set up the appointment with Bodkin. This is a routine security background investigation.

LEWINTER: But he's already had one of those. When August first came out here, they did that.

GROTTEN: I know, Miss Lewinter, but we're updating it. Strictly routine, I assure you. Now, if I could trouble you to answer a few questions?

LEWINTER: You have nothing to do with the alimony?

GROTTEN: That's right. Nothing.

LEWINTER: I see.

GROTTEN: I am interested in the fact that he is behind in his alimony payments, though. You mentioned earlier that he was three months behind. How come you waited that long to file a complaint with the courts, Miss Lewinter?

LEWINTER: If I went to a court every time August missed an alimony payment, I'd look like a fool. You have to understand August. He's a very forgetful person. He's always forgetting birthdays and anniversaries and dinner dates and bills—and alimony payments. He simply doesn't have a head for details.

GROTTEN: Did you attempt to remind him, about the alimony payments, I mean?

LEWINTER: Oh, I tried, I tried, Lord knows I tried. I sent him registered letters and telegrams. I did everything but actually go there. I couldn't bring myself to do that, not with that *woman* living there. I'm not angry, mind you. August has a right to a life of his own. But that woman. I don't know what he sees in her.

GROTTEN: You've met her, I take it?

LEWINTER: Only once, before we were divorced, at a party. I know what you're driving at. No, I don't know her very well. But anyone who has met her says the same thing. In a word, she's a shrew.

GROTTEN: I don't mean to open old wounds, Miss Lewinter, but what led to the divorce? What went wrong?

LEWINTER: Oh, it's very complicated. You're not pressed for time, are you? Ha. Well, let me see if I can make a long story short. I think the thing that really broke the camel's back, so to speak, was that August used to exaggerate his own importance. It wasn't exactly that he lied, you have to understand. But he sort of created his own image of himself with a web of fabrications. Take the business about the waste-disposal scheme. I suppose it was a genuine enough scheme. But the way he talked about it, you'd think he was Leonardo da Vinci offering the world the steam engine or whatever it was da Vinci did invent. August wanted desperately to be important. He was always searching for things that could make him important. This involved a lot of half-truths and exaggerations. And when you punctured one of his pretenses, he seemed to fall apart in your hands. It was very sad, really.

GROTTEN: Was he involved politically?

LEWINTER: Oh, no, never. August political? He never gave it a second thought. He was interested in practical things—his work, his schemes, but never politics.

GROTTEN: Was he happy with his work?

LEWINTER: As far as I could tell, yes. He seemed to think that he had made a very good impression on whoever it is that's in charge of his section at M.I.T. He seemed to feel that they were receptive to his new ideas.

GROTTEN: Did he ever talk about the Soviet Union?

LEWINTER: The Soviet Union? Good God, I don't even think he knew where it was.

Edited transcript of conversation between Agent T. Blumenthal and Doctor Donald Fishkin. 13 August. Subject was Lewinter's dentist.

FISHKIN: Lewinter! That son of a bitch rabble-rousing bastard. Why the hell are you asking about Lewinter? He get caught with his fingers in the till or something? Boy, would I like to get my hands on that crazy maniac. That's right, maniac. He's off his rocker, crazy, insane, a good-for-nothing son of a bitch. What he needs is a custom-made strait jacket. Look, take a tip from me, steer clear of that raving madman. Four years I treated him, four years. Right. Four years he comes in here telling me how pleased he is to have found such a good dentist. Right. Then one day he waltzes in, calls me a prick to my face, and waltzes out with his X rays. Right. With a waiting room full of patients, too.

BLUMENTHAL: Did he ever—

FISHKIN: The bastard, he's a walking loony, if you ask me. Skipped out of here with his X rays just like that. Son of a bitch never even paid the hundred and twenty-five dollars he owes me. Four years. Right. Four long years. I'll tell you something, from me to you, he's around the bend. Right around the bend.

8

"HE SOUNDS PARANOID," yawned Kaplan.

"Lewinter?" asked Billings, a frown tugging at the corners of his thin, dry lips.

"What's his name, the dentist."

"We're not here to analyze what's-his-name, the dentist," Billings said coldly, the frown deepening. He removed his horn-rimmed glasses with both hands—someone had once told him the frames lasted longer if you took them off that way—and placed them on the sheaf of transcripts. "I take it, then, we can dismiss the possibility that the subject of this C.P.P. is insane?"

Kaplan let the silence drag out until it was uncomfortable before he answered. It was a technique he had developed in his medical practice; never shoot from the hip, appear thoughtful, weigh your words, lure their minds out across the silences to meet you halfway.

"There's no such thing as insanity in psychiatry," he said finally, definitively. "It's really a legal term, insanity, implying the inability to distinguish between right and wrong. Since this is not a legal proceeding, and since you're not concerned with rights and wrongs, perhaps we should stick to terms that have some psychiatric relevance."

They had not got on from the start: Billings, the prissy intelligence pro committed to the gospel that achievements in his field, as in any field, came from discipline, obedience to the imperatives of the pecking order and paper work; and Kaplan, the brilliant young psychiatrist who associated discipline with mediocrity and reveled in leaps of intuition. "Good God, can't we come up with a psychiatrist who isn't Jewish?" Billings had complained when an aide handed him a list of the people on the Comprehensive Personality Profile. "They're inevitably so sloppy."

Billings had meant *sloppy* in the mental sense, but his first glimpse of Kaplan convinced him that the term could be applied in the physical sense too. Kaplan had a large nose, a prominent Adam's apple which bobbed like a buoy when he talked, and long hair that looked as if the wind had recently blown through it. The vest of his $400 suit was unbuttoned to the waist, revealing an eighty-nine-cent red polka-dot tie that Kaplan had bought at Tie City.

"All right, let's not use the word *insanity,*" Billings was saying. "Naturally, I realize that there's not much to go on yet—the major portion of the interviews have yet to come—but we have to start somewhere. Perhaps we can hammer out a preliminary estimate . . ."

"Sounds, eh, anal compulsive to me," said Erich Schindler, the physicist on the C.P.P. A squirrelish man with jutting, nicotine-stained teeth, he had a habit of talking with his head angled down, as if peering over eyeglasses he neither wore nor needed. His biggest contribution to the conversation before he weighed in with "anal compulsive" had been to hold forth, apropos of nothing in particular, on the "Cartesian distinction between mind, the essence of which is understanding, and body, the essence of which is motion." Peering over the nonexistent glasses, he entered the lists again. "Look here, my boy, eh, don't mean to step on toes and all that—you're not sensitive about territorial imperatives, are you?—but I learned a long time ago that you can't miss the mark, well at least you can't miss it by much, if you, eh, label someone anal compulsive, can you?"

"God damn right," Kaplan agreed. He liked Schindler despite his meandering mind and exaggerated professional airs. Kaplan had been surprised to find a scientist of Schindler's prominence taking part in one of these affairs; he guessed, partly from his own experience, that the honorarium, as they called it in the academic world, had been too enticing to turn down.

"Anal compulsion is the ragweed of psychiatry," Kaplan continued. "It's everywhere. It's a fancy way of saying uptight, and who isn't these days." He looked pointedly at Billings. "Listen, it's too soon"—Kaplan waved toward the pile of transcripts—"for anything but the most vacuous generalities."

"Perhaps you'll be so kind as to try anyhow," Billings said.

Silence. At the instant it became painful, Kaplan spoke up.

"That's what you're paying me for. O.K., let's start with the basics. There are roughly three reasons why people defect from our side to their side. First"—Kaplan leaned forward and began to speak intensely, his Adam's apple bobbing, the words tumbling out like eighth notes—"they are running away from debts, divorces, entanglements, job troubles, crimes that are about to catch up with them, pressures they can't stand, the sticks and stones of outrageous fortune, life in general. They have no idea where they're going and couldn't care less. They have no place to go but up. Now there is some evidence that could place Lewinter in this group. His job couldn't have been all that satisfying or he wouldn't have put so much time and effort into that garbage scheme of his. Then there is the business of the debts. And I get the feeling from the first batch of interviews that he was about to get hooked to a girl who sounds in many ways like a wax model of the wife he left. Maybe he realized this and skipped before it was too late."

"So you think it's a classic case of a man running away from troubles, then?" Billings summarized. It was a conclusion he personally found congenial.

"I didn't say that. I said there is some evidence that he *may* fit into this category. But there is evidence that could put him into either of the other two categories also."

"What are these, eh, other two categories?" asked Schindler, puffing away at the cigarette dangling precariously from his lips.

"The first batch are your runaways. O.K. The second batch are suffering from schizophrenia, which, technically speaking, is a functional psychosis characterized, among other things, by private fantasies. Occasionally one of these fantasies takes the shape of a person seeing himself as a symbol who, by his example, can remake the world. Jesus, I think, was suffering from schizophrenia. Anyhow, you find a lot of this among radicals. They see themselves as cogs in the machine, and fantasize about that single act—assassination, suicide, self-immolation, defection—which can elevate them into a symbol. Now if Lewinter were really moving in radical circles, as his brother suggests, he may have seen defection as a dramatic symbolic act that could thrust his life and ideas into the spotlight."

Kaplan suddenly became aware of his own intensity. As if to sap it of its strength, he leaned back and stifled a yawn. "Then there is the third category, which is by far the most interesting, at least to me. To people in this group, defection is a kind of get-rich-quick scheme, or the psychic equivalent of it, which is to get status quick. And there is more than a hint that Lewinter could fall into this grouping too. What little we know about his life so far can be read as a frantic search for status: experimenting with a new name every few years until he winds up with initials, which are the trimmings of status; his concentration on an earthshaking scheme to save mankind from being overpowered by garbage; even his flight from his wife to another woman. Remember what his ex-wife—who didn't have a very high opinion of him—said. Wait a second, here it is. Quote: August used to exaggerate his own importance, unquote; and again, quote: sort of created his own image of himself with a web of fabrications, unquote. Now of course all of us have an exaggerated image of our own importance"—again Kaplan made it a point to look at Billings—"but we have to find out how serious a theme this was in Lewinter's case. If it was considerably exaggerated, and everything we know so far is compatible with this supposition, and if his achievements within this society were such as to give the lie to this image, then he could have skipped, or defected, as we say in the trade, in order to—and here I'll use my term again—get status quick. He'd do that by taking something of value with him, something that would catapult him immediately upon arrival into a position of status in the eyes of his hosts. Now, whether this description fits Lewinter, and if it does, whether that something of value was his own warm body or a garbage-disposal scheme or secret ceramic nose-cone information or whatever remains to be seen."

"Bloody confusing, eh? What you say"—Schindler, the physicist, interrupted himself to chain-light another cigarette—"only reinforces my impression, or should I say prejudice, that the whole thing, the transcripts, they, eh, read like something out of Rashomon—you know the Japanese Rashomon theme?

—or Durrell's *Alexandria Quartet?* Marvelous books, the *Alexandria Quartet.* A heterogeneous group of people look at the same set of circumstances or the same person, and each comes up with a different version of the truth. Ha! Lewinter appears to change from person to person, or should I say perspective to perspective. What I mean to say is that Fishkin's Lewinter isn't anything like the brother's Lewinter, who in turn isn't anything like the wife's Lewinter. And so on. How in heaven's name, or anybody's name for that matter, are we supposed to pick out the real Lewinter from this, eh, what shall I call it, garbage heap? Ha! Yes, garbage heap will do very nicely. That's what I would like to know. How, eh, to find the real Lewinter?"

"By cutting through the contradictions, the role playing, the posing and posturing, the conceits, to the quintessential Lewinter," Billings offered. "That's what the C.P.P. is all about—to strip away the outer layer and make some rather educated guesses as to whether he was the kind of person who could bring himself to harm his country, and whether, if he wanted to harm his country, he had the wherewithal to do so."

"That's a mighty tall order, that there is," said the fourth member of the group, Fred Farnsworth, a retired chief of detectives from Houston who was the C.P.P.'s nuts-and-bolts cop.

"Let's plod on, gentlemen, if you don't mind," Billings said, glancing at his watch. He turned back to Kaplan. "Do you get any general feelings about his childhood? The brother had a lot to say on the subject, you'll remember."

Kaplan appeared to weigh the question for a moment.

"You can discount almost everything the brother says," he finally replied. "The one thing that came through with striking clarity was his jealousy of his sibling. The younger brother got everything the older brother had been denied, and he resented it. He still resents it. Observing Lewinter through the prism of his brother's jealousy is a risky business, at best."

"That doesn't get us very far, does it?" Billings realized that he probably should have waited for another batch of transcripts to accumulate before beginning the round-table phase of the C.P.P.

"He was obviously fucked-up," Kaplan went on, uninvited, beginning to enjoy the sound of his own voice. "Question is, how was he fucked-up?"

"What d'ya mean, how?" asked Farnsworth, the cop.

"I've got a theory about child rearing," Kaplan said, winking at Schindler to indicate he was putting Farnsworth on. "It's important to know whether his parents fucked him up spontaneously, without malice aforethought as it were, or whether they deliberately set out to fuck him up, which is the case a good part of the time in your average nouveau upper-middle-class families."

Farnsworth snapped at the bait. "What's the difference?" he asked.

"Good God, don't you know? When you're fucked-up premeditatedly, you wind up with an identifiable syndrome; you're a manic depressive or a cleptomaniac or a sexual pervert or a sadist, or something a shrink can wrap up and put into a neat little package. But when you're fucked-up spontaneously, you're eclectic; you dip into this neurosis or that psychosis. Your shrink has just about pinned one label on you when you're off and running, the shrink, textbook in hand, clamoring after you in a desperate attempt to follow your psychic footprints. Which he is never able to do. A lot of people who've been fucked-up spontaneously are mistakenly taken for geniuses. Take me. But that's another case history. Hey, get a load of this"—Kaplan was thumbing through the ad section of *The New Republic*—"'Attractive, athletic, highly intelligent black female intellectual, educated, warm, isolated, lonely, seeks dialogue with group of male intellectuals with eye toward communal living. No qualms about color.' Why don't we strike up a correspondence, sort of an indoor sport, if you know what I mean. What d'ya say, huh?"

Billings was furious. His thin, aristocratic features turned crimson—all except his lips, which, drained of color and moisture, looked like a slab of sidewalk. At that instant, he hated Kaplan and all the brainy young upstarts like him, inside and outside the department, who paid no allegiance to seniority, who showed no deference to experience, who forced those in a position of leadership to prove themselves over and over again. "Mr. Kaplan," Billings said shortly, biting off the words. "I realize, of course, you are extremely entertaining—but your brilliance is not moving the puck off center."

"But it's certainly making the time pass!" Kaplan said. Schindler and Farnsworth chuckled. Kaplan wondered if he had gone too far. After all, the money wasn't to be sneezed at. The smugness began to fade from his face.

That was it, the last straw, and Billings was on the verge of sending the wise-cracking Jew psychiatrist packing when Leo Diamond—looking casually elegant and cool, and feeling every bit as confident as he looked—strode into the room.

"Bob," Diamond said, nodding in turn at Billings and the men scattered around the room. "Gents."

"Leo," Billings said—but with a barely detectable instant of hesitation, as if he wasn't sure of his name. It was one of those little things that meant so much—the minute signal of who was to give ground.

"Well, I s'pose you haven't gotten down to brass tacks yet," Diamond offered, settling gracefully into a leather swivel chair. "I got my dupes of the interviews last night. There really isn't very much to go on, is there, until we get some more raw material in."

Kaplan sat back onto the couch and studied the ceiling. The smugness returned full force.

Billings took his eyeglasses from the stack of papers and, using both hands, his finger tips feeling for his ears, levered them onto his head. "We've been nibbling at the edges a bit, hunting for some themes and threads, as it were." Billings was damned if he'd give Kaplan the satisfaction of agreeing with Diamond.

"You're Kaplan, aren't you?" Diamond said, swiveling toward the figure on the couch. Without waiting for an answer, he plunged on. "I read your article in *Esquire* on—how do you pronounce it?—the Ki-*butz*-ing Syndrome. Absolutely brilliant. I couldn't put it down."

Kaplan beamed at the compliment. "You're pronouncing it wrong—it's Ki-*bitz*-ing Syndrome, with the emphasis on the first syllable. That's Yiddish."

Diamond tasted the word two or three times to make sure he had it right. "I want to tell you, since I read that article, I've seen the syndrome a thousand times—even in myself. It's damned difficult for a spectator to keep from intruding in the game in some subtle way, isn't it? How d'ya come across the idea?"

"Intuition, I guess. My family gets together every Wednesday evening at my mother's apartment in the Bronx for penny ante poker, dealer's choice. Have for years. Sort of an institution, if you know what I mean. Anyhow, for the last year or so, my mother has sat out—she's getting old and slows the game down. One night I noticed her flitting from one player to the next, glancing at the cards, whispering, advising, laughing, scowling, screwing up her face. It got so you wouldn't watch the player so much as my mother's face to get a line on anyone's hand. Turns out she was having more fun kibitzing than playing. After that, I began to notice the same thing everywhere I turned—it always seemed to me that people in business, in the arts, what have you, were gathered around some invisible poker table, telling the players what to do, having all the fun but taking none of the risk. There you have it, the Kibitzing Syndrome."

"Well, I'm speaking as a layman, of course, but I thought it was absolutely brilliant."

Diamond knew that he could count Kaplan as an ally now.

"Was Lewinter a"—Diamond said the word slowly and correctly—"kibitzer?"

"No question. His relationship with the radicals that his brother obliquely referred to was in the nature of kibitzer to players. You can see it, too, in . . ."

Kaplan droned on, doing in essence what he had refused to do for Billings—poke among the meager clues to pick up the threads of Lewinter's psychic life. As Billings listened, he sensed the unspoken alliance between Diamond and Kaplan, and knew he had to assert himself before Diamond completely dominated the session. God damn the Diamonds, he thought. It seemed as if his whole career had been spent jockeying for position with them. He himself had spent the war years behind a desk, committed to the colorless, thankless, work-a-day routines of espionage, laboring in an environment that nourished, and was nourished by, the notion that the side that kept the best records would inevitably emerge as the victor. Then the war ended and the field men returned, like pilgrims toward the church which sent them forth, to the desks, squirming into the pecking order ahead of those who served by sitting and filing. It wasn't fair, Billings knew, but there was nothing to be done about it except to fight them every inch of the way.

". . . gets the feeling also that the father was a doer, or player, and that this . . ."

Billings made his move. "Not all of us have had the pleasure of reading your article in *Esquire,* Mr. Kaplan. Perhaps you can say whether your syndrome sheds some light on why our subject defected—and whether he took any juicy secrets with him, which after all is the main business of this enquiry."

"Aw, come off it, will you?" said Kaplan, aware that there was little that Billings could do as long as Diamond was running the show. "You've been ball busting all morning."

At this point the game ended, for Leo Diamond did the single thing that sealed his right to dominate Bob Billings, the C.P.P., and the entire department: he came to Billings' defense. "With all respect to your professional credentials," he told Kaplan in a tone of voice that left no room for argument, "Bob Billings has been in this business a long time. What he understands is the element of time. His ball busting, as you call it, has saved a great many lives. We're dealing with a hot potato this time out. The Ruskies have taken our fine feathered Lewinter to their bosom, and we've got to find out why and we've got to find it out fast. If Bob here is overeager, it's because he understands what's at stake." Diamond looked around him and smiled. "Look," he began again afresh, "let's put these initial frictions down to overeagerness"—it wasn't lost on Kaplan that Diamond, albeit in a kindly voice, was blaming Billings—"and start over again, huh? What d'ya all say?"

Outside the French windows, a robin gripping the branch of a mangled sycamore chirped away at another who was trying to intrude on his territory. It reminded Diamond of the birds he and Sarah had seen in the Central Park Zoo the day before—their contrapuntal bird barks echoing through the tiled chambers where they lived in imposed asylum from the world of trees and spaces between trees. Suddenly clutching his arm, Sarah had said, "I detest zoos."

Diamond broke into his own thoughts. "There are a couple of items we can pin down today. The first—I noticed it the moment I read the transcript last night—is who the hell took Lewinter's papers from the Sinclair woman's apartment?"

"Since we're the only ones, so far as we know, conducting an investigation," said Billings, "one can only assume, as our investigator Wilson did, that it was one of our agents who got his signals crossed." Billings tried to put the old firmness back into his voice—and almost succeeded.

"But that's just it, Bob, are we the only ones investigating Lewinter?" Diamond asked. "After all, there is one other party who would be extremely interested in Lewinter's past."

"The Russians, huh?" Farnsworth asked, filling in the blank. I'll be damned. It's not far fetched. We had a biological warfare specialist defect two or three years ago, remember, guy name of MacComber, and there were some few of us who were convinced the old Ruskies were a-backtracking on him. Well, I'll be damned."

"At least it's a possibility," Diamond said. "Obviously, the first thing to do is find out if one of our people lifted those papers. If the answer is no, that should narrow it down to the Russians."

"God damn," said Farnsworth, who was still caught up with the idea that an honest-to-goodness Russian agent had waltzed in off the street and stolen Lewinter's papers. "Listen, I'll put a Bravo sixteen forty-two Charlie out to all city, state, and federal bureaus right off. If'n one of our people took it, we'll have a positive reply within twenty-four hours. By God, this is something."

"All right," Diamond said, and moved on to the second item. "The other thing that struck me as one that we can profitably deal with now, if you agree, Bob, is the memory business."

"What memory business is that, Leo?" Billings asked, coating his words with some of the old blandness.

"I noticed it, too—the memory," Kaplan said, ignoring Billings and speaking directly to Diamond.

But Billings was not to be denied that easily. "Of course we all noticed the memory business—it stuck out like your proverbial sore thumb. But you'll remember, I'm sure, that the brother said Lewinter had lost it in a fall when he was seven or eight years old. And this bit of evidence is entirely consistent with his standard printout, which makes no mention of a photo-memory ability, and more importantly, with the testimony of his former wife, who complained that—how did she put it—that he had no head for details, that he was always forgetting dates and, later, alimony payments. Lewinter, gentlemen, was a forgetful man. Quite obviously, his ability to retain material—which, I grant you, could be important if it were proved he had it—was certainly not remarkable."

"First off—" from Kaplan.

"To begin with—" from Diamond.

The two laughed like conspirators. The color began to drain from Billings' lips again.

Diamond waved Kaplan on. "Go ahead, what were you going to say?"

"First off, I think it's important to distinguish between one's ability to retain information or experience, and one's ability to recall what has been retained. In general, the human mind retains almost everything, or at least a great deal more than it can recall under normal stimulus; under psychiatric treatment or hypnosis, we can usually dredge up—that is, get someone to recall—a lot of fodder that was retained but buried. So what we're really interested in here is not Lewinter's ability to retain but his ability to recall. And apropos of this, a couple of things should be noted."

Kaplan could have argued the other side of the memory business as effectively, but he was out to cut the ground from under Billings. "One is that he apparently did have a photographic memory up to whenever it was he fell off the garage roof. Two is that as far as I know it is possible to lose this ability and then regain it later in life, either permanently or for short or prolonged periods of time. Three is the impressive piece of evidence which demonstrates that he in fact did regain the ability of total recall."

"If you're referring to the poem—" Billings began.

But Kaplan had up too much steam to do anything but

keep talking. "Of course, the poem. According to his girlfriend, he only read it through once. Eight months after this casual encounter with an obscure poem, when he is on the verge of deserting a girl he has promised to marry, he wants to send her a token of affection, of guilt, if you will. And so, in Japan, presumably far away from any copy of the *Kenyon Review*—"

"That remains to be seen," Billings said, but he was drowned out by Kaplan's persistent voice.

"—he dredges up the poem. I'd say that was quite a performance."

"What about the ex-wife's comment about him not having a head for details?" asked Farnsworth. "And why isn't it on his security record if'n he had a photo memory?"

"Mr. Farnsworth, people with the ability of total recall can recall anything they want to recall. But like everyone else, they have the ability of total—what shall we label it?—repression too; that is, they can bury, or fail to recall, things which they find cumbersome or tedious or a waste of time, things such as anniversaries and birthdays and"—Kaplan stressed the next item as if it were some kind of argument clincher—"alimony payments. As for the security record, you'll remember his brother's testimony—that he conveniently hid his photo memory when he was trotted out in front of the doctors. It's simple—he didn't want to be thought of as a freak. Lots of people with photo memories react the same way."

"Look, there's no question this is worth pursuing," Diamond said. "If he had a photographic memory, then he wouldn't have had to photograph anything or copy it or steal it or memorize it or even understand it to take the material with him."

"Why, naturally, all he would have to do would be to glance at it," Billings offered, taking refuge in the last haven of the defeated, sarcasm.

"Precisely," said Kaplan, coolly taking the sarcasm at face value.

"O.K., then we're agreed, I take it," Diamond said. Billings remained silent. "Let's cue in on the poem. I, for one, accept his girlfriend's intuition—that he would have spilled the beans if he had memorized the poem before his trip to Japan. But could he have stumbled across a copy of the *Kenyon Review* in Japan? And let's pin down the medical facts about losing and regaining photo memory, huh? I think we may be on to something."

9

Comprehensive Personality Profile 327

Subject: Lewinter, A. J.

Director: Billings, Robert

Staff: Kaplan, Dr. Jerome S. Farnsworth,

              Frederick F. Schindler, Prof. Erich T.

Enclosures: Transcripts of field interviews conducted:

              15–17 August

TOP SECRET

Unedited transcript of telephone conversation between Agent A. Bodkin and Professor Whitman Finch, Chairman of Department of Literature at Kenyon College, Gambier, Ohio.

15 August. Subject has no known connection with Lewinter.

FINCH: It's not a very good poem, actually. You understand that these things are supremely subjective. What I mean by that is that someone may reasonably take a poem such as this on its own terms and actually like it. That is, it may *say* something— I believe that's how my students would put it—the poem would *say* something to them. But I dare say, I should think that the vast majority of experienced critics who are prepared to comment judgmentally would quite agree that the poem is eminently mediocre. The form is entirely derivative. There is very little originality in it. The theme is hideously confused. First the poet talks about the psychic relationship between man and sexual congress. Then he appears to meander into a treatment of cyber-netics. There is a distinct separation—and it would appear to be inadvertent, which is to say unartistic—between the form on the one hand and the content on the other. The cadence shows some small promise. But, on the whole, I would have to say, yes, it is quite, I would have to say it is quite undistinguished.

BODKIN: I don't want you to think I'm not interested in this, Professor, but what I'm really trying to find out is, has the poem ever been reprinted outside of this particular issue of the *Kenyon Review.*

FINCH: Oh, my good heavens, no. Why would anyone want to do that?

Unedited transcript of Top Secret cable from Richard Mathews

Harding, cultural attaché in the American Embassy, Tokyo. Received and decoded morning of 15 August. Subject has no known connection with Lewinter.

> EXHARDING REUR 121352Z
> THIS HAS TO BE STRANGEST REQUEST WE EVER FIELDED STOP CHECKED ALL LIBRARIES WITHIN HUNDRED MILES OF TOKYO AND FOUND ONLY ONE DASH UNIVERSITY OF KYOTO DASH THAT STOCKS BACK ISSUES OF KENYON REVIEW STOP KYOTO REPORTS THAT SEPTEMBER NINETEEN SIXTY FOUR ISSUE MISSING BUT CANT REPEAT CANT SAY WHEN IT WAS TAKEN STOP INFORMATIVELY FACT THAT IT MISSING NOT EXTRAORDINARY AS LIBRARIAN REPORTS THAT HUNDREDS OF BACK ISSUES OF ENGLISH MAGAZINES BEEN TAKEN FROM STACKS BY LAZY READERS STOP NATURALLY IMPOSSIBLE TO CHECK PRIVATE COLLECTIONS DEFINITIVELY BUT ASKED AROUND EXTENSIVELY AND UNABLE LOCATE ANYONE WITH BACK ISSUES OF KENYON REVIEW STOP TRUST THIS FILLS THE BILL
>
> =HARDING

Edited transcript of interview between Agent R. Grotten and Dr. Louis Krimenger, Director of the Krimenger Clinic for Psychiatric Disorders. 16 August. Subject has no known connection with Lewinter.

KRIMENGER: (cough) You smoke? I know they're poison but

I can't give them up. (cough) Now, where were we. Oh, yes, the answer to your question is simple. It is extremely rare—but it is certainly possible. (cough) There was a famous case in 1934— a woman name of Evers or Evans or something of the sort lost and regained her photographic memory. Well-documented, as I recall. Say, listen, if you have another one, I'd be glad to check it out for you without a fee. It'd make a hell of a paper.

Edited transcript of interview between Agent F. Luftwell and Dr. Gerhard Grueneberg, Chief of Psychiatry Service at Bellevue Hospital and Director of the Freud Archives in Washington. 16 August. Subject has no known connection with Lewinter.

GRUENEBERG: I suppose it's always possible. I'd be a fool to say it wasn't. But I've never heard of a single instance of anyone regaining a photographic memory.

LUFTWELL: I understand there was a case in 1934—

GRUENEBERG: Ah, yes, that's the one case everyone cites. The Evak woman. A complete hoax. She worked in a circus demonstrating her powers of total recall. The business about her losing and regaining her photographic memory—she used to pull that all the time to get publicity. In 1934, some poor doctor took her seriously . . .

Edited transcript of interview between Agent S. Eckart and Congressman Fred Walters at his New York City office. 16 August. Subject was reported to have interviewed Lewinter concerning the latter's proposals to establish a national solid-waste-disposal corporation.

WALTERS: I'm glad to cooperate with you fellows whenever I can. I was in Army Intelligence during the war, you know. Now frankly, I just don't remember that name. I vaguely recall someone bugging me a few months back—ha-ha, I don't mean that literally—with some harebrained scheme to pump glass and iron and steel waste through pipes to regional centers for recycling. But it was purely pie in the sky. Listen, if it's important, I could have my people check the files for you.

Note: A subsequent check of the files turned up a mimeographed report bearing Lewinter's name and proposing the establishment of a national solid-waste-disposal corporation. The report is marked Exhibit 17 Charlie, *and bears my initials on the upper right hand corner of the title page and the fourteen pages that follow it.*

Edited transcript of interview between Agent A. Bodkin and Thomas A. Osborne, Branch Director of the Consol-O-Debt office in Boston. 17 August. Subject was reported to have interviewed Lewinter concerning the latter's application to borrow money.

OSBORNE: You understand, we usually don't reveal information about our clients. We like people to feel that they can confide in us as they would a priest or minister.

BODKIN: I can appreciate that, Mr. Osborne, and it is nice of you to waive the rule for us. We appreciate it. Your government appreciates it.

OSBORNE: Yes, well, I have his application right here. I got it out when you phoned. Here it is here, see? Initial A, initial J. Lewinter, capital L, small W.

BODKIN: Yes, that's the one.

OSBORNE: Yes, well, this is a classic case of a guy who makes decent salary—eh, question 12, ah here, $17,500 a year—yes, quite a decent salary and doesn't know how to handle it. That is, he doesn't know how to handle money. We do a good deal of business with this sort of customer, giving them one loan to consolidate their debts. I'll tell you something, Mr. Bodkin, it makes this job satisfying, helping people out of financial difficulties. You know, we're not your average shylock moneylender. We're a business with a heart.

BODKIN: How much of a loan did you give Lewinter?

OSBORNE: Yes, well, in the end we decided not to take him in as a customer.

BODKIN: You didn't lend him money?

OSBRNE: No, we didn't. Actually, the reason isn't on the application. But there was something about the guy, I remember there was something about him that set off alarm bells in my head. We have to rely on our intuition a lot in this business, Mr. Bodkin. And my intuition said: Watch out, this guy is an unstable character. May I ask why you're asking bout him? Has he reneged on a loan? I'll bet my last dollar he has reneged on a loan.

Unedited transcript of interview between Agent A. Bodkin and James George Styron, Associate Professor of Chemistry at Boston University, Charter Member of PEACE (Professors Eager about Changing the Earth). 17 August. Subject knew Lewinter while the latter was associated with PEACE.

STYRON: So Mr. Bidkin or Bodkin or whatever your name is, you've finally cornered me.

BODKIN: Bodkin, my name is Bodkin. I gathered you were reluctant to see me.

STYRON: Of course I'm reluctant. Though I must admit I've been expecting this. You don't mind, do you, if I put on my tape recorder too. How the hell do you get this damn cassette in?

BODKIN: Twist it around. That's it.

STYRON: Well, let me guess why you're here. You think that our PEACE is some sort of Communist plot to take over greater Boston and subvert the youngsters and put LSD into the city's water system. Have I got it right? Your masters just don't understand radicals like myself who are committed to working within the system to change the system.

BODKIN: Mr. Styron—

STYRON: Professor, if you don't mind. Don't get the wrong impression from the name of our group. I'll admit that PEACE is about as corny as they come; I was personally in favor of something less catchy but also less corny. You know, maybe it's a good thing you cornered me. Perhaps you'll go away with some understanding of our humanist roots, and the delicate chemistry that turns a humanist into an activist. Are you familiar with the humanist tradition, Mr. Bidkin?

BODKIN: It's Bodkin, Professor Styron. B as in bravo, O as in Oscar, D as in diamond, K as in king, I as in India, N as in November. Bodkin.

STYRON: You're pretty sensitive about your name, aren't you?

BODKIN: Professor, I don't know what your secretary told you, but I haven't come here to talk about PEACE, not directly anyway. I'm trying to find out about one of your group's former members, Professor Lewinter from M.I.T.

STYRON: Lewinter?

BODKIN: Initial A initial J Lewinter. Did you know him very well?

STYRON: Well, that is a helluva thing, you coming all this way to ask about Lewinter. Know him? Nobody knew him. He never really joined our group. He sat in on four or five sessions, and we were glad to have him because we welcome participation on the part of our scientific colleagues over at M.I.T.

BODKIN: Was there anything unusual about him? Was he outspoken?

STYRON: Well, that's the funny part. He never said a single solitary word until the last time. We were discussing starting a chain letter in scientific circles. As usual I took the activist position, I'm not ashamed to tell you. If we could deluge the White House with 100,000 or even half a million letters signed not by the average slob in the street but by the scientific elite, he'd have to sit up and pay attention. Anyhow, Lewinter got all agitated about the idea—

BODKIN: Agitated how?

STYRON: He just started waving his arms over his head and calling us elitists. He left me with the impression that he had more radical things in mind than we were willing to entertain. He never showed up again after that night, and I must say I'm not sorry about that. It's difficult enough to get something concrete done without people like him around.

BODKIN: Did you hear anything more about him after that?

STYRON: It's only rumor, of course, but someone told me that Lewinter had taken up with the MDLers crowd at Harvard. Now those are the people you fellows should really be after, not us.

Edited transcript of interview between Agent G. Brandt and Nancy Mitgang, currently being held in lieu of $50,000 bail in Charles Street Jail awaiting trial on charges of possession of explosives. 17 August. Subject was member of Militant Democratic League during period that Lewinter was reported to have been associated with group.

MITGANG: Up yours. Those are the last two words you're going to get out of me. If you think I'll tell you any more about Hank than I told the rest of them, you're full of crap. So stop sucking around me. Fuck off.

BRANDT: I didn't come here to talk about you or Hank or the MDL.

MITGANG: What then? The theology of William Blake? The sexual imagery in the metaphysical poets? What then?

BRANDT: Lewinter. A. J. Lewinter. Do you remember him?

MITGANG: (prolonged laughter) Lewint . . . (more laughter). You have to be . . (more laughter).

BRANDT: May I ask why you're laughing?

MITOANG: Lewinter. It's so incongruous, a fuck face like you asking about a creep like him. Jesus shit, what did he do? Put a six-cent stamp on an eight-cent envelope? (More laughter)

BRANDT: I thought—

MITGANG: (Laughter)

BRANDT: I thought—

MITGANG: You thought what? You thought you would come sucking around me and get information. Well, there is no information. There's nothing to tell. Lewinter was never really involved in the movement. He was on the fringes for a while, that's all. You're sucking up the wrong tree. He was so uptight he would have scared a shrink half to death just stretching out on a couch. Someone brought him along on one of our sensitivity-training sessions down on the Vineyard once and he almost jumped out of his skin when we all went swimming in the raw. One of the girls went to ball him later and said he wouldn't even take his clothes off till she turned the fucking light off. Funny part was she said he wasn't half bad once he got going. You never know, do you? I'll bet you ball with the lights off too!

BRANDT: Did you ever see him again after the session on the Cape?

MITGANG: He hung around a while I guess. But he never got involved in anything.

BRANDT: How come?

MITGANG: How come what?

BRANDT: How come he hung around a while? How come you let him if he was such a square?

MITGANG: I guess it was Hank. He thought Lewinter had great potential. Can't pick them right all the time, can you?

10

HUNCHED LOW, knees flexed, left hand extended fingers first like an antenna, right hand retracted and wrapped loosely around the pistol-grip knife handle, Harry Dukess sucked air into his lungs in wheezing gasps. All the while his instincts and fingers probed, like the point of a spiraling rapier, for the opening that would allow him to kill his opponent. But Dukess was form without content; a shopworn spring that coiled without tension and uncoiled without temper. When the opening came, Dukess lunged clumsily toward it. The younger man deflected the thrust with a whiplash flick of his wrist and arced in and up with his knife arm to stab the older man under the armpit.

"Fuck," said Dukess as the rubber blade bent against his skin. And then, between gasps for breath, he said: "Once more."

The trouble, Dukess consoled himself, was not so much the body as the mind; confronted with Van Avery's clean-cut, upwardly mobile face, it didn't believe there was any real danger here. This time, Dukess thought, he would supply the danger from his own storehouse of memories; he would substitute someone else for Van Avery, the way a man sometimes makes love to one woman but thinks of another. He hunched down again and tried to recall what the face of the Shiptar had looked like just before he killed him. Except for the mustache, be couldn't remember the features, only the chilling sense of menace. He tried to summom the menace, but all he got was a detached glimpse of the moment, not its texture. No matter how hard or how often he tried, Dukess couldn't recapture the curious admixture of fear and exhilaration that had surged through him the few times in his life he had had to fight for his life.

Van Avery grunted, faked a kick, then feinted toward Dukess' eyes with his left hand. Dukess' knife arm came up to block the blow that never came. He started to lower it again when Van Avery's rubber blade slashed down, leaving a red welt across the thick blue veins of Dukess' wrist.

"The first ten minutes," Dukess said. He was breathing easier now, stretched out alongside Van Avery on the wrestling mat that filled one corner of the attic. "If it ever comes to it again, I'll have to take 'em in the first ten minutes. I run down too fast after that."

It was a professional discussion, and Van Avery made a professional criticism. "I don't think so, Harry. If you're up against a pro, he'd figure you for ten minutes and hang back till you had nothing left. Anyone with training would do that. Know what I'd do?"

"What would you do?" Youth, Dukess thought cynically, was faster—but not smarter. But then, given its speed, it didn't have to be.

"Assuming the guy doesn't know who you really are, your best bet is to play possum. Stand flatfooted, throw your fists up kind of thing, come on like a stumblebum. Then zap him, *swoosh*"—Van Avery drew his forefinger across his throat in a slicing motion—"before he knows he's dealing with a pro."

"Couple of things wrong with that," Harry Dukess said. He tightened his stomach muscles and looked down the length of his body and saw that his middle still bulged. "Why's the guy trying to kill me if he doesn't know who I am, tell me that, huh? If he's out to kill me, chances are he knows my name, rank, serial number— and age. Me, I'd put everything I had into the first ten minutes."

"And if that didn't work?"

"If that didn't work, I guess I'd give up." Dukess felt depleted by the workout with Van Avery in his attic, by the prospect of giving up. "Funny how it creeps up on you. One day you're doing two, two and a half, maybe even three hours of hand-to-hand with Curley at the shop. Then before you know it you can't go half an hour without feeling as if your lungs are bursting." Dukess sat up, peeled off the shirt of his gray sweat suit and leaned back against the wall. "Let's finish off these gin and tonics, what d'ya say, Fred, then we'll shower and light up the charcoal. Glad you could bring the family over today. Got some London broils that are going to make your mouth water." From somewhere outside came the shrill squeals of children wrestling in the grass. "Knock off the rough housing before someone gets hurt," Dukess yelled toward the open attic window. The squeals subsided. Dukess turned back to Van Avery. "Damn kids never grow up, do they?"

But Dukess was still chasing his youth. He held up his right hand, palm out, studied it—a big hand grown pudgy. "I killed three men with this hand"—Dukess was speaking quietly now—"two with a knife, and one I held under water until the bubbles stopped coming. Any one of them would have done the same to me. Funny to be sitting here in an attic getting ready for a Sunday barbecue and remembering that. Funny."

"I never killed anyone personally—came in too late for that kind of thing," Van Avery said. There was a suggestion of regret in his voice.

"You could, you know. You're cool enough and quick enough and detached enough. I'm sure you could if you had to."

"Thanks for saying that, Harry. But they say you never know till you do it."

"Well, those days are gone forever. Nobody fights to the finish anymore. We live in an era of pulled punches."

"Har-ry!" Dukess' wife, trying to mask her annoyance behind a bantering singsong delivery, called up through the floorboards. "It's half-past five and the charcoal takes a good half-hour. Har-ry, you hear me?"

Dukess cupped his hands. "Right down, Clara," he yelled. But he didn't move a muscle.

Van Avery stood up and began doing Tai Chi Chuan exercises he had picked up from a Nationalist Chinese agent during a Saigon tour. It was a graceful posing performance, a kind of manual of Karatelike blows delivered in agonizingly slow motion. "How . . . things . . . go . . . in . . . Bangkok . . . Harry . . . huh?" he asked, spacing the words so that they punctuated the motions.

"No sweat," Dukess answered. "Like I said, just another fuck-up that nobody'll ever hear about—I hope. Bangkok Control put a 'terminate with prejudice' out on a local fellow who had a couple of friends too many."

"Did . . . you . . . terminate . . . the . . . friends . . . too?"

"One we bought, one we terminated." Dukess watched Van Avery pivot on his heel and punch his fist straight out from his shoulder like a slow-moving piston. "D'ya line up a professor for the trip to China, Fred?"

Van Avery sank back to the mat. "Would you believe we went from A to Z in the file and all we came up with was an art history guy at Berkeley who said he'd think about it? We'll find someone, but we may have to pay more than we bargained for."

"Shit," Dukess said. "I remember the days when they used to come sucking around for assignments. We weren't pariahs then. It was easy to get favors done—you arranged to get a book or an article published, maybe you even lined up a job at a university for them. Times are really changing. It's not only the academic types. When's the last time we took on a first-class agent, huh? The bright young people aren't going into intelligence work anymore. There's too much money to be had elsewhere."

"I don't think it's that so much, Harry. It's that our sort of work is too collective for all those individualists the colleges turn out these days. They don't know what a team effort is."

"All I know is that they expect me to pull off big coups with second-rate people—present company excluded, Fred. Shit, I shouldn't have to be reading the daily summary of Soviet press. I have better things to do with my time. We just don't get sharp people anymore. I remember when you first came around for a job. Why, you practically knocked the door down, you were so anxious. You didn't bitch if you had to work late a couple of nights or pass up a vacation."

Dukess shook his head. "It's the academic types who really piss me off, though. They sail with the wind, whichever way it's blowing. I'll bet you couldn't get to anyone on Diamond's C.P.P. either, could you?"

Van Avery sank to the floor in a cross-legged position, his back ramrod straight, and began doing isometric exercises with his clasped hands. "I got somebody—but don't ask me how much it cost."

"More than twenty-five hundred?"

"An even three grand."

Dukess whistled. "You could have bugged the whole god damn townhouse for that kind of money. Who'd you get?"

"Schindler, the physicist. Remember he did a favor for us

four years ago during one of those Pugwash symposiums in Belgrade?"

"Couldn't you use that to get him to work for nothing? Threaten to leak it to the papers—"

"I started to, but he's a smart old bastard. Said if anyone went to the papers, it'd be him and we'd never get an academic type to work for us again. The last thing we want is another flap with an academic type, so I paid up."

"And?"

"And what?" Van Avery asked.

"What's happening at the C.P.P.?"

"Oh that. It's really weird, Harry."

"How, weird? Aren't the vacuum cleaners coming up with any information?"

"They've got plenty of information, all right—but so far nobody knows what to make of it. Seems like Lewinter was in debt up to his elbows. Courts are after him for back alimony."

"So he skipped to avoid debts, huh?"

"There's more to it. He's been gravitating toward some of those radical groups in the Boston area—first the PEACE people—"

"We have a file on them, don't we?" Dukess clasped his hands the way Van Avery did and strained to pull them apart.

"Local FBI's got an agent on their executive committee. Don't strain so hard, Harry, just keep up a steady pressure; that's it. Lewinter was also in with the MDLers, but it's not clear how deep. Then there's the nutty garbage business."

"The garbage business?"

"Seems like Lewinter's been pushing a scheme for a multi-billion-dollar federal solid-waste-disposal program. Even took it to someone up on the Hill. Apparently the scheme meant a lot to Lewinter, and—here comes the good part—his brother, who comes across pretty levelheaded, says that Lewinter thought Russia might be receptive to the scheme."

"That would really take the cake—defecting to give the Reds a garbage-collection program!"

"There's still more. And this is the part that confuses me. Turns out Lewinter had a photographic memory which he was supposed to have lost when he was eight or so. Then just before he defected, on the same day, he mailed a postcard to his girl-friend quoting a poem in it."

"So he's an egghead," Dukess said. "What's so unusual about that?"

"Apparently he only saw the poem once in his life and that was eight months before. And he was still able to repeat it."

"Which brings us back to the photo memory, huh? Maybe he found the poem in Japan—they got libraries there, you know."

"No. The C.P.P. checked. The cultural attaché in Tokyo says there was no copy of the poem around town. Just to con-fuse the issue more, the C.P.P. got statements from doctors about photo memories. One said you can regain it, the other said you can't."

"What'd the C.P.P. do with all this?"

"That's just it. Billings, who's supposed to be running the show, is obviously out to make the best case—that Lewinter skipped because of debts or something like that, and didn't take anything with him. It's easy to see why Billings takes this line. He identifies with his department and doesn't want any black marks against it. And he doesn't want to risk losing the MIRV security portfolio to us or another agency, which they might if it turned out that Lewinter was a serious MIRV leak. I can read it O.K. up to here. But along comes Diamond—he's been sitting in on most of the C.P.P. sessions, and according to our three-thousand-dollar source, he just about runs the show. And he apparently is out to make the worst case stick. It was Diamond, for instance, who pushed the whole business about the photo memory and is hot to trot about Lewinter's radical affiliations. And the shrink in the group is supporting Diamond right down the line for no better reason, at least this is what our physicist says, than he seems to hate Billings' guts."

"A can of worms, huh?" Dukess said.

Van Avery was genuinely puzzled. "I understand Billings wanting to make a best case, but why is Diamond pushing the worst case? You know him, Harry. Maybe you can figure it?"

His head back against the attic wall, Dukess thought about the question for a while. Suddenly he stood up and motioned Van Avery to follow him. "Want to show you something." The other corner of the attic, near the staircase, housed Dukess' work space. It included a small wooden table, a bookcase packed with Foreign Service journals, a desk lamp, and a small office safe. Dukess spun the combination lock, opened the safe, and took out a scrapbook with clippings and photographs. He put it on the desk and began thumbing through the pages. "See this, this is Diamond and me taking parachute training in England. This one here, it's Diamond and Viktor—remember I told you about Viktor, the one who died in Czechoslovakia?—in occupied France. Here's one of the three of us on the Croisette in Cannes."

"That a German soldier in the background?"

"Yeah. I ran Diamond from London for a while, and then I joined him in the Alpes Maritimes. That was taken just before the Germans broke our ring. Here's one taken just after the war—Viktor, Diamond, and me again. I don't even remember where it was—we were just bumming around at the time."

Dukess looked at the now brittle photographs with eyes that were at once hard with anger and moist with nostalgia. "You understand now, Fred."

"Maybe I'm just thick, Harry, but you'll have to spell it out."

"Diamond's concocting the worst case because he's like me. Both of us long for the good old days when we could go without sleep for forty-eight hours and not feel it, when we could run on nervous energy and pep pills for a week, when we were in the thick of the action, when we invented gambits and played them out on sheer nerve. I've still got some of this at the Agency—but Diamond was farmed out after the Cernú affair. The Lewinter business is giving him a new lease on his old life.

Mark my words, Fred, he's not only concocting the worst case. Oh no, it won't end there. That son of a bitch is going to try to turn this into an operation. He's going to come up with another Cernú."

Later, much later, after gin and tonics and London broils, as Van Avery was rounding up the family to leave, he took Dukess by the arm and pulled him aside onto the screened-in porch.

"You boys always talk shop," one of the wives complained. "What's so interesting about shop?"

"I forgot one thing," Van Avery said quickly. "While you were away, I had one of our people pick up some of Lewinter's papers. Thought we'd take a look-see ourselves. Anyway, Diamond's on to the fact that somebody took them—but he thinks that maybe the Ruskies are running a parallel backgrounder. He put out a Bravo sixteen forty-two Charlie tracer on it. What do you think, Harry, should we 'fess up?"

Dukess considered the problem. "I'd hate to give Diamond a chance to accuse us of meddling—let's hold off on it for a while and see how this thing plays out, huh?"

11

Comprehensive Personality Profile 327

Subject: Lewinter, A. J.

Director: Billings, Robert

Staff: Kaplan, Dr. Jerome S.Farnsworth,

              Frederick F. Schindler, Prof. Erich T.

Enclosures: Transcripts of field interviews conducted:

              19 August

Edited transcript of conversation between Agent A. Bodkin and Doctor Simon Kastner, Ballistic Nose Cone Research and Development Section Chief. 19 August. Subject was Lewinter's superior at M.I.T.

KASTNER: I assume you're here because of Lewinter. He's missing, isn't he? Un-huh, I thought so. I knew something was up. No Lewinter, no letter, no telegram, no word, no nothing. Did he skip?

BODKIN: I'm afraid that's not my end of it, Doctor Kastner. You probably know as much as I do.

KASTNER: Yes, of course, I understand. You fellows are pretty close mouthed about this sort of thing. O.K., what can I tell you?

BODKIN: Well, first off, you can tell me what kind of work he did for you and how well he did it.

KASTNER: You want specifics or generalizations? The specifics are rather technical.

BODKIN: I'll settle for generalities.

KASTNER: Smart man. Wish I could. O.K. Lewinter was— should I use the past tense or the present tense?—is, was, a specialist in ceramic engineering, and an extremely competent fellow, naturally, or he wouldn't be here in the first place. His specific area is ballistic nose cones, which involve the discipline of ceramics. He is—was—part of a team which is trying to develop a ceramic material that can absorb rather than reflect electronic transmissions. What we're looking for is something that is porous electronically. Needless to say, the first country to come up with such a material will have an enormous advantage. It will mean that the nose cones will be undetectable by enemy radars. The radar pulses won't bounce off the nose cones. In layman's terms, it means you get no echo, no pip, on the radar screen. And hell, if the Ruskies can't find them and track them, they can't shoot the nose cones down. You follow me so far?

BODKIN: I think so. Have you come up with anything yet?

KASTNER: Wish to hell we had. No, I'm afraid that a quote porous unquote nose cone is still a consummation devoutly to be wished, so to speak. The most promising materials don't come anywhere near withstanding the heat of reentry. We've almost used up our initial budget—some $17 million—and the only concrete thing we've come up with so far is a material that can distort the doppler effect of an incoming cone about 7 percent, which isn't worth a damn because the other side doesn't rely on doppler for anything more than a fast confirmation of which way the missile is headed.

BODKIN: So Lewinter had no secrets in his own field to give away then.

KASTNER: I see we're down to the nitty-gritty, huh? That's correct. He had nothing to give away except perhaps the formulas we've tried and discarded.

BODKIN: That could be something, couldn't it? Help them narrow the field, kind of thing?

KASTNER: Theoretically, you're right. But, in practice, they'd have' to cover the same ground themselves—if they haven't done so already—to make sure we didn't goof. No, Mr. Bodkin, if I were offered a Russian Lewinter I'd say thanks but no thanks.

BODKIN: Was that all Lewinter worked on, porous-nose-cone development?

KASTNER: On my time, yes. A few months ago, just after he finished a three-month course in astrophysics, he worked up a series of MIRV trajectories, the kind of thing that had the decoys tracking like the real thing and the payload tracking like a decoy. I passed them on to the trajectory section.

BODIUN: What happened to the trajectories?

KASTNER: They turned them down. Amateurish, they said. Strictly amateur stuff.

BODKIN: Anything else? Did he work on anything else?

KASTNER: Ha. Ha. Ha. Just his garbage hobby. You fellows know about that?

BODKIN: Solid-waste-disposal project, right?

KASTNER: That's it. Strictly extracurricular. And nonconfidential.

BODKIN: How about access? Could he have had access to any material outside his own special area?

KASTNER: We run an airtight shop, securitywise, Mr. Bodkin. It would have been impossible for him to see anything, anything at all, outside his own lab. And, as I told you, his lab has so far scored a big fat zero.

BODKIN: If he had seen some classified material, how would he have gained access?

KASTNER: As I say, it's impossible.

BODKIN: But hypothetically?

KASTNER: Well, hypothetically, he would have had to apply for the material in the documentation stacks in the vault downstairs. He would have had to have a signed "right-of-access" check to draw any particular folder. Which he didn't have except for Category 7 stuff—that's ceramic-nose-cone data.

BODKIN: And if he had managed to draw material from the stacks, what then? Could he photograph it or copy it?

KASTNER: Again, impossible. I told you we run a tight shop. He would have had to take it to the reading room off the stacks, where he would have been under constant surveillance by one of the reading room guards. Anything he copied down would be noted in the log and reported to the security section, which would have asked me why he was copying something down.

BODKIN: I see. You don't mind if I take a look at the stacks and the reading room for myself, do you?

KASTNER: Help yourself, Mr. Bodkin. But you're wasting your time. We run an airtight shop. Hell, when you come right down to it, the only thing Lewinter had to offer anyone were those amateurish trajectories of his and some garbage-disposal nonsense. Hardly enough to put him across a border, huh?

Edited transcript of conversation between Agent A. Bodkin and P. J. Noble, Documentation Stacks Librarian for Ballistic Missile Research and Development at M.I.T. 19 August. Subject has no known connection with Lewinter.

BODKIN: I'm not sure I understand. I thought you were the permanent stacks librarian.

NOBLE: But I am, you see. I was moved up from Permanent

Assistant Documentation Stacks Librarian after the accident—

BODKIN: The accident?

NOBLE: Our Mr. Marmsbury. He was very near-sighted, you know. One of life's little twists and turns, *n'est-ce pas?* We'd been chatting about vacation, he and I. Poor Mr. Marmsbury was a widower, you know, and he planned to take one of those swinging singles cruises. To the Caribbean. Not ten minutes after we parted, he lay dead under the wheels of a truck. Can you imagine, not ten minutes.

BODKIN: How long ago was this?

NOBLE: Now let me see, today's the nineteenth, isn't it? Nineteen, eighteen, seventeen, sixteen, fifteen, fourteen, thirteen, twelve, eleven, ten, nine, eight, seven, six. It was the sixth, just two weeks ago tomorrow.

BODKIN: So you've only been librarian for two weeks, then?

NOBLE: Permanent Documentation Stacks Librarian, we call it. That's correct. Of course, I was Assistant Documentation Stacks Librarian for fourteen years before, so I know my way around here. I'm not what you'd call a babe in the stacks.

BODKIN: Tell me, Mr. Noble, do you remember one of the staffers here named Lewinter, initial A initial J Lewinter?

NOBLE: Oh, I'm afraid I didn't have much contact with the staffers, that is until two weeks ago. You see, the Permanent Assistant Documentation Stacks Librarian, which is what I was, spends all his time in the stacks filing, so he doesn't get to see many of those bright faces. And I'm afraid I don't remember a Lewinter visiting us during the last two weeks.

BODKIN: Un-huh. Let me try a different tack. Was your pred-
ecessor, Mr. Marmsbury, a careful man?

NOBLE: He was Mr. Meticulous. I admired him for it, really.
He was a librarian's librarian, Mr. Bodkin. That could stand as
his epitaph. Here lies a librarian's librarian.

BODKIN: A librarian's librarian.

NOBLE: Absolutely. In all the years I knew him, he slipped up
only once. Do you know anyone who has only made one teeny
mistake in fourteen years of exacting service, Mr. Bodkin?

BODKIN: I'm afraid not. No, that's quite a record. By the way,
what was that slip-up?

NOBLE: Oh that. Just one of those silly errors that reminds us
we're all human. One of the staffers came down a month or two
ago with a handful of trajectory formulas and asked to see the
trajectory folder to make some comparisons. If he hadn't had
his own trajectory formulas in his hand, I'm positive Mr.
Marmsbury would never have given them to him. But it threw
him off his guard, I mean having his own trajectory formulas in
his hand like that. And it was only a matter of minutes.

BODKIN: Minutes?

NOBLE: Yes, minutes, before Mr. Marmsbury determined that
the staffer didn't have a right-of-access check. I'm sure he
never even got the folder open in the reading room. Can you
imagine the nerve, walking in here with a Category 7 clearance
and asking for trajectory material?

BODKIN: Hell of a nerve. Did Mr. Marmsbury report the incident?

NOBLE: He noted it in the log, of course. He was meticulous

in these matters. But since he retrieved the folder before the interloper could read it, I don't think, no, I don't think he made what you call a federal case out of it. Ha, that's a good phrase, don't you think? A federal case!

BODKIN: Quite a good phrase, Mr. Noble.

Edited telephone conversation between Agent A. Bodkin and Lieutenant Merton Frank of the Boston Police Department. 19 August. Subject has no known connection with Lewinter.

FRANK: Marmsbury, Arthur, initial R, Caucasian male, age 62, height 5 foot 7½ inches, weight 155, eyes brown, hair gray, that the one?

BODKIN: That's it, Lieutenant.

FRANK: Right. It was a hit-and-run, all right.

BODKIN: Did you catch the guy?

FRANK: No, we didn't. I remember this one. Strange. He was hit by a small van with a logo stenciled on both sides in bright yellow letters. Half a dozen people identified the logo. It was so clear nobody bothered with the license plates. Fairfax Dairies. That's what the logo said. Fairfax Dairies.

BODKIN: What was so strange?

FRANK: There is no Fairfax Dairies, not in Boston, not in Massachusetts, not anywhere on the eastern seaboard as far as we can determine.

Edited transcript of conversation between Agent A. Bodkin and

Louis Mendelini, Reading Room Security Officer. 19 August. Subject on various occasions kept Lewinter under normal surveillance in the reading room.

BODKIN: When did you retire?

MENDELINI: A year ago September. Thirty years on the force. With all those long-hairs and perverts and drugs, I'm not sorry to be out. I put in my time.

BODKIN: This is quite a change of pace.

MENDELINI: It drags, sure. But at least the people here are gentlemen. Oh, I get bored stiff. But it's a good way to stretch the pension check, you know what I mean.

BODKIN: I'll probably wind up the same way. Listen, give me a rundown on how you operate, will ya?

MENDELINI: Sure, it's simple. When a guy draws anything from the stack, he can only come into the reading room. Chuck—that's the officer on the door—Chuck checks their badge and I.D. and the label on the folder and reads them to me on the intercom system, this thing right here. Then I copy what he says into this running log, with the time in and the time out, like here, see, this one here. Then I just sit and watch what they're doing through this window. It's a mirror on the other side, what they call a one-way window. We used to have a regular window, but all those eggheads got nervous about someone watching them, so they put in this one-way window. Funny thing is they all know it's there, all right—some of the old-timers even wave at the mirror when they walk in—but you should see what some of them do.

BODKIN: What, for instance?

MENDELINI: Like pick their noses, or scratch their ass. One of these days I expect someone to jerk off. And I'll log it. Arrived such-and-such a time, jerked off, departed such-and-such a time. Ha!

BODKIN: Listen, do you remember a guy named Lewinter, 39, medium height, balding, paunch?

MENDELINI: I really don't remember these guys by name. It's not my job to. But it'll be in the log here. Lewinter, huh?

BODKIN: Initial A, initial J, last name is Lewinter with a capital L small W.

MENDELINI: See, I've got them indexed alphabetically, and next to the names the pages of their visits. I invented this system myself.

BODKIN: Can I see his last visit.

MENDELINI: Last visit coming up. Page 245. Here, 44, here it is, 45. Ah, here, Lewinter, see. He comes in here at 1535 with a folder marked *Payload Trajectories,* whatever that means.

BODKIN: What's *rused* mean?

MENDELINI: It's my own shorthand for "perused." Means he just sort of thumbed through the stuff, as opposed to *trate* which is short for "concentrated study" and means that they really got involved in the stuff. Now, see here, at 1542, which is seven minutes later, Marmsbury came into the room and grabbed the folder back.

BODKIN: Marmsbury came into the room and grabbed the folder back! Do you remember the incident?

MENDELINI: Jesus Christ, no. Marmsbury was always bursting in and grabbing folders. He was very near-sighted, you know. They said you could draw the formula for the atomic bomb if you flashed a PTA card in his face. It's none of my business, you know. I only work here. But it's a hell of a way to run a security stack, isn't it?

BODKIN: I guess it is.

12

LEO DIAMOND WASN'T STARTING a new life; like an engine coupling with a boxcar on a siding, he was picking up an old one where it had been left off. And the first order of business, so it seemed to him, was to divest himself of the dead weight he had carried around through the interregnum—the habit of doing things by habit, the indifference with which he sugar-coated his perceptions to make them palatable, above all the clock that ticked away in his brain to remind him, the few times he glanced over his shoulder, that midway through the journey of a life was too late to search for old sidings.

The clock was no longer ticking when he and Sarah boarded the shuttle for New York two days before the start of the C.P.P. In the cool half-light of a Washington twilight, with the remote city backing and pivoting away from the airplane, picking up where you had left off seemed a perfectly reasonable thing to do.

". . . feels like to be a member of an oppressed minority," Sarah was saying. The smoking light blinked on. Searching through a khaki fisherman's sack crammed with one of everything, she produced a cigarette and lit it.

"And what oppressed minority are you a member of?" Diamond asked banteringly.

"Why, the left-handed minority, of course," Sarah said. "Your security people didn't tell you I was left-handed, did they? We're the most discriminated against group in the world, we lefties. Everything is made for righties—guitars, can openers, gear shifts, rifle bolts, cameras, you name it. We're outcasts, Leo. D'ya know that a left-handed oath is one you don't have to keep, huh? That the evil eye is the left eye, d'ya know that? When the French say someone is *gauche,* they mean he's awkward. When the Italians call someone *mancino,* they mean he's deceitful. Even the Russians are against us—when they do something *na levo,* they're doing it on the sly."

Her laughter, at once tender and triumphant, wrapped itself around them like a cocoon, and it made Diamond feel private and warm and one of the chosen.

Across the aisle, a middle-aged weights-and-measures bureaucrat fidgeted with a slide rule and glanced enviously out of the corner of his eye at the cocoon, aware that it was there, resentful at being excluded from it.

It was the same in New York. Sarah had the use of an East Side apartment—a model spending the summer in the Aegean had given her the key—so she and Diamond had a good deal of privacy. But for the first time since they had become lovers, they sought the company of others. It was like bringing a plant nurtured in darkness out into the sunlight. The overall effect of the change in environment was to deepen the attachment between Diamond and Sarah with a fragile cement—the elitist, two-against-the-world feeling.

"Did you hear her?" Sarah said after the press party at the photographer's studio for the group, Sarah included, that would be going to Russia to model American ready-to-wear fashions. "She's an absolute dictator at her magazine. Rips off memos with things like 'Is there anything more beautiful than a single delicate pearl? Positively no!' She's always doing that—ending with a question, and then answering it herself." And Sarah mimicked her perfectly: "'What do you think of growing old, my dear? It's simply ter-rible, isn't it? Growing old, I mean. It's so, well, how to phrase it, unavoidable, don't you think? I do. I console myself by telling myself that it's unavoidable. Do you have a philosophy? That's mine. If it's unavoidable, why, then, one can't really be expected to avoid it, can one?'" And again Leo found himself safely inside the cocoon of Sarah's laughter.

"This Russia thing," Diamond said, "do you really have to go?" He had known about the junket, of course, but somehow the idea that Sarah would be away for a week had not bothered him until now.

It was after the press party when he brought it up. Sarah and Diamond were sharing a small table with the Kruzmans, John and Joan, at a crowded, noisy, dingy East Side pub presided over by an enormously fat lady who corked the door with her body when all the available space inside was occupied. There was a scuffle at the next table—an intoxicated fag trying to crash a dinner party was being shouldered toward the door by the boyfriend of a man he had been pawing. The Kruzmans —she was a fashion editor, he a copy writer on Madison Avenue—had been to the studio party also, and, for lack of anything better to do, were dissecting it. They talked haphazardly, their fragmented sentences overlapping, neither paying much attention to the other, each fighting off interruptions by the other, he by raising his voice when she tried to break in, she by cutting down on the space between words and rushing on when it would have been natural to pause for a fresh breath or a fresh thought. All the time their eyes roamed back and forth across the restaurant as if they were on patrol.

". . . the one with the handlebar mustache, you couldn't miss him," John Kruzman was saying. "Met 'im in Amagansett, at Lull's barn, 'member? . . ."

". . . Lill's barn, as you call it, happens to be . . ."

John fought Joan off by going up half an octave and some decibels. "It's a god damn barn . . ."

"—difference . . . remodeled . . ."

"—anyhow . . . not the point . . . handlebar mustache is telling some naïve chick with no bra that he's following

132

Fitzgerald's advice, F. Scott, that is, writing his novel as if he were going to be beheaded the day he finishes it—"

"—girl happens to be Beatrice Joiner . . . her layouts are the smartest things in—"

"—gave me idea for short story—"

"—you met her ex-husband—"

John went up another quarter-octave and plunged on: "About guy on death row writing a book. See—"

"What do you mean no bra . . . body stocking—"

"—governor agrees to delay the execution until he finishes it . . . get it? He writes the novel as if he were going to be beheaded the day he finishes it! So he never finishes it." John Kruzman made the mistake of laughing at his own fantasy, and his wife used the lapse to get up a head of steam.

"—you men all the same never look at a girl when you can look through her any part of her button holes armpit holes body stocking's greatest invention since . . ." She plunged on, pauseless, while her husband waited for the crack that would allow him to wedge himself back into the conversation.

Inside the cocoon, its walls soaking up the conversation that hung in the air like moisture, Diamond repeated the question: "This Russia thing, do you really have to go?"

Sarah's finger tips rested lightly on the back of his hand, an understated intimacy that drew emotion like an electrical charge across a gap. "If you don't want me to go, Leo, I won't."

"I don't want you to go."

"I won't then."

Diamond brought up the subject again that night in bed.

"You sure you don't mind?"

"Am I sure I don't mind what, Leo?"

"Going to Russia," he said. "You sure you don't mind giving up the trip?"

Again she told him that if he didn't want her to go, she wouldn't go.

The intimacy, always understated, always overpowering, was there all the time now—the pressure of her breast against his arm as she leaned close in the zoo to tell him, "I detest zoos"; the quiet half-smile that came when the conversation lagged, as if to discredit words as a means of communication.

Slowly, effortlessly, Diamond began to accumulate the details of her life that served, like caulking, to join together the main events he already knew about. He discovered, for instance, that she had once wanted to be an actress and had gone so far as to spend two stifling hot months doing summer stock on Cape Cod. "The high point of my career," she said merrily, "came when I played the title role in 'Tea and Sympathy.'"

Diamond bit: "That's not bad, the title role."

And Sarah yanked home the hook: "I played the tea—I was the only one in the company who could whistle like a teapot coming to boil, so every night I stood in the wings and, on cue, played the tea." And she demonstrated, starting on a low note and sliding into a steamy high-pitched whistle that she held until her lungs were drained of air and her eyes bulged.

Then she collapsed in a spasm of laughter that sent tears spilling down her cheeks. Later, Diamond remembered the tears and recognized in them the salty residue of once bitter disappointment.

Another time Sarah told about being decked out in middy blouse and a navy blue pleated skirt and packed off to boarding school, where she spent most of her free time writing desperate letters to her father begging him to let her come home. After eight months, he finally gave in—but the patina of loneliness acquired in the interim clung to her still like some faint fragrance that wouldn't wash off.

"What did you do in boarding school?" Diamond asked.

"When I wasn't writing long self-pitying letters home, I sat on a bed talking about sex and acne with a room full of pimply faced virgins."

"What do girls talk about when they talk about sex?"

"At one time or another, just about everything—virginity, oral sex, how many calories there are in sperm, whether during intercourse you would guide him in or let him do it himself. That was a big question, I remember, whether you should guide him."

"What did you decide?"

Sarah smiled innocently. "Don't you know?"

Gradually the intimacies and insights began to give Diamond a new perspective of Sarah. What he had taken for childlike innocence—a one-dimensional figment of his own naïveté, he now saw—was neither childlike nor innocent, but rather a determined, almost teeth-gritting openness. It was this quality, Diamond now decided, that had attracted him—her refusal to protect herself lest she fend off some experience. "I never got to somebody without battering down walls," he told her during one soft, musing moment. They were walking back to the apartment from the zoo, heading east on Sixtieth Street past the dust and debris of subway construction, past the rows of workmen sulking on the sidewalk, their backs against buildings, eying girls. Around Sarah and Diamond, people flowed in cross-currents or milled in eddys waiting for lights or moods to change. "It's almost . . ."

"Almost what?" Sarah prompted.

"Almost as if I spent my life dealing with walls, and you're the first flesh-and-blood person I've actually confronted."

Just before they arrived at the apartment, Diamond came back to openness. "Everytime I made love with my wife"—he had to keep himself from wincing at the word *wife*—"I had the feeling she was doing me a favor. With you, I have the feeling you're doing yourself a favor."

Sarah thought about that. Presently she said: "Which is another way of saying I'm a selfish bitch."

"No, not that, not that at all. Everyone's selfish, everyone is occupied with himself. But you, you're a glutton for experience." After a while Diamond added: "Sometimes I'm afraid I'm just another experience for you." He wanted her to contradict him, to protest that he was much more than that. But she took in what he was saying and what he was wishing and remained silent.

There was another layer to Sarah, and Diamond perceived it when he telephoned from the brownstone to tell her he had just got hold of the second batch of C.P.P. interviews and wanted to read them before coming back to the apartment.

"Can't you do it tomorrow, Leo—I'm in an awful funk." Her voice, sullen and without inflection, had moved beyond asking; it was on the edge of pleading.

"I'd rather do it now," Leo said quickly, his eyes already skimming the top sheet. "I don't want to let them pile up."

"I'm sorry, Leo." It was an apology without an explanation. "Forget the whole thing." And she abruptly hung up.

"What got into you?" Diamond said when he finally arrived at the apartment.

"I get like that sometimes," she said. This time it was an explanation without an apology. "Suddenly everything seems so gray on gray—the sky, the street, the future, the past, the present, my life, you and me, everything. I needed something to hang on to for a moment—the sight of you. It's over now. Forget it."

But Diamond couldn't forget it; it dawned on him that there was within Sarah an echo of a sound he was familiar with—a half-note of desperation. Like Don Quixote leveling his lance at the windmills within himself, she was battling a very persuasive despair. Her almost manic openness, Diamond now saw, was a last-ditch defense against indifference—and indifference was the outer edge of despair. Even her collection of things—her roots, as she called them—were part of the picture, for they created a familiar home ground from which she could wage her war, and to which she could retreat when the battle went against her. In one of those instants of icy detachment of which he was capable, Diamond saw himself not as a lover but as a bollard to which she had tied up—for a day or a week or a month, until the despair overwhelmed her and compelled her to move on.

"I'm sorry about before, Leo"—here it was, a full-fledged apology—"hanging up like that, I mean." Suddenly Sarah switched moods. She spread her arms wide, palms out—she was wearing blue jeans and was bare from the waist up—smiled coquettishly and asked: "You're not angry, are you?"

"Not angry," he agreed, matching her mood.

"You still want to go out tonight?"

"Not if you don't," he said.

"I don't," she said. "There are some eggs in the fridge—how about an omelette for dinner?"

"An omelette will do me fine—I used to eat *fines herbes* in France all the time during the war. Lived on a farm outside of a town called Plascassier. They had lots of chickens and lots of eggs, so when everything else was scarce, we ate omelettes."

"I can't picture you in the war," Sarah said, and she smiled and kissed him on the mouth and went off to prepare the eggs. Later, after dinner, she asked him how he could put catsup on an omelette. "It kills the taste," she said.

"That's the general idea," Diamond replied gravely. "Since France, I hate eggs."

"Why the hell didn't you tell me?"

"I did—sort of. I told you I ate eggs all the time."

"But you didn't say you didn't like them."

"Well, for Christ's sake, don't you have any imagination?" Still later, Sarah caught Diamond staring out of the window downriver toward the tip of Manhattan. The sun was setting behind the towers on Wall Street, throwing into sharp outline the architectural features of the bridges that connected the island with Brooklyn and turning the East River into a lacework of quicksilver and shadows.

"A penny?" Sarah said, and when he looked confused, she added, "For your thoughts."

"Oh, I was thinking about Lewinter—you remember, the guy who defected to the Russians."

"How's the C.C.P. going?"

"It's C.P.P.—for Comprehensive Personality Profile. Unfortunately, it's going just where I thought it would go."

"He took secrets with him, huh?"

"It looks that way. Of course, we'll never really know, but it all adds up to the fact that he may rate as the most serious defection this country's ever had." And Diamond went on to select those details available to the C.P.P. which seemed to prove his point. "Apparently Lewinter had nothing worth giving away in his own field, but he got a glimpse of some extremely sensitive material in another field."

"But a glimpse, Leo—what good is a glimpse? He would have had to copy it or photograph it or memorize it, wouldn't he?" Sarah was playing amateur to Diamond's professional, throwing quick questions at him the way a straight man feeds one-liners to his comic.

"Normally, yes—access is nothing unless you have the ability to take it with you. But it turns out there is a strong possibility that our friend Lewinter was endowed with a photo memory." Diamond told her about the poem and about the doctor who said it was possible to lose and later regain a photo memory. "So he simply read the material and that was that—he could probably give it back to you formula for formula."

"There's more to it, isn't there, Leo? You wouldn't be so sure if there weren't more to it."

Diamond watched the shadows smother the pinpricks of light on the river. "There's a lot more to it—the pieces fit together so well one way that it's hard to see how else to assemble them. First off, shortly after Lewinter defected, someone went to his apartment and lifted all of his personal papers. We checked to see if it was one of our agents. It wasn't, which means it was one of theirs. Obviously, *they* were going to great lengths to see who it was they had—a sure indication that they thought they had somebody important. Then there is the business of the librarian, Marmsbury. Three days after the defection—remember, by then they would have held an initial debriefing—the librarian who gave Lewinter access to the secret formulas was run down and killed by a truck from Fairfax Dairies."

"Coincidence," said Sarah unconvincingly.

"The police checked it out—there is no such animal as Fairfax Dairies on the eastern seaboard."

"But why would they kill the librarian?"

"To cover up the fact that Lewinter had access to very sensitive material. If we didn't suspect he had access, we wouldn't get worried about the defection—and we wouldn't change the formulas he swiped."

"You really think they murdered the librarian?" Sarah asked in a low, awed voice. Suddenly the whole thing was very frightening.

"In my business, Sarah, there's no such thing as coincidence."

"What are you going to do about Lewinter?"

Diamond laughed, revealing more than a trace of bitterness in his voice. "Chances are *I'm* not going to do anything about it. Unless I come up with some pressing reasons why I should follow through, it'll probably be dumped into the Agency's lap."

"You'd like to keep it, wouldn't you?"

"I'd like to keep it, yes—this kind of operation is very, well, challenging. It's almost like a game. You figure out a move. Then you figure out how they'll interpret your move and what response they'll make. And you try to psych out whether they'll think you've figured out their next move. Then you figure out another move. It's kind of like chess, Sarah. There are obvious, logical moves and sometimes you make them. But you're always looking for the brilliant innovation, the flash of imagination or intuition that comes once in a hundred games. You remember, I told you about the Cernú affair—that was like that; it was a great move which might have succeeded . . . might have succeeded . . ." Diamond let the thought trail off into unspoken regret. Then he started up again, fresh with a second wind. "Do you play chess?" She shook her head no. "Not many girls play chess. It's a man's game—it's really a vicious game, chess, cunning and vicious. It's war and aggression and gamesmanship and nerve all wrapped up into one. You know, I've often dreamed of playing chess with live people. The ones that are taken off the board would be killed—"

"Could you do it?" Sarah interrupted in a low voice. "Could you really do it?"

"I know I could. I could even sacrifice—give up one man in order to gain a position or advance a gambit. I know I'd have the nerve."

The conversation lagged as Sarah absorbed this information. Presently she said: "What would you do about Lewinter if it were yours to handle? I know what I'd do."

Diamond, preoccupied with his human chess game, was only faintly interested. "What would you do?"

"Well, it's simple. I'd change the formulas he stole; I'd use new formulas. That'd make the information he gave them obsolete."

"It'd cost too much money—something in the neighborhood of sixty or seventy billion. Try again."

It had become a game between them, and Sarah was

determined to defend her amateur standing. "O.K., I'd confuse the Russians by sending them a second defector with a different version of the same information. What's wrong with that?"

"Too slow; it takes years to work up a good plant. And if he slips just once—say he gets the name of the high school he was supposed to have attended wrong—all you've done is convince them that the first defector is a very important guy with very important information. But don't be discouraged. Try again for the Kewpie doll? Think of the headlines if you win: BEAUTIFUL MODEL SAVES MIRV."

"What's MIRV?"

"Forget I said that—go on and try again."

"MIRV has something to do with what he stole, doesn't it? All right, try this one." Sarah looked up at the ceiling and closed her eyes as if she were doing some difficult mental calculations. "I've got it this time. It's really very elementary. The object is to discredit Lewinter, right? It's no skin off our nose if they have him as long as they don't believe him. Well, all you've got to do is convince the Russians you're trying to convince them he's a real defector. When they see you're trying to convince them he's real, they'll naturally conclude he's some sort of fake. What's wrong with that, huh?" She was sure he'd find something wrong.

"Go through that one again, will you?"

She did, ending up again with: "What's wrong with that?" Diamond looked off again toward the river, by now a current of coal-black liquid. "Offhand I can't see anything wrong with it. Let me think about it a while."

The next day was to be their last in New York, and so they went to bed early to make the most of it. Long after Sarah had fallen asleep, Diamond lay with his eyes wide open staring into the blackness of his mind. At 2 A.M. he went into the kitchen and made himself a cup of coffee, which he forgot to drink for a while. When he remembered, it was too cold. At 5:45 A.M., with the first shoots of light gray protruding above the window sill, Diamond shook Sarah awake.

"What?" she asked, her eyes swollen with sleep.

Diamond smiled down at her as if he were enjoying a private joke. "How would you like to take up chess?" he said.

PART III
THE MIDDLE GAME

13

I T RAINED most of the afternoon, long strands of chain-linked tear drops that snapped the leaves back and forth like punching bags, accumulated in the discolored copper gutters and gushed to the ground below. By the time Pogodin and Lewinter arrived, well after dark, the rain had stopped, but the hundred yards or so from the end of the paved *cul de sac* to the dacha was a sea of mud.

"I've been meaning to put down planks, but somehow I never seem to close the gap between thought and action," Zaitsev laughed as he waved them indoors.

"That's a common enough sin on earth . . . I forgive you," Pogodin said solemnly, and he etched a cross on Zaitsev's forehead with his thumbnail.

"Well, welcome, Pope Pogodin," Zaitsev bellowed, and he

threw an affectionate arm over Pogodin's shoulder. "Tell me, how does one say 'welcome' in English?" When Pogodin told him, Zaitsev turned formally to Lewinter, thrust out a hand and said: "Vel-cum." There was a strong odor of alcohol on Zaitsev's breath and it made Lewinter wince. Zaitsev turned back to Pogodin. "Your companion has the look of an over-nourished fairy, but the hell with it, tell him I welcome him despite his weakness of character—to my cottage, to Russia, et cetera, et cetera, et cetera."

Inside, the dacha smelled of wet wood and wet wool and bare feet. Mud-caked shoes were strewn in the doorway where Zaitsev's guests had abandoned them to dry. The room itself was twice as long as it was wide, in the style of the eighteenth-century Russian manor houses. The ornate carved wooden shutters were open to the moist night air. There were no panes in the windows because Zaitsev only used the house in the summer; once the warm weather was over, he never strayed far from the creature comforts of his centrally heated Moscow flat.

At the far end of the room, the still-wet branches of a sycamore poked through an open window. A spider web, so fragile it looked like threads of light, connected two of the leaves. A dozen or so people, as mixed a lot as any Russian intellectual could gather under one roof in August, were sitting or standing or leaning around. Empty and half-empty bottles of Glenfiddich Scotch and Remy Martin cognac and Polish vodka (the kind you have to finish once you open because the bottle has no stopper) littered the tabletops. Saucers overflowed with cigarette stubs and ashes and ash-coated apple cores and cherry pits. Next to what used to be the fireplace but had been fitted with doors and turned into a liquor cabinet, a very beautiful and very intoxicated ballerina sat cross-legged on the floor sobbing uncontrollably. When anyone tried to console her, she sobbed even more bitterly, because, she explained between hiccups, the only thing keeping her from becoming a prima ballerina was that her husband—also a dancer—was a homosexual. Homosexuals were the outcasts of Russian ballet.

"Introductions!" Zaitsev boomed, clanging a knife against one of the vodka bottles for attention. His eyes were bloodshot and red-rimmed, his face was flushed with drink and heat; he was in top form.

"Translate for me, Yefgeny," he ordered Pogodin. "Don't worry about the names too much, because your American will never remember them anyhow. But be meticulous about my oral marginalia. As usual, they will be priceless." Anticipating another Zaitsev monologue, the dull hum of spiritless conversation faded into silence; the party had perked up.

"The crybaby is Valentina Berezhkova," Zaitsev began, gesturing toward the ballerina on the floor. "When she's not blubbering, she has the face of an Odette—and the soul of an Odile." Everyone laughed, even the ballerina through her tears. The audience was warming.

"Here meet Alexandr Timoshenko, mediocre translator, gutless editor, fading liberal light on the editorial board of *Novi Mir,* the slowest gun in the back rooms of the Writers' Union."

In fact, Timoshenko was one of the most influential liberal literary figures in the country, and much respected by Zaitsev. "Alex, greet Yefgeny Mikhailovich Pogodin, ambivalent intellectual, ambivalent humanist, ambivalent Marxist, ambivalent bureaucrat. On the surface, he is all Communist. Scratch the surface and you'll find, not Lenin or Marx, but Taras Bulba. In this, he has a lot in common with Russia. Ambivalence, Alex, is the key to our souls. The English author Thomas Carlyle captured this, didn't he, in his character Diogenes Teufelsdröckh—Diogenes for 'God-born,' Teufelsdröckh for 'Devil's dung.' The ultimate in ambivalence. Did you know you have to have a chit from the Ministry of Culture to draw translations of Carlyle from the Lenin Library? Pity. He really understood the relationship between material things and spiritual things. So it goes. Here, Alex, greet also one of the few people in the world who has gone out of his way to get into Mother Russia, the American defector Lewinter."

Zaitsev used the word *defector* as if it were a job classification. Pogodin, leaning over Lewinter's shoulder, translated only part of the monologue—enough to account for the laughter, but not enough to insult. Timoshenko, a thickset, totally bald man with a warm smile, shook hands all around.

One by one, like a teacher calling the roll, Zaitsev introduced his guests. There was Solomon Kaganovich, the renowned Yiddish novelist who had spent fourteen years in a Siberian prison camp and worked nowadays as a handyman in Dom Modeli, Moscow's central fashion studio. Earlier in the day, Kaganovich had flooded the only toilet in the house, and so Zaitsev, to everyone's glee, introduced him as "the master plumber"—which was also the name of Kaganovich's famous unpublished book about Stalin. There was Sergei Yevdokimov, a composer of children's songs who churned out bawdy ballads for the underground circuit on the side. Zaitsev introduced him as "Russia's foremost specialist on toilet graffiti." Zaitsev's ex-wife, a gone-to-seed woman with a flashing gold tooth and an embarrassingly flat chest, was there with her latest husband, a little-known journalist named Bubnov. Zaitsev purposefully mispronounced his name when he introduced them, and Bubnov was too embarrassed about being there in the first place to correct him. Zaitsev's current mistress, the Fat Cow—as he privately called her—was next. "Here," Zaitsev said, molding his palm over her right breast, "meet the goddess of hay fever, who has transformed the common sneeze into an aria. My Katrina." On cue, she produced a sneeze, and Zaitsev said, "Dear lady, may God bless you."

In one corner, near the window with the sycamore jutting through it, sat Shliapnikov, a wiry, quiet, dead-drunk carpenter from a nearby village. Yevdokimov, the graffiti specialist, had come across him in a coffee house and brought him along to show how unclass-conscious he was. But as Zaitsev pointed out, it merely showed how class-conscious he *really* was. Right next to the carpenter sat a grim-faced man in his late thirties, a biochemist named Andrei Antonov-Ovseenko. His father had been an army general destined for great things until Stalin had him executed in the 1936 purge. Antonov-Ovseenko, who had never protested against anything in his life, had recently been coaxed into signing a manifesto demanding that the government reopen the case of one A. Axelrod, an outspoken poet who was thought to be languishing in a mental institution reserved for unharnessed liberals. Just that morning, Antonov-Ovseenko had learned that the manifesto, with his name prominently displayed, had turned up in the *New York Times*. "Andrei here is an amateur ice skater," Zaitsev said by way of introduction. Smiling wanly, Antonov-Ovseenko saluted the newcomer. "Right now," Zaitsev added, "he's skating on very thin ice."

"There but for the grace of God go you," a voice piped up from one corner.

This evoked a general round of laughter.

"What does he mean by that?" Lewinter asked when Pogodin translated.

"I don't know," Pogodin said, a puzzled look in his eyes. There were a handful of other people in the room: a couple of Bolshoi musicians, another man whom nobody had ever met before—Zaitsev introduced him as "the unknown guest"—and a junior diplomat whose last name was Krestinsky and whose first name had been irrevocably lost—at least to the host— when he walked through the door. Krestinsky, just back from a tour of duty in Cairo, had brought along a tin of hashish, which some of the guests had tried before dinner. After half a dozen puffs, they laughed nervously and switched back to hard liquor.

"Zaitsev, darling," the Fat Cow called, her voice still

musical in a nasal sort of way, "if you're finished with the roll call, give us another record."

"I'll put one on for the American," Zaitsev said. Painstakingly, he lowered the diamond needle onto the groove. "Tell him, Yefgeny, tell him it's to make him feel at home. Atmosphere is everything. I understand it's a classic of sorts."

The record Zaitsev put on was an eight-month-old rock hit by an American group called the Sins of Omission. It began:

Ashes to ashes, and yeah
Shit to shit, oh yeah
Everyone's hung up, oh my good christ yeah
On the mirror bit.

Around the room, Zaitsev's guests listened in rapt silence to words they didn't understand. Lewinter had never heard the song before and couldn't make any sense out of it either, but he nodded appreciatively.

The party had reached a plateau; it could turn deeply serious or uproariously funny—or both.

Absent-mindedly, the Fat Cow dipped into a huge handbag at her feet and pulled out a new French antibiotic throat spray she had bought at an outrageous price from a friend recently back from Paris. She inserted the pressurized capsule in the plastic dispenser, put the whole contraption in her mouth, then pushed and sucked in at the same instant. The spray, which smelled like an insecticide, coated the back of her throat and worked its way up her nasal passages, clearing the congestion that plugged them. Katrina blew her nose, first one nostril and then the other, into a paper dinner napkin. "Ah, I feel better," she said. "These French drugs really work."

"You've just seen Katrina at her hobby," Zaitsev explained "Some people accumulate paintings or stamps or money or lovers, but our hay-feverish hypochondriac here collects medicines. And not just any medicines, but Western medicines. You should see the chest upstairs—a veritable pharmacy of American pills and English ointments and French sprays."

"My prizes are my West German birth control pills and a Swiss laxative—the chocolate tastes divine," Katrina chimed in.

Pogodin, translating furiously to Lewinter, thought of the hay-fever pills the American had brought with him.

"Zaitsev, old fart," said Timoshenko, the *Novi Mir* editor, "are you against collections of medicines—or collections per se? It sounds from your tone as if you're making a reverse acrobatic leap from the particular to the general."

"No amount of mental acrobatics could leave you behind, Alex," said Zaitsev. He plucked the French throat spray from Katrina's hand and went through a pantomime of spraying his throat, then his nose, then his ears, and finally his behind. Everyone was convulsed in laughter.

"Your friend," Lewinter whispered to Pogodin, "is quite a clown."

"I'm against collections of any kind," Zaitsev began, obviously on the verge of a reasonably long discourse. "They are antithetical to Marxism-Leninism, which is a melange that currently goes by the name of Communism."

The audience oohed and aahed, egging Zaitsev on. "More precision, Zaitsev," the Yiddish novelist Kaganovich called.

"You're right—more precision is needed. I'll sharpen my tongue. To collect things—to collect anything—is a form of perverse materialism, an admission that in this land of plenty, something could someday be in short supply." Zaitsev spoke sardonically, and everyone understood it as such—except Katrina.

"But Zaitsev darling," she chimed, "there are shortages. When's the last time you found hundred-watt light bulbs?"

"You know what the peasants say?" asked Kaganovich. "The shortage will be divided among the peasants."

"Exactly," Katrina said with no logic at all. "And what of a person who collects things of beauty, art objects and the like? That's not the same as collecting medicines which you may have to use someday."

"Dear lady, it's all hoarding, whether art or armpit spray," Zaitsev answered. "What difference if you hoard objects of beauty against the day when there is no more beauty in the world. Hoarding is hoarding; it's antisocial and antisocialist, and that's an end to it."

"And you, Zaitsev, if you were to hoard, as you put it, what would you collect?" This from Timoshenko, who sat hunched on the edge of an old sofa, his knees wide apart, his hands clasped between them.

Zaitsev rested the bridge of his nose between two fingers and thought a minute. His eyes fell on the delicate strands connecting two leaves of the sycamore. "Cobwebs," he said. "I'd hoard cobwebs against the day when the spider becomes extinct."

"But why cobwebs?" Pogodin asked.

"Ah, my dear friend, because they stand as a rebuke to all manmade constructions. The stresses and strains are perfectly calculated. The design is utilitarian. The building materials are cheap and readily available. And one never tires of seeing them, as opposed to those post–neo-Stalin monstrosities they are throwing up in Moscow. Did you hear about the new office buildings on Kutuzovski Prospekt? *Kosomol Pravda* ran the story. They constructed it so the windows couldn't open, and then fitted it with undersized air conditioning. The metallurgical combine moved into it in June. For a few weeks they generated so much sweat that the bureaucrats who record such things were convinced that the metallurgical people were working at a fantastic pace and gave them all bonuses. In July the workers refused to come to work, bonuses be damned, and the combine had to move back to its ancient spaces on Gorky Street—so ancient that the windows actually had hinges on them."

It was a bravura performance, the kind Zaitsev could be counted on to give when any party showed signs of flagging. Some of his quips would be making the rounds for weeks to come. The only thing the audience had to do was listen appreciatively—and spur him on with one-line questions. It was an old indoor sport.

"Is your friend catching any of this, Yefgeny?" Zaitsev asked. "After all, we want him to think well of our party."

The play on words wasn't lost on the guests.

Lewinter, who had been getting bits and pieces of the monologue from Pogodin, mumbled something in Pogodin's ear. "He says," said Pogodin, "that Katrina's problem may be in her head, not her nose. He says her compulsion to collect medicines suggests to him that she should see a psychoanalyst."

It was as good a one-liner as any.

Zaitsev responded with a theatrical roar. "Thank God," he said, throwing his hands in the air in mock surrender, "for the incompatibility of Marx and Freud. But for that, we'd have those insane hyenas of psychiatry hanging out their shingles in our part of the globe. No, none of it for me. There is a fundamental difference between East and West, Mr. Lewinter. In your world, it isn't capitalism that's king, it's psychiatry. We, on the other hand, live in a world where psychiatry is a defrocked country priest. When *you* get a cold, it's because you hate your job or your wife or your life; when we get one, it's because of germs, pure and simple. Your psychiatrists have created an atmosphere where the ordinary everyday emotions of worry, anxiety, depression, boredom, love and hate, et cetera, et cetera, et cetera, require medical treatment. Here we simply take another drink. And thank God for that. If you ask me, the basic flaw of psychoanalysts is that they assume it is a good thing to be normal."

"But isn't it, Zaitsev darling? Isn't it good to be normal, I mean?"

"Normality, my dear Katrina," Zaitsev pontificated, "stifles creativity. What great chess player was ever normal? Have you heard that some of the factories that have gone over to the New Economic Plan are picking plant managers the way they do in the West; giving them psychological tests. Holy mother of hell, there's not much use testing people to find out if they will make good managers unless you know what it is that makes the good ones good!"

Shliapnikov, the drunken carpenter, had missed most of the conversation. But the mention of "psychological tests" had tripped a wire, and now, from the corner of the room, he blurted out: "Most of our nuts are in the loony asylums. God keep it that way." He looked around for someone to second the motion.

"There are a lot of people in asylums who aren't nuts, friend," Timoshenko said quietly, coldly.

"Like Axelrod," said Antonov-Ovseenko, happy to have a cause.

"You're a fool," Zaitsev exploded, glaring at Antonov-Ovseenko, "a god damn fool. Axelrod is stone dead. Has been for some time."

There was utter silence in the room; only Timoshenko, who kept abreast of such things, had known Axelrod was dead.

"What did he say just then?" Lewinter asked Pogodin.

"They're talking about a mutual friend," Pogodin answered evasively.

"How do you know he's dead?" Antonov-Ovseenko asked in an almost inaudible voice.

Timoshenko interrupted. "This is a conversation for another time and another place. Please."

Zaitsev poured himself another bourbon and downed it in one smooth, straight motion. "Another time, another place," he repeated. "Good title for a book."

"It's funny," Lewinter told Pogodin, "I don't understand a word, but I can sense the atmosphere has changed."

But Zaitsev was off and running in a new direction.

"Did you know," he said, "that Xerxes had myopia? That's why he sat on a hill over Salamis and watched fifty Greek ships beat his five hundred Persian ships without changing his tactic. He couldn't *see* properly."

"Didn't his generals tell him what was happening?" asked the unknown guest.

"Xerxes had another disease common to great men," said Zaitsev. "He didn't trust the people around him."

"Lots of great men have suffered from physical defects," said Pogodin. "It would make an interesting thesis."

"I hear Brezhnev has hemorrhoids," Zaitsev said. His ex-wife and the Fat Cow laughed hysterically. "Why are you laughing, dear Katrina? Do you have a pill for that?"

"As a matter of fact, I do." She giggled. "An Italian suppository."

"Talking of great people, did you ever notice, Zaitsev, that nearly all great writers love cats?" said Yevdokimov, the graffiti expert. "Our own Turgenev, Tolstoi, Pushkin—the list is end-less. You have one back in Moscow, don't you?"

"I do. I call him Chichikov, after the rogue in Gogol's *Dead Souls* who roamed the countryside buying the souls of serfs who were thoughtless enough to die, thereby depriving the masters of their property. Cat lovers are a special breed. You can tell a lot about a person by his attitude toward dogs and cats. Napoleon and Mussolini hated cats. Hitler loved dogs. Authoritarians and sadists, as in Germans, and masochists, as in homosexuals, love dogs. Sexy, independent, freedom-loving people love cats."

"Don't forget Kublai Khan, Julius Caesar, and Richard Coeur de Lion—they also loved dogs, Zaitsev," Pogodin said. "There's a common denomination there."

"Yefgeny certainly knows his history," said the Fat Cow. "It runs in his family," Zaitsev said. He suddenly felt very tired and very bored and very cruel—and his monologue took on a cutting edge. "He is the great-great-grandson of Mikhail Petrovich Pogodin, who pasted together a seven-volume history of Russia and did back flips defending Nicholas I."

Pogodin gasped in open-mouthed astonishment; he had known Zaitsev since their days at the university together, but he had never traded family trees with him.

"If you're implying that Mikhail Petrovich was an apolo-gist, I take exception," said Pogodin.

"Take exception then. Take two. Nicholas was a tyrant and anyone who tried to defend him was as great a rogue as

Chichikov. Even your great-great-grandfather. On the first day of his reign Nicholas crushed the Decembrists. He spent the rest of his tour of duty, so to speak, shitting on the national minorities, suppressing liberals who dared to criticize him, building up the secret police. Nicholas was a paternalistic fungus on the Russian body politic."

"You find no redeeming features?" asked Pogodin. He was on the edge of anger; Zaitsev seemed to be putting him down for the exercise.

"Just one—he provided the background tapestry for the golden age of Russian literature; out of Nicholas' Russia came Pushkin, Lermontov, and Gogol."

"Ah, Zaitsev darling, you manage to find redeeming features wherever you look," said the Fat Cow.

"True enough—even in you."

There was an embarrassed silence. Tears welled up in Katrina's eyes. Zaitsev had gone beyond good clean fun. Timoshenko, the *Novi Mir* editor, came to the rescue. "What do you think, Zaitsev, has the Cyrillic alphabet hurt or helped Russia?"

"In a political or literary sense?"

"Literary."

"Then of course the answer is that it has hurt us, in the same way that the change of the railway gauge between Russia and the West hurts us; it has slowed movement of intellectual freight across this frontier—and we are the worse for it."

"I agree," said Timoshenko, "but I think the West has suffered even more than Russia. Imagine having a literature that has never really absorbed Pushkin or Tolstoi or Dostoevski or Gogol? The idea is absurd."

"Let's do a test case," Kaganovich said. He turned to Lewinter. "Have you read the Russian giants?" Pogodin translated.

"I read Dostoevski's *Crime and Punishment* in college, but I suppose that's about it," Lewinter answered. He hoped they wouldn't get into a more detailed discussion; he remembered reading the book, but he could recall little beyond the title.

"Zaitsev darling, ask him some penetrating questions about America," the Fat Cow said. She was her old self again, a half-empty glass in one hand, a cigarette in the other.

"Yes, tell us, Mr. Lewinter, is it true that Americans hate black people?" asked Yevdokimov, the graffiti expert.

"How can they allow thirty million people to live in starvation?" asked Bubnov, the journalist.

"How could you allow Kennedy—two Kennedys—to be murdered?" asked the Fat Cow, pointing with her cigarette. "That's what I want to know. How?"

"My dear, beautiful, simple-minded Katrina, Lewinter here was not personally responsible, was he?" said Zaitsev. "He might just as rationally ask: how could you allow Lenin to be shot in the head by an assassin's bullet. Come, one question— one reasonable question—at a time."

Timoshenko began the interrogation of Lewinter. "Can you give us some picture of what life is like in America?

Living, as we do, in a fundamentally different society, I'm not sure we have a clear idea."

With Pogodin translating, Lewinter tried to describe life in the United States. He spoke slowly, haltingly, as if searching for the right words; actually he had anticipated the question and knew very well what he was going to say. "How can I sum up a country that is three thousand miles wide and two hundred million people deep?" he began. "If I had to go to the heart of the matter, I'd say 'impersonality.'"

There was a momentary discussion when Pogodin translated that; Zaitsev wondered whether Lewinter was talking about being an "unperson," which was something he had thought was more or less a Soviet phenomenon. The misunderstanding was quickly straightened out.

Lewinter went on.

"Several years ago, a woman was attacked and murdered in a section of New York. It happened on a street late at night. The newspapers later discovered that thirty or forty people had heard her cries for help or observed the attack from their bedroom windows; yet not a living soul went to her assistance, not a soul opened a window and shouted for help, not a soul even telephoned the police. I think this is the essence of America; two hundred million private worlds, surrounded by two hundred million moats of fear and distrust. In a word, overpowering isolation."

It was an interesting answer, interesting because it supported what the Russians in the room had always read in their own newspapers—and because they read it in their own news-papers, mistrusted.

"And what do you expect to find here that you couldn't find in America?" Timoshenko asked. As Pogodin translated the question, some of the people in the room leaned forward, anticipating an intriguing answer.

"Bridges," Lewinter answered. And he added lightly: "Perhaps a spider web or two."

Lewinter was aware that he had made a very good impression.

"Be prepared for a disappointment, my American friend," Zaitsev said. "It was one of your Anglo-Saxon poets who said that every man is an island. In the end, it is as true here as anywhere." Zaitsev picked at his ear, thought a second, and added casually, "And our cobwebs are more often than not the cobwebs of fear."

"He's nothing at all like you described," Zaitsev said. "When you first came in, I thought he looked fairyish, but I liked him in the end."

The last of the guests had left; the ballerina, unable to find one of her slippers, had thrown away the other one too and tip-toed through the mud in her bare feet. Now Zaitsev was stretched out full length on a couch, his eyes covered with a damp dishtowel. Pogodin, his shirt sleeves rolled up to his elbows, sat at a table munching on a piece of stale black bread and goat cheese. Lewinter and the Fat Cow were soundly asleep upstairs, Lewinter in a wickerwork chair that would leave crosshatches on his flesh when he awoke; Katrina curled up in a ball on one corner of the huge mattress that she shared with Zaitsev.

It was time for post-mortems.

"Actually, I never really expected you to turn up," Zaitsev said. He submerged the dishtowel in a bowl of water at his side, wrung it out, and folded it over his eyes again. "When you called and said you were coming with *him,* I was astonished. How come they permitted it? Is this some new technique of debriefing?"

Pogodin took a sip of Bulgarian white wine. "Cooped up too long . . . getting itchy . . . getting temperamental . . . sleeping badly." Pogodin was chewing and talking at the same time now. "Good therapy. My idea, actually. Had trouble convincing them until they heard it was you who was giving the party . . ."

"And when they heard it was me?" Zaitsev prompted. "They said absolutely no." The two men burst into laughter—a laughter that cemented the bonds between them.

"You couldn't resist, could you?"

"With you, never," Pogodin said. "You generate a chemistry . . . I'm curious—how did I describe him?"

"Describe whom?" Zaitsev asked.

"Our Mr. A. J. Lewinter."

"Ah, yes, Lewinter. You left me with the impression he was one of the shallower specimens of *Homo sapiens* around, someone who talked in slogans and skimmed the intellectual surface. But I thought that he spoke movingly. Oh, one must forgive him his naïveté about Russia; he's been fed his share of propaganda too."

The two men fell silent for a while. Zaitsev, relaxed and under no pressure to entertain anyone, concentrated on trying to erase the memory of light from his eyes; Pogodin leaned back in his chair and enjoyed his tiredness. Outside, it had begun to rain again, and the first drops were spattering against the sycamore leaves.

Zaitsev broke the silence. "I can't understand defection. I can understand the alienation that sets the stage for it. Who in his lifetime hasn't experienced it? But starting a new life . . . giving up the little things . . . he probably doesn't even know how to dial one of our telephones, let alone have someone to call. Wait till he finds out there is no such thing as a telephone book in Moscow!"

"Zaitsev, before you go to sleep under that dishtowel, tell me who Axelrod is—or rather, was?"

Zaitsev didn't stir for a moment. "Would you believe me, Yefgeny, if I told you I'd rather not talk about it." Zaitsev sat up abruptly and wiped his face with the dishtowel. "Perhaps you would be better off, you would find it easier, not knowing such things."

"Perhaps. Who is to say." Pogodin was very troubled. He wanted to know—and he didn't want to know.

Before he could press the point, Zaitsev changed the subject. "Did you enjoy the party? What did you think of Timoshenko?"

"I was surprised to see him here. I didn't know that the two of you were friends. I met him, did he tell you, when he came to Japan two years ago on vacation; the ambassador gave a cocktail party for him. He's a real maverick, isn't he?"

"Did you ever hear how he discovered Solzhenitsyn?" Zaitsev asked. "He was scanning manuscripts for *Novi Mir* at his flat late one night when he picked up one called *One Day in the Life of Ivan Denisovich*. He told me the story himself. He read a dozen pages into it, then got up and put on his tuxedo. He lit a candle, opened a bottle of champagne, sat down in his easy chair, and stayed up the rest of the night reading the book. He said he knew he was reading a Russian genius—and that he was witnessing the renaissance of Russian literature. He put his neck on the line publishing it. He has a lot of guts."

"How long have you been friends?"

"We've been good friends only a few months. We . . . well, sometime I'll tell you the whole story. It's too late right now. But you tell me, Yefgeny, how did things go at Obninsk?"

"I knew you'd get around to that. You're curious, eh? Let's strike a bargain. Tell me about Axelrod and I'll tell you about Lewinter and Obninsk."

"God, back in Russia, what is it, less than three weeks, and you're already in the swing of things." Zaitsev couldn't help but laugh—but the laughter had a bitter note to it, bitter because of the story to come. "Axelrod. Yes, Axelrod. You're sure you want to know? It's not complicated. This time last year Axelrod stood up at the Party Congress and made a speech. He said that the censors had refused to pass his latest manuscript for publication, had demanded deletions—imagine country bumpkins telling Axelrod what words he can and cannot use. He said he had been harassed by the police. He said that the manuscript of a work in progress had been seized and not returned. He said that he had been denied a visa to travel abroad. He denounced censorship, he denounced the Union for putting up with censorship, he denounced the system which permits uneducated Communist Party flunkies to edit—can you imagine?—to edit the great writers of our country. And all of the people who submit, in one way or another, to the editing, all of those *who edit themselves before the editors get to their manuscripts,* all of them simply sat there and listened without so much as a nod of support. Axelrod knew what he was getting into, of course. They put him in an asylum outside of Leningrad—one that is supposed to be packed with Leningrad writers and poets. About three months ago I heard on the grapevine that Axelrod had hanged himself. They say that he was on latrine duty, that he took apart the mop and made a noose out of its strands and hanged himself from the curtain rail of a shower stall. Did you ever read his novel *One Step Backward?* No, you couldn't have; it was never published. One of his characters, I think a half-wit named Dmitri, kills himself the same way."

Now there was only the sound of the rain outside the windows. "I hear they're planning to announce he died of cancer or something of the sort—they're waiting until after this

Writers' Congress so there won't be a fuss. As if there would be a fuss."

The rain sounded louder than ever. Zaitsev spoke again: "For all I know, he probably was insane!"

Zaitsev poured himself a shot of bourbon and studied his reflection in it. "Now, my friend, it is your turn to deliver—tell me how things went at Obninsk?"

"This is not material for cocktail chatter, Zaitsev, you understand that. I'm a fool for telling you."

"Ah, Yefgeny, would I broadcast state secrets? Don't take me for an idiot. Now talk!"

"Well, the debriefing went smoothly enough. Our friend Lewinter checked out in every possible way. He was questioned and cross-examined and cross-questioned and examined again. God, was it boring."

"And they believed him?"

"Yes, I'd say they believed him. The only trouble was that the whole thing was so fantastic. He claimed that he had found a master carbon with the trajectory formulas on it in a mimeograph room. Can you imagine, he simply picked them off the floor of a mimeograph room. He memorized them, so he says, and then walked down to the department's library and drew out the originals to see if he really had what he thought he had. He had his hands on the originals long enough to convince him that he really had the MIRV trajectory formulas. Then he says the librarian discovered that the name Lewinter wasn't on the access list and took away the originals."

"So the Americans will know he had access to the formulas?"

"Not necessarily. Lewinter suspects the librarian might have hushed the whole thing up. He would have been fired if he had admitted giving 'eyes only' material to someone not on his authorization list."

"So there was no hitch to the story at all?"

"There was one hitch—but we don't know what to make of it. One of the sixteen formulas he gave us doesn't plot; that is, it isn't a trajectory formula. Either Lewinter remembered it wrong . . ."

"But he double-checked them against the originals?"

"No, he only had the originals for a few minutes and couldn't check every last one of them."

"Ah."

"So either it was a normal lapse of memory—he memorized it incorrectly to begin with, or memorized it correctly and then forgot part of it. Or he is lying. Or the Americans have a warhead on one of their MIRVs that goes straight up and never comes down . . . which is extremely unlikely, but, in this world of ours, not impossible."

"It seems to me," said Zaitsev, "that the fact that one formula didn't plot is testimony to his genuineness. After all, the Americans wouldn't be dumb enough to send a plant to us with fifteen good formulas and one that didn't plot."

"And I thought you were a devious person." Pogodin laughed. Espionage was his game and he played it well. "What better thing to do if you want the other side to fall for your plant than to mix in a really stupid mistake with the material. No, in the end; the fact that one of the sixteen formulas didn't plot tells us nothing whatsoever."

"Where to from here?" Zaitsev asked. "The game grows intriguing."

"I wish to hell I knew." Suddenly Pogodin's façade of crisp confidence seemed to dissolve. He plunged across the room to the window with the sycamore poking through it and pushed the branches roughly out, destroying the cobweb in the process. "This bastard's been bothering me all night," he said.

The abrupt change in the tone and tempo of the conversation brought Zaitsev around in his seat to stare at his friend. He remembered seeing Pogodin stalk a room like a caged lion once before; it was the night Pogodin's wife had died in childbirth. Unable to control the situation or influence its outcome, unable even fully to understand what was going on, Pogodin had almost come apart at the psychic seams. Now something of that same mood was upon him again.

"What is it, Yefgeny Mikhailovich?" Zaitsev asked. There was no trace of banter or irony or liquor in his voice now.

"The plain, simple, elementary fact is that I don't know what to do. You know how these things work as well as I do, Zaitsev. One mistake, that's all it would take. One mistake and all those years of work will go down the drain. If I screw up this one . . . I'm really scared. My ambition scares me. But the possibility that I won't achieve my ambition scares me even more. I've always been so sure before . . . but who can say what is right? Who is this Lewinter? I mean who is he really? What should we do with his information? My God, sometimes I wish to hell I'd never laid eyes on him. I've never gotten involved in politics before . . . I don't know how to play it."

All Zaitsev could think of to say was: "Maybe it will blow over." And so he said it.

"No, it won't fade away. There is one hell of a battle brewing. Every bureaucrat in Moscow is coming out of the woodwork on this one. The army, the navy, the missile people, the New Economic Plan people, probably your perspiring metallurgical people too. If we accept Lewinter's information and act on it, we'll have to build an antimissile system from the ground up. And it will cut deeply into everyone's programs. But if we do have the secret of the American MIRVs, we'd be fools not to use the information."

"I'm only an amateur, you understand, Yefgeny, but it seems to me that people in your line of work always make the same mistake. They assume that the best course is to use the information they get. Else why get it? And this need not be the most rational way to proceed. I can conceive of instances where the best thing is to get the information—and forget it."

"That's the line Avksentiev has taken."

"Don't tell me Avksentiev's involved."

"Precisely. Comrade Minister Avksentiev is afraid that his pet economic reforms, which are going along slowly enough as it is, could be ruined by a crash military program such as this. It's Avksentiev who's leading the attack in the Politburo against

Lewinter. As a matter of fact, I'm to see him tomorrow morning." Pogodin hesitated, and then added: "I guess I'm in over my head."

"Don't let it worry you too much," Zaitsev shot back. "You're in a place where that is the human condition."

14

FOUR-LANE HIGHWAYS are a fairly new phenomenon in the Soviet Union. As such, they generally have all the modern conveniences—one of which is road signs. Every bump or curve or crossroad is marked a half-mile or so in advance to warn that a particular bump or curve or crossroad is dead ahead. A second sign is planted like an X to mark the spot. But there was no sign of any kind where this particular single lane, well-paved road met the main Moscow-Smolensk highway—a clear hint to anybody who turned off that he had better know where he was going or he had no business being there.

Shortly before 10 A.M. a black Zil with a dented fender and rusted chrome swerved off onto the side road. "They'll be checking I.D.'s just ahead, Comrade," the chauffeur told the passenger in the back seat. Pogodin took his identification out of his wallet and looked at the photograph. It showed him in the full uniform of a lieutenant colonel of the KGB. He tried to peer through the eyes in the photograph to see what he had been thinking when the picture was taken, but he got no further than the expressionless stare that is the trademark of all official photographs.

Pogodin toyed with the I.D. card and stared out the window. He was sorry now that he had spent the night at Zaitsev's dacha. The party and the post-mortems had done little to prepare him for the interview with Avksentiev; a good night's sleep would have been more in order. And Pogodin was tired, there was no doubt about that. He had been under an enormous strain in the nineteen days since returning to the Soviet Union with what he thought was a big catch—perhaps the biggest intelligence catch since the end of the war. Somewhere along the way Pogodin's career had become inexorably intertwined with Lewinter's fate. Pogodin had discovered Lewinter (no matter it was by sheer accident) and brought him home; ergo he was responsible.

The responsibility had weighed heavily on Pogodin during the debriefing at Obninsk. He had sat in on the nightly round-up sessions listening attentively as the experts went over Lewinter's story with a fine-tooth comb. Everything had gone smoothly until the inquiries started to come in from Moscow. Then, suddenly, Lewinter was no longer a trophy for the intelligence community to flaunt; he was political. It was at that point that Avksentiev had come into the picture.

And Avksentiev was someone to reckon with. Pogodin knew Avksentiev, or at least he used to know him. Avksentiev had been his section chief in Prague some years back. Since then he had gone on to bigger and better things, as everyone knew he one day would. Pogodin wondered if Avksentiev had changed any since Prague. In those days he was a meticulous planner, a man who did his homework and then confronted problems the way he crossed bridges—one at a time. He was especially good in dealing with sensitive matters; he spoke in metaphors and never stepped on toes and he generally got his way. Pogodin would have to watch for the metaphors.

Beyond the first curve in the side road, well hidden from the highway, the Zil pulled up at a railroad-crossing gate. An old woman sat on a chair in front of a small shack. A framed photograph of Lenin hung over the door. The woman was there to turn back anyone who took the road by accident—or out of curiosity. Nobody had. Ever.

The first of two military checkpoints came a quarter-mile beyond that. Four miles into the road, on the edge of a flat, fertile shelf that stretched as far as the eye could see, stood Avksentiev's estate. The main house, a gray, square, spare stone mansion, had been built in the seventeenth century by a Russian count who considered himself a patron of the theater. The central hall was actually a miniature proscenium stage upon which the count's serfs had performed plays—some of which the count, who fancied himself a genius, had written. The stable, a long, low building tucked away behind a small rise, had been converted into a bunkhouse for the military unit permanently attached to the estate. Immediately behind the main house stood the ruins of a small chapel; some of the walls still had fragments of frescoes on them. The chapel had been blown up by local peasants in the burst of antireligious fervor that followed the Bolshevik Revolution.

A formal garden had been added to the estate in the mid-nineteenth century by one of the count's descendants who had come across a painting of Versailles. Smack in the middle of the garden stood the four-foot-thick roof of a steel-and-cement air raid shelter, a relic from what the Russians called the Great Patriotic War. There was a story to the shelter. The Germans had used the estate as a divisional command post during their drive on Moscow in 1941. At the high-water mark of the campaign, the German general staff had ordered all divisional commanders to construct massive shelters in case Hitler decided to visit the front line. He never did. Later, during the Cold War, the shelter was provided with modern air conditioning and communications equipment in case Stalin decided to visit the estate. That visit never materialized either. Avksentiev had only recently turned the bunker into a storage cellar for wine and potatoes.

Pogodin's car swung past the shelter and drew to a stop on the gravel driveway next to the front door. A very old man, whom Pogodin took for a servant, stood on the steps. The man was well over six feet tall and very thin. He wore loose fitting trousers and a rough, collarless peasant shirt buttoned to the neck. His eyeglasses were thick as magnifying lenses. Walking with a slight shuffle, his backbone curved like a bow, the old man led the way into the house. He kept his eyes on the ground, following—or so it seemed to Pogodin—some invisible path marked out on the tiles.

The trail led through the proscenium hall lined with gilt-framed oil paintings and marble statues. There were six huge columns in the room that looked like reddish-brown porphyry but were actually made of balsa wood so they could be easily rearranged for different plays. At the far corner, near a large wooden contraption that had been used to re-create the sound of wind and thunder for the count's theater, two small girls sat cross-legged on the floor playing pick-up sticks. Both of them looked up at Pogodin and smiled and went back to their game. The old man opened a small door—so small that Pogodin had to duck under the lintel—and motioned Pogodin through. The door closed behind him, and Pogodin found himself alone on the top of a steel ladder that spiraled down into darkness. The air was filled with the faint odor of sulphur. At the bottom step, Pogodin paused, the way one does when entering a movie theater, to wait for his vision to adjust. The only light came from a half-dozen slit windows high in the walls. Slowly, the blacks and grays started to fall into place and Pogodin began to make out his surroundings. The room was directly beneath the proscenium hall and about the same size. At one end, yellow beads of electric light frow another room seeped under a curtain. Odd pieces of theatrical equipment—mock trees, a row boat with saddles in it, a large straw basket full of armor, a fake well—were lined up against the far wall beneath the windows. Hanging from the ceiling from pieces of string of various lengths were dozens of cutouts made of paper and straw and colored wool. Some looked like birds in flight, some like houses or castles, some like floral designs, some like nothing Pogodin had ever seen before.

"They're called *pajaqi;* Polish peasants decorate their homes with them. Have you seen the floor yet?" The voice, speaking a precise, almost classical Russian, came from beyond the curtain with the light seeping under it. It belonged, unmistakably, to Avksentiev.

"It's too dim to make out, Comrade Minister."

"Ah, yes, of course. Try scraping your shoes against the floor then."

Pogodin rubbed his right foot back and forth and heard and felt sand. He crouched very low and looked more closely; the floor was covered with a sand drawing, an intricately etched geometric pattern of circles and squares and triangles that spiraled out from the center of the room like ripples in a pond.

Again the voice of Avksentiev. "It's quite unique, I'm told. There probably aren't a dozen men alive that can still do that sort of thing. Come, join me in here, Yefgeny Mikhailovich."

When Pogodin made no move to go, Avksentiev added: "Don't worry about disturbing the floor. Come ahead. The first step is the hardest." And Avksentiev laughed good-humoredly at the psychology that invariably kept his visitors rooted to the floor.

"It's like walking on a great painting, Comrade Minister," Pogodin said, and he tiptoed across the room toward the beads of light, trying hard to put his toes inside the patterns and keep his heels off the ground.

The glare from a naked electric bulb struck Pogodin's eyes as he pushed aside the curtain. Now the odor of sulphur was overpowering. He stood inside the room, blinking, uncertain, waiting again for his vision to return.

"You haven't changed a bit, Yefgeny, not one bit," Avksentiev said. "You still look so American it makes me nervous to talk to you. I haven't seen you since . . . where was it?"

"Czechoslovakia."

"Quite right, I should have remembered. Czechoslovakia."

Pogodin could make out Avksentiev now. He was sitting, stark naked, on a wooden bench, covered from head to toe with a thin coat of dried mud.

"Will you join me, Yefgeny? I have it flown in specially from the Black Sea. The mud there is extremely rich in sulphur. Excellent for arthritis. But then, I don't expect you have arthritis, do you? Join me anyhow. There are probably other ingredients in it that will do you good."

"Thank you, Comrade Minister, but I think of mud as something one wipes off, not on."

"You always did have an orthodox mind. Well, Yefgeny Mikhailovich, it is pleasant to see you after all these years. You look well, tired perhaps, but well. Sit down, help yourself to a drink. I'll wash off the mud and we'll talk." Avksentiev moved to a tiled corner and turned on a shower nozzle full blast. The caked mud began to dissolve into rivulets and run down the drain.

Boris Avksentiev was one of the rising stars in the Soviet Communist Party hierarchy. At fifty-one, he was already a candidate member of the ruling Politburo, the deputy minister in charge of overall implementation of economic reforms and secretary of the supersecret committee that supervised the country's external security organs. During his Komsomol days, he had been a champion wrestler; at one point there had been some talk of sending him to the Olympics, but the idea had been shelved when Avksentiev expressed an interest in going into security work—which he did for some time. The people who think about such things didn't want him to become too conspicuous too soon. As Avksentiev hosed down, Pogodin could still see the wrestler in him; sturdy shoulders tapering to a narrow waist and muscular thighs. If Avksentiev's body had a defect, it was that his legs were, proportionately, short for his torso; people who saw Avksentiev sitting down invariably came away with the impression that he was much taller than he actually was.

Avksentiev wrapped himself in a white terry-cloth robe and, patting his body dry, took a seat opposite Pogodin. "How do you like the house? It's quite a rarity, really. The theater, I mean. Did you see the wooden contraption upstairs? If you turn the crank, it produces the sound effects of a storm."

"I was wondering what it was," Pogodin said. He understood that there would be some ice-breaking small talk.

"This level has the prop room; some of the original scenery is still here. Way in the back there is a trap door to the stage. It's really charming—a genuine piece of Russian history."

"I thought you lived in Moscow—I was surprised when the car headed out of the city," Pogodin said. He edged his chair around to face Avksentiev. The legs squeaked across the floor and sent a chill up his spine.

"I have an apartment in Moscow, but when I can get away, I prefer to come here. I like to commune, though with what or whom I'm not quite sure." Pogodin laughed politely, nervously.

"Who does the sand drawing? It really is a masterpiece."

"Ah, that's a long story. But I'll tell it to you. Did you take notice of the old man who met you at the door? He does it. He makes the *pajaqi* too. He learned the art in Poland; he's Polish peasant on his mother's side, and was raised there until the family moved to Odessa in nineteen oh seven. He was sixteen, I believe, at the time."

Absently, Avksentiev poured himself a glass of mineral water. "In the morning, long before anyone else is up, the old man sweeps the sand on the floor into a bucket. He rolls a sheet of newspaper into a funnel, pinches off the end and fills the funnel with sand. Then, bending at the waist, he begins his new design. He always works from the center out in expanding circles, and ends up at the foot of the spiral staircase. Every day, three hundred and sixty-five days a year, there is a different design on the floor; he never does the same one twice. He's going blind doing it, but he keeps at it."

"It probably takes him back to his youth," Pogodin offered. But Avksentiev went right on as if he hadn't spoken. "It may surprise you to learn that the old man is my father. Ah, I see you are surprised. He has an interesting story, my father. He grew to manhood in Odessa. One of his boyhood friends was a seminary student named Joseph Vissarionovich Dzhugashvili, whom we of course know as Stalin. When Stalin joined the Communist Party, my father tagged along with him. In the early days before the Revolution, the two of them robbed banks in Odessa together. During the Civil War, Stalin stayed in Moscow but my father took on a job nobody else wanted: executing deserters. He traveled from front to front, putting his pistol to the heads of quaking men and puffing the trigger. He had read somewhere that condemned men were entitled to a choice, so he always carried two pistols—a large smooth-bore revolver and a small caliber pistol—and he let them pick which one he was to use. When Stalin consolidated his power in the late twenties, he decided to reward his old comrades. One bright day he rang my father up on the telephone and gave him this estate. In the thirties, Stalin purged all his cronies, all his bank-robbing friends, the Odessa Party people, everyone—everyone except my father. He used to sit on the stage, his feet dangling, waiting for them to come. I remember that every night he used to embrace me and say 'good-bye,' not 'good night.' After a while he began clutching at the paraphernalia of his youth, things which took him back to the days in Poland when he didn't have the thought of an irrational death hanging over his head. That's when he began with the *pajaqi* and the sand drawings. He doesn't speak much these days. He's not really insane; he's just living in another, simpler world."

Pogodin listened in silence, torn between embarrassment and curiosity. Curiosity won out.

"And did you ever learn why your father was spared?"

"Ah, no, some years ago I made discreet inquiries, but nobody knew. Perhaps his name was simply overlooked. Perhaps Stalin remembered some favor my father had done him and spared him for it. Perhaps they set out to arrest him and couldn't find the road. Who can say?"

Pogodin had heard many stories about the days of Stalin's terror—one from his own father, who had been summoned home from an overseas assignment to what he thought would be prison or execution, only to find he was being promoted. But the story of Avksentiev's father was particularly moving. "There's something very melancholy about using sand to create art. It's so . . . well, transient. There will be nobody to continue the tradition when your father is gone."

"Ah, but there will be," Avksentiev said. "You see, I've taken up the art. The actual drawing is not that difficult, something like putting frosting on a cake. It's developing your own patterns and maintaining the concentric symmetry that's hard. I can do a fairly simple thing of linked circles, and I'm trying to develop the complexities."

"How fascinating," Pogodin said. "I envy you your commitment to tradition."

"My commitment, Yefgeny Mikhailovich, is to the status quo, whatever that status quo may be." Avksentiev said the words coldly, like an instructor who had finally arrived at the theorem. And Pogodin understood the story of the sand drawings was not small talk—but metaphor.

"I owe you an apology, Comrade Minister," Pogodin said. "I didn't realize we were engrossed in a serious discussion."

"If you are up to your old standards, Yefgeny, the point will not have been lost on you."

"You are telling me the answer is no."

"Precisely. On the merits, anyone would think that we were foolish not to act on the information that the American defector has offered us. But you must understand that I and my colleagues are committed to the status quo—out of instinct, out of habit, out of inclination. It really doesn't matter very much what that status quo happens to be. Our country has been through decades of turmoil and terror. Now at long last we've come to a period of peace and stability and consolidation. When we do move off center, as we are now with economic reforms in some industrial enterprises, we move slowly, deliberately, hesitantly—and only after long and meticulous study. If we accept the defector's information at face value, we must move off center quickly. It would bring on an enormous amount of dislocation, involving money, priorities, reputations, areas of influence within the government and, more important, within the party. You can appreciate, can't you, that it would be no easy matter."

Now Pogodin understood why he had been summoned for this private meeting with Avksentiev. He was being told to lay off. Avksentiev and those members of the ruling circles for whom he spoke felt more comfortable doing nothing.

"Yefgeny, you have shown yourself to be a resourceful and tactful intelligence officer. Now it would seem that you've jeopardized your impartiality. You've become a partisan—and that puts you on dangerous ground. You have a bright future ahead of you. Only bear with us. Some of us, quite genuinely, don't trust this American defector. Our fears about abandoning the status quo are reinforced by our instinctive doubts about a man who walks in off the street, uninvited, and offers us one of America's most closely guarded secrets. We are inclined to mistrust him. We are sitting on the fence now. Perhaps the Americans will push us one way or another. Do you know who is handling this on their end?"

"I haven't been in touch with that side of the operation, Comrade Minister."

"An old friend of ours, the one who ran the Cernú operation in Czechoslovakia when we were there—Leo Diamond. Odd, isn't it?"

"Is that what makes you think Lewinter is an operation?"

"Partly. Diamond has an operational mind. It's precisely the kind of thing he would think up."

"So we write Lewinter off, then. That is your conclusion."

"Not quite, no. We will harvest some propaganda from him. After all, we have on our hands a man who has defected from America because he can no longer tolerate life there. The very least we can do is let him speak out on the subject. As for the rest, we will wait and see."

15

"OF COURSE, if it's too much trouble . . ." Lewinter said, and left the sentence hanging unfinished in the air.

It was an awkward moment. The waitress, a matronly woman who hovered over Lewinter like a bird about to pounce on a worm, waited for someone to tell her what to do. Boris Miliutin, the Propaganda Ministry Chief of Section who had been called in to handle the press conference, held his breath, his fork and knife poised over the 250-gram portion of beefsteak on his plate.

"I don't understand," Avksentiev said when Pogodin translated. "If *what* is too much trouble?"

"It's the meat, Comrade Minister," Pogodin explained quietly. "I believe it is too rare for him. He would like it put back on the fire."

Avksentiev snapped his fingers, pointed at Lewinter's plate, and said a few words in Russian. The waitress leaned over Lewinter's shoulder and snatched it away. Miliutin, a thin, imperturbable functionary with a beak nose and eyeglasses that rested a third of the way down on it, tucked his fork and knife under the overhang of his plate and lit a cigarette. He pinched it between the thumb and forefinger, with the burning end pointing up, and had to twist his wrist completely around to smoke.

"You were giving us your impressions of Moscow?" Avksentiev said. Out of politeness, Avksentiev, Pogodin, and Miliutin ignored the food in front of them. Lewinter never thought to invite them to eat.

"Well, Mr. Av-sen-tev, I hope I will not be stepping on anyone's toes if I say that my first impression of Moscow is that it is a singularly dreary city."

"What does that mean, 'stepping on toes'?" Avksentiev asked when Pogodin translated word for word.

Millutin, who had never traveled outside of the Soviet Union but spoke textbook English, explained. "Excuse me, Comrade Minister, but it is an expression that means 'to annoy.' I step on toes, I annoy, that is the logic behind it."

His khaki eyes narrowing competitively, Pogodin threaded his fingers through his kinky hair. "He's using it in the sense of 'offend.' *Annoy* will do, but *offend* is more precise.

"I can never understand translations," Lewinter said. "Everytime I say something, you have a discussion. Hey, don't translate that, I'm not complaining, it's just interesting."

"What does he say?" asked Avksentiev.

"He says everytime he says a word, we have a discussion," Pogodin said.

"Then let him learn Russian," snapped Avksentiev. He was hungry and the food in front of him was getting cold.

"What did he say?" asked Lewinter.

"Comrade Minister Avksentiev asks if you've had any luck with Russian," Pogodin said. "We must find you a tutor soon."

"Yes, by all means. I would like to try my hand at it. If I'm going to live here, I'd better. When in Rome . . ."

"Ah, I take it he is comparing Moscow to Rome," said Avksentiev, who had caught a single word. "Tell him I've been to Rome too, twice in fact, and I also like it."

Pogodin was having trouble making the two conversations mesh. He was about to try a new tack when the waitress returned with Lewinter's plate. Lewinter sliced experimentally into the middle of the meat and announced that it was fine. Suddenly he noticed the other three men had been waiting for him. He blushed, confused, embarrassed. "Please, Yefgeny, don't wait for me; eat."

For a while the four men ate in silence, Lewinter meticulously arranging each forkful so that it contained an equal portion of meat, green beans, and stringy fried potatoes, the other three more or less toying with cold, soggy food or sipping Bulgarian wine.

"Ask him, Yefgeny, if he's given any thought to where he would like to settle and what he would like to do."

"I appreciate him raising the subject," Lewinter said. He had been wondering when someone would get around to it. "I'm quite happy where I am up on the Lenin Hills. Of course, I wouldn't need a whole house; a four- or five-room flat will do me nicely. As for work, I would very much like to get involved in the field of pollution, or more specifically the question of solid-waste disposal. I believe I can make some important contributions in this area."

Avksentiev took this in. "Well, Yefgeny, whose house shall we give him? Podgorny's or Kosygin's? Lenin Hills! I'd like to live up there too. He has a lot to learn, your American friend. Explain to him, will you, that the Hills are reserved for senior members of the government and important visitors, like himself. Tell him we will provide a nice flat for him somewhere in the city, along with a car, and a reasonable stipend. The usual sort of arrangement. As for the work, well, we shall see where he can contribute most to the growth of our socialist society, eh?"

There was silence as the waitress brought custard and coffee.

"Can you ask about the hay-fever pills, Yefgeny?"

"What does he say now?"

"Comrade Minister, Mr. Lewinter suffers from a severe case of hay fever. He brought some American pills with him, but we naturally took them away until we could analyze them. Now they seem to have disappeared."

"Yes, of course, how extremely interesting. Perhaps Miliutin here should begin briefing our American friend on the press conference. It is a matter of some importance that it come off well."

"What does he say about the pills?" Lewinter asked. "I hate to bother him . .

"Mr. Lewinter," Miliutin said in English, "if I could own your attention for a short space of time." He lit another cigarette from the stub of an old one and opened a small notebook on the table. "You will meet the representatives of the press, including some representatives of the capitalist press, in a conference room off the Great Hall of Mirrors here on the Kremlin grounds. It's only a short walk from where we sit. I myself will be with you to help you, to guide you, to clear up any misunderstandings.

"I should warn you now," Lewinter said, "I get very nervous before large groups of people."

"So, there will be no need to be nervous, Mr. Lewinter. In most instances the questions will be friendly. I can, in fact, with some accuracy, deliver you an idea of what those questions will be—and perhaps you, in sequence, can deliver us some idea of how you will answer them."

And so they began the dress rehearsal for the press conference.

"The first question will more than probably be a general one dealing with conditions in the United States of America, the conditions which presumably encouraged you to seek asylum with us. And what will you answer to that, Mr. Lewinter?"

In his mind's eye, Lewinter could see the journalists waiting for his answer, and he became nervous at the thought. "I, eh, well, I guess I, eh, would begin"—he cleared his throat and started to tell Miliutin what he thought Miliutin would want to hear.

". . . imminent collapse of capitalism as we know it. It simply can't keep tearing people and society apart and last. I'd talk about the repression, about the concentration camps for dissidents, about the economic and cultural chaos. I'd tell them about the enormous disaffection of the middle class in America, about all those people who have found that cars and television sets and washing machines on credit do not make a utopia. I'd say that it is the middle class that is the backbone of the revolution brewing in America."

Lewinter was sure that he had answered very well indeed.

Miliutin took another puff of his cigarette and looked coldly across the table. He knew his business. For a moment he didn't say a word. Then: "Mr. Lewinter, I will make three criticisms of your response, two minor and one major. I hope you will take them inside you. First the two minor ones: You made no mention of racism and moral depravity among the younger generation. Our Russian people are educated to these problems, and would think it extraordinary if you overlooked them. Then, you talk about the middle class bringing on a revolution. This is something our people are not familiar with. In the writings of Lenin, the middle class does not figure in the downfall of capitalism; rather it is the polarization of the middle class into proletarians and exploiters and the subsequent struggle between them that will overturn capitalism. Your answers should take this into account—though not in those words, of course."

"You take a very catholic position, Comrade," Pogodin said. He was toying with a demitasse spoon, stirring the coffee that had spilled into his saucer.

"I'm not quite sure in what sense you use the expression *catholic*," Miliutin said, holding his ground. He tilted his head downward and looked at Pogodin over the top of his eyeglasses.

"*Catholic* in the sense that you accept things as dogma that were written fifty years ago. There *is* an enormous middle class in the United States and, as Mr. Lewinter points out, it *is* the source of most of the dissatisfaction in the country. Neither Lenin, nor Marx for that matter, correctly assessed the role of the middle class in an advanced capitalist society. Ignoring the existence of the middle class won't make it go away, will it? Surely we can do better than that."

"I should think, Comrade Pogodin, that we could do better than waste our few moments here in the technical discussion of the role of the middle class in a capitalist economy."

The discussion was in English, and Avksentiev looked from one to the other as if he were watching a Ping-Pong match, comprehending nothing.

"But there is a larger issue here, Comrade Miliutin."

"A larger issue?" Miliutin said coolly.

"Exactly, a larger issue. It is extremely important, in my view, for Mr. Lewinter to establish his credibility. To do this, he must answer the questions candidly, not like some record that the Propaganda Ministry puts on a phonograph. I would even think it advisable if he complimented America—or at least distinguished between the American people, who are, after all, a great and freedom-loving proletariat, and the ruling circles."

Miliutin leaned forward and looked at Pogodin through the middle of his eyeglasses. He was extremely near-sighted, and they made his eyes seem like two small rivets. This time Miliutin spoke in Russian. "You have crossed departmental boundaries, Comrade Pogodin, and that puts you on dangerous ground."

It was the second time that day that someone had used that expression.

Avksentiev waded into the conversation. "I gather you are having some sort of disagreement."

Speaking quickly, quietly, Pogodin filled him in. Lewinter, ignored for the moment, leaned back in his chair, bored. Since his arrival in Moscow, he had been the center of attention. Now he realized that he was—and would remain—the odd man out.

Avksentiev listened to Pogodin, and delivered his verdict without an instant's hesitation. "You are correct, of course, Yefgeny, about the middle class. I've no doubt that Comrade Miliutin here, in other circumstances, would be the first to concede the point. But he must have his way. You see, you fail to understand what audience we are addressing. We are not talking to the people in capitalist countries. They will inevitably assume that Lewinter is insane, or they will believe the stories that the Americans will undoubtedly fill their newspapers with—something to the effect that Lewinter is a debtor or a wife-beater or a pederast. No, we are talking to our own people,

which is something Comrade Miliutin understands, since it is
his business to understand that. We are presenting Lewinter, not
to make converts out of capitalists, but to reinforce what we
have always told our own people: that things are better here
than in the West. To put it in the terms of the conversation we
enjoyed this morning, this is a case where candor could undermine the status quo. Comrade Miliutin here is the faithful
defender of the status quo; let us leave Mr. Lewinter in his
skilled hands."

Miliutin edged his eyeglasses up the bridge of his nose
with a forefinger and turned back to Lewinter. "And now, Mr.
Lewinter, if I can anticipate the second question . . ."

"And now, if I can have the second question?" Miliutin's
long, bony finger stretched across the table toward a man in the
second row. "Mr. Vlasek, the representative of *Rude Pravo*."

His legs crossed, his pencil tapping against his lined note-
pad, the Czech correspondent from *Rude Pravo* put his question. Was it true, could Mr. Lewinter tell him, that the great
majority of American university professors had been co-opted
by the Establishment into doing all sorts of military and intelligence chores, both on and off campus?

Yes, Lewinter said, it was true. He himself had been more
or less forced to work on a military project in order to get
his teaching fellowship at the Massachusetts Institute of
Technology. Oh yes, it was a subtle business. Nobody came
right out and said work on such-and-such a project or no job.

But one was made to understand from the start that the teaching position, and subsequent promotions and pay raises, depended on contributing to the government projects, which, in turn, funneled vast sums of money into the university treasuries. In the old days, publish or perish was the rule in American universities. Now it was produce or perish. Does that, asked Lewinter, answer your question?

The answers were coming smoothly now; even Miliutin had begun to relax. There had been a horrible moment when Lewinter, on the threshold of the conference room, caught sight of thirty or forty journalists and the batteries of klieg lights and cameras. He had actually backed off a step, his mind racing wildly to find some plausible excuse why he couldn't walk into the room and meet the press. But there was no turning back; from the moment he first entered the Soviet Embassy in Tokyo, there had been no turning back. And so, encouraged by Miliutin's palm flat against his shoulder, he crossed the threshold and took his place at one side of a desk and listened as Miliutin introduced him to the world. Here meet a man, said Miliutin, who has fled from capitalist oppression and been granted political asylum in the Union of Soviet Socialist Republics.

Then came the first question—the one about conditions in the United States—and Lewinter stepped into the spotlight. Coughing and clearing his throat to hide the fact that he kept running out of breath halfway through each sentence, he talked about the imminent collapse of capitalism, about the repression and concentration camps, about the economic and cultural chaos in America. He remembered to mention racism and the moral depravity of the younger generation. And he described how the middle class in America was polarizing into the haves and have-nots. The more he talked, the more confident he grew.

Miliutin's fingers swept in an arc and designated a woman reporter from a Bulgarian daily newspaper, *Narodna Mladege.* "What impressions does Mr. Lewinter have of the life in the socialist sphere?" she asked.

"I have of course only been here a short time," Lewinter said. Nothing like this had ever happened to him before, and he was beginning to enjoy watching journalists scribble down whatever he said as if his words had some great value. "But I'll be happy to give you my impressions. I think, first of all, that the normal social intercourse between people is less complicated and more honest. That is to say, everyone isn't looking to get something for nothing . . ." Lewinter's voice droned on, filling the air with observations he had come by secondhand.

Miliutin squinted into the klieg lights and selected the next questioner, a Frenchman who ran a small wire service to English language Communist newspapers. "How have you been treated, sir?" he asked. "Do you have any complaints?"

"I've been treated with every courtesy," said Lewinter. "My only complaint is that I seem to have misplaced my hay-fever pills I brought from the States, but I'm sure my hosts have adequate remedies for hay fever." The remark drew a laugh.

A Soviet journalist asked Lewinter if there were others

like him in the United States who were dissatisfied enough with conditions there to flee.

"A great many, I think," said Lewinter. "The exodus is on."

Miliutin designated a fat East German journalist who had been in Moscow almost twenty years. But before he could get his question out, a brash young Reuters man sitting next to him popped up. He was already in a good deal of trouble for maintaining contacts with literary dissidents. Miliutin suspected that it was this particular Englishman who had smuggled out the first published account of Axelrod's heretic speech to the Party Congress.

"Let's get down to some unrehearsed nuts and bolts, if we may, Mr. Lewinter," the Englishman said. "Comrade Miliutin here introduced you as a scientist. What sort of scientist are you? And did you bring any information with you?"

There was absolute quiet in the room; even the Soviet and East European journalists were curious what Lewinter would answer.

Miliutin smiled thinly in the direction of the Englishman and nodded. It was a question he had anticipated.

"Well, what sort of scientist am I? A good one, I hope." Laughter. "I am basically, which is to say by training if not by inclination, a ceramic engineer, someone who knows how to make dishes. I told you before that I was co-opted by the military-industrial complex. They had me working on the nose cones of ballistic missiles. Nothing really very secret. But in the course of my work I came to believe that the American military establishment, aided and abetted by the giant economic interests in the country, were constructing a first-strike missile force which could be used—and in my opinion, would inevitably be used, once it existed—to launch a preemptive war against the Soviet Union. I wanted no part of this—and so I came here. Naturally, I feel obligated to share what little knowledge I have of ballistic nose cones with my Soviet counterparts. But as I say, there was nothing really very secret about what I was doing; my sharing is more in the nature of a gesture."

Several of the Soviet journalists in the room applauded Lewinter's statement of conscience. Miliutin pushed his eyeglasses up with his index finger. His face was expressionless; those in the room who had dealt with him often and knew him well could only guess at the satisfaction he felt.

"Next question, please," Miliutin said, and his finger hovered in the air.

Moscow, August 22 (Reuters). The Soviet Union announced today that it has granted political asylum to an American expert on ballistic missiles.

1945 Moscow standard time

Moscow, August 22 (Reuters). Moscow today granted political asylum to an American scientist who helped construct nose cones for nuclear missiles. In a rare press conference held in the Kremlin, the Soviets introduced the defector, A. J. Lewinter, 39, to Soviet and Western journalists. "The American military establishment is constructing a first-strike missile force to launch a preemptive war against the Soviet Union," Lewinter declared. "I wanted no part of this, and so I came here. Naturally, I will share what little knowledge I have of ballistic nose cones with my hosts."

1949 Moscow standard time

PART IV

THE GAMBIT

16

WHEN IT CAME to Intelligence matters, this was (for all practical purposes) where the buck stopped—a conspicuously inconspicuous Foam Rubber City conference room on the third floor of the Executive Office Building, a stone's throw from the White House. The only marking on the door was the room number and a badly typed note on an index card put up so long ago the Scotch tape was dry and peeling. The note said:

> *POsitively* No ADmittance
> WithouT
> Written AUthorization

When Committee 303 (which took its name from the room number) was not in session, the door was double-locked and the area was checked for electronic bugs twice daily by security technicians. When the committee met, generally on Thursday nights, there was supposed to be an armed guard posted at the door. In practice, however, the committee borrowed any warm body that was handy to ward off accidental visitors. There never were any. Ever.

On the Thursday that 303 took up the Lewinter affair, a girl from the evening typing pool had been commandeered. Engrossed in her book *(Games People Play),* she didn't look up when Buzz Martin stuck his head out of the room. "Sorry to interrupt," he said with a trace of cynicism. "There's a gentleman waiting downstairs—tall, fortyish, name of Diamond—ask him to come up, will you, honey?"

"Sure thing," she said, and headed for the lobby.

Committee 303 was essentially a clearing house for the U.S. Intelligence community. It came into existence in 1961 when President John F. Kennedy, smarting from the fiasco at the Bay of Pigs, cast about for ways to put a tighter rein on American Intelligence agencies. Thereafter, all covert Intelligence operations—especially those of the C.I.A.—had to be channeled through 303 for approval.

Despite its crucial role—or perhaps because of it—Committee 303 was shrouded in secrecy; in all of Washington, there were only a few hundred people who were even aware of its existence. Buzz Martin's wife wasn't one of them. Her husband was that kind of man: in his private life, a stickler for propriety; in his career, a stickler for security. It was this tight-lipped quality that had caught the eye of the President years before when he was looking for a special assistant for national security affairs. Now Buzz Martin (the nickname dated back to his salad days when he won a reputation for cutting through knotty problems like a buzz saw) was the President's man on 303, a no-nonsense, middle-aged whiz kid who spent almost all of his waking hours weighing options, and who seemed to have a single passion in life—to protect the power and prestige and person of the President of the United States, come what may.

Martin demonstrated this once again at the start of the session when Harry Dukess, the regular nonvoting representative of the Central Intelligence Agency on 303, had reported on the "fuss" in Bangkok. "We spread a little money around and set things right," Dukess had explained, trying to gloss over the incident.

"That plain won't do," Martin had said, cradling a puffy cheek in the palm of his hand. He rated everyone in government according to his ability to embarrass the President—and the C.I.A. people stood high on the list. "You guys spend more time playing games and toying with disaster than anyone I know

"That's not quite fair," Dukess had begun to protest. "If you're going to bring up the Indonesian affair again—"

But Martin cut him off with a wave: "One of these days you're going to give us another full-fledged U-2 incident. Well, if anything embarrassing surfaces from the Bangkok business, the first priority is the President, which means we may have to throw one or two of your people to the wolves."

"Won't bother him none, a-throwin' someone to the wolves, long as 'tisn't him that's a-bein' throwed," chuckled the senior senator from North Carolina, another permanent member of 303. William Jennings Bryan Talmidge was a pearl-handled pistol of a man, courtly and decorative when it suited his mood, but explosive when riled. And at seventy-two, Talmidge was still easily riled, especially by the C.I.A. "God damn, mah subcommittee don't even know how much money they spend, no less on what," he often complained. "Time someone took 'em down a peg or two."

Talmidge looked as if he could do the job too. In the nation's capitol, he was a power broker par excellence. It wasn't so much that he knew where the bodies were buried—though he had, as he allowed, "more than an inklin'." The source of his power was the military and his relationship to it. Arguing passionately that sufficiency was no substitute for sheer overpowering mathematical supremacy, he pressed on the military establishment installations of all sizes and shapes and descriptions. Not surprisingly, more than a share somehow wound up in his home state. "If'n he puts one more thing down here," one of Talmidge's Republican opponents privately complained, "the state's gonna sink."

On paper, Talmidge and the other members of Committee 303 were equal, but Buzz Martin, being the President's man, and Senator Talmidge, being his own man, were (as the saying goes) the most equal. It was a state of affairs the other members and the organizations they represented had learned to live with gracefully, if not happily. The only potential dissenter, Lieutenant Colonel Pruchnik, a representative of the Joint Chiefs who combined second-generation drive with third-generation patience, was content to bide his time. The other members —Deputy Undersecretary of State Kenneth Foss, G.O.P. Representative Howard Snell, Deputy Secretary of Defense Richard Kunen—deferred judgments until the big two had reached agreement and then followed along behind.

With the Bangkok business out of the way, Dukess had brought up another matter. The Agency wanted a final go-ahead on Operation 85 Bravo, which had been approved in principle by Committee 303 the previous month. Operation 85 Bravo called for aerial drops over Cuba of arms, ammunition, false documents, and bogus money to espionage teams that didn't exist. The idea was to gradually make the Cuban authorities aware that the Americans were running phantom drops—an old ploy, used to advantage against North Vietnam—so that if and when Washington put in real espionage teams, they would be much easier to resupply, the Cubans presumably having lowered their guard by then.

"Ah for one think it might be a spankin' smart idea to hold off on this a tiny bit," Senator Talmidge had said, and Buzz Martin had chimed in: "As far as the White House is concerned, we have to weigh the possibility that one of the planes will eventually be lost. What then?"

"I thought we've been all through that," Dukess had said. "The planes will be piloted by Cuban exiles, not Americans, and they'll operate from bases outside the country. And the con-tractees know that if they're shot down, they're on their own."

"They know that now," Martin had said. "But when they're in that Cuban jail, you can bet they'll spill everything—who paid them, where they trained, who they were working for. Since we have no plans to put in live teams for a while, why don't we put this one on the back burner." There had been a general nod of agreement.

"Well, then, if that's outa the way, let's move on to this Lewinter business," said Senator Talmidge. "What d'ya say, Buzz, why don't you stick your head out the door and get this Diamond fella up heah."

"Gentlemen," said Diamond, striding into the room. His eyes flitted over the committee members and came to rest, like a latch locking into place, on Dukess. "Harry, didn't know you were in on this," he said evenly—without a trace that he was talking to a man he hated.

"I represent the Agency," Dukess said flatly.

"I never assumed otherwise," Diamond answered. He hefted his briefcase onto the table and clicked it open. "Augustus Jerome Lewinter, gentlemen," he said, introducing a thick file folder as if it were the man in question.

"Ah take it from the fact that y'all are heah that we're in a mite of trouble, son?" Talmidge squinted across the table at Diamond as if he were blinded by light—or getting ready to pounce.

"You take it correctly, Senator," Diamond said. And he

proceeded to give 303 a detailed account of the defection of A. J. Lewinter.

Diamond had spread the folder on the table in front of him, but he didn't bother to glance at it. "There you have it," he wound up. "The Russians trotted him out—you saw all the stories, I take it—and squeezed him dry for internal propaganda value."

"How did our cover story go over—I mean, did anybody believe it?" This from Kunen, an overeager, overripe political scientist.

"That was handled fairly well," Diamond said. "We knew what was coming, so we arranged for the Boston police to have a warrant out for Lewinter—exposing himself to some teenage girls. Three witnesses, too. And the Boston courts were after him for back alimony—that was the real thing, by the way. Since the police warrant predated the Soviet press conference, the boys in the press more or less swallowed the story and printed it as a fact."

"That about brings us to what the folks back home call the core of the apple, the pit of the prune, don't it?" asked Talmidge.

"You mean, what did Lewinter take with him?" said Diamond.

"Exactly, my boy, what did this heah Lewinter fella stuff into his kit bag when he decided to head for greener, or should I say redder, pastures?" Talmidge folded his hands behind his head and leaned back into the linked palms.

"It isn't what was in the flight bag, Senator. It's what was in his head. And we have good reason to believe . . ."

Leaning forward with his elbows on the table, speaking as if he were taking them into his confidence, Diamond reconstructed his "worst-case" theory: the indications that Lewinter had regained his photo memory lost as a child, the evidence that he had access to a top secret MIRV trajectory file long enough to imprint the heart of it in that photo memory.

"How about motive?" asked Martin. As Diamond spoke, Martin jotted notes on a yellow legal pad. He did it out of habit; before he left for the evening, he would deposit them in the burn bag and brief the President from memory on those matters he thought the President should know about. Martin wrote *Motive* and put a colon after it and then waited for Diamond to go on.

"You can take your pick," Diamond said. "The psychiatrist on our C.P.P. decided finally that Lewinter was after status. The defector, our psychiatrist tells us, especially the one that brings some valuable information with him, stands out in a crowd. And Lewinter wanted to stand out in a crowd. I myself am inclined to search for the motive in Lewinter's leftist—perhaps *radical* is a more appropriate word—activities. He apparently had become very disillusioned with the United States. Anyhow, we have enough motive for three defections."

"O.K., let's go back to the MIRV folder you say he saw. What was in it?" Martin wrote *MIRV* and a colon and waited for Diamond's answer.

"The United States, gentlemen, has something like eleven hundred and seventy missiles in its arsenal—the great bulk of them either land-based Minutemen in silos or Polaris missiles in nuclear submarines. You probably know the figures better than I do, but I understand that by the end of this month, almost all of these missiles will have been fitted with MIRVs—Multiple Independently Targetable Reentry Vehicles. Now, MIRV, as I understand it, is basically a nose-cone package or pod which puts three payloads where there used to be one, thereby multiplying our fire power and the chances of penetrating the enemy's antimissile defense. At a given point from the target, the pod opens and dispatches the payloads toward preselected targets. There are sixteen basic MIRV payloads in the U.S. arsenal; some are actual nuclear bombs, some are decoys designed to look or act like nuclear bombs, and some are antiradar devices designed to jam their antimissile system. So far, so good. Each of the sixteen basic MIRV payloads has a signature trajectory—that is, depending on what it is and what it does, it follows a given trajectory once it leaves the pod. Now obviously, anyone who knew these trajectories could program a computer so that it could tell within seconds, using inputs from tracking devices, which incoming blips were real warheads, which were decoys, which were jamming devices."

The roof of Diamond's mouth felt dry. He paused to collect some saliva.

"This is what Lewinter took with him," Diamond went on.

"Or at least this—it seems to me, gentlemen—is what we have to assume Lewinter took with him."

"In other words," Martin said grimly, "he gave them the key to our missile system." It was worse than Martin had expected; he was already weighing the potential consequences to the President—and the options.

"'Pears to me as if he plain disarmed us," said Senator Talmidge. An indecipherable smile-frown played on his face.

Across the table, Kunen let out a long, low whistle.

Only Dukess—who had known all along what was coming—took Diamond's presentation calmly. "I think . . ." he began tentatively, and when he saw the heads swivel toward him, he began again, this time with more strength. "I think perhaps the Acting Deputy Assistant Secretary for Security Policy"—Dukess dragged out Diamond's title until it sounded faintly ridiculous—"has put an unnecessarily grim interpretation on the available facts."

Dukess had hesitated before joining the conversation; Talmidge and Buzz Martin, sitting on either side of him, looked like Zealots ready to squeeze the nonbeliever between them. But even as he hesitated, he had caught sight of Diamond's face—the impersonal eyes that looked both liquid and black, like inkwells; the smug mouth turned up at the corners in the beginning of a smile. And so Dukess, drawn in by remembrances of things past, plunged in to deal with the realities of things present.

"The Acting Deputy Assistant Secretary"—this time Dukess put the emphasis on the word *acting*—"has given us the worst case, which seems to be based largely on his long-standing inclination to believe the worst in any case." Dukess turned toward Diamond and spoke directly to him: "Is there a single shred of outside evidence you can muster to support this worst case of yours?"

Diamond turned and looked out the window, sorting out his facts. "You want corroboration, that's fair enough. Tell me, Harry, what would you do if a Russian turned up at the American Embassy in Japan requesting asylum? Unless he were a big fish, like Svetlana, you'd tread carefully, right? You'd think of all the possibilities—you'd think about plants and double agents and a rigged defection designed to explode in your face. Before you gave him the time of day, you'd make him prove that he was worth taking risks for. If he proved it, you'd give him the asylum he asked for. O.K., run this scenario backward—the Russians had Lewinter in their hands a few hours when they whisked him off under escort to Moscow. *They took him.* Quite obviously, *they* at least were satisfied that he was worth taking." Diamond turned to the other members of 303 the way a lawyer turns to a jury. "It seems to me, gentlemen, that all our attempts to understand the significance of Lewinter's defection must"—Diamond lowered his voice and whispered the word *must* again—"begin with this simple fact: they took him. There are other pieces of the puzzle that corroborate the worst case. Remember, the Russians stole Lewinter's personal papers as a part of a background investigation of their own—something they only run on very important defectors.

Remember also, they probably murdered the librarian to cover their tracks. And it is of more than passing interest that Avksentiev himself now seems to be involved in the whole affair—"

"How do you know that?" Dukess challenged.

"Our military attaché in Moscow came up with that tidbit," said Dick Kunen. "Seems like Lewinter had lunch with Avksentiev before the press conference. We got it by pouch today—you'll probably find it in your interoffice when you get back to the Agency."

Dukess glanced at Diamond's impassive face—and returned to the attack. "There's another side to all this. Let's assume for the moment that friend Diamond's worst case holds up. As I understand it, our experts estimate that two hundred nuclear hits could devastate the Soviet Union—in the official lingo, render damage to property and human life that would be unacceptable to any rational Soviet leadership. The experts also say that, given the present state of Soviet antimissile defenses, even if they knew which of the thirty-six hundred incoming payloads were warheads, they still wouldn't have a hope in hell of sustaining less than eight hundred hits. In other words, even if it's true, the worst case is a meaningless case. In the end, we can always saturate their antimissile defenses with MIRVs, so our second-strike deterrent retains its essential credibility, Lewinter notwithstanding."

Kunen rocked back in his chair so that his weight was balanced on its rear legs. "That's with today's technology," he said.

"If the Soviets decide to invest some time and money in antimissile research and development, they might develop a better kill ratio. That, combined with the ability to pick out the warheads from their signature trajectories, could keep the hits below the two hundred level. What then, huh?"

"The Soviets have shown no inclination up till now of going all out on antimissile technology," Dukess shot back.

"The Soviets didn't have the trajectory formulas up till now," Kunen retorted.

"There's no proof they have them now," Dukess said angrily.

"Gentlemen," Buzz Martin cut in.

Kunen rocked back, almost lost his balance, regained it. "I'd like to ask Diamond a question," he said. "Since you're so close to this affair, you must have some idea on what we might do to neutralize Lewinter's defection." Kunen posed the question quietly and casually, without the slightest hint that the script had been written before Diamond walked into the room.

"Wait a second," Dukess said, cutting off Diamond's answer. "The Acting Deputy Assistant Secretary was invited here to account for a defection that his department is responsible for—not to tell us what to do about it."

The oil of Talmidge's Southern drawl coated the turbulent conversation: "Well, now, surely nobody can object if'n someone as close to the whole business as Mistah Diamond heah gives us the benefit of his thoughts on the subject—always assumin', of course, that he has some thoughts on the subject."

"As a matter of fact, Senator, I do have some thoughts on the subject," Diamond said. And he told the members of Committee 303 how he proposed to neutralize the defection of A. J. Lewinter.

When he finished there was absolute silence in the room.

"I think we're moving too fast," Dukess said presently. "We need to slow down, we need to weigh these signals of yours carefully. But the assassination part is out of the question; it'd take our people three to six months to mount an operation like that, and by then it would be pointless."

"I can do it in ten days," Diamond said flatly.

"You'd never succeed," Dukess sneered.

"That's the beauty of my scheme," Diamond answered. "I wouldn't have to succeed—just make a credible attempt."

Kunen rocked back on his chair again. "As far as the Defense Department is concerned," he said, "we'd be willing to let Diamond, operating out of the Defense Intelligence Agency, run such an operation, if the committee deems it appropriate to proceed."

Suddenly Dukess saw more clearly how the lines were drawn.

"I'd be curious to know how you propose to attempt to assassinate Lewinter within ten days," Dukess said.

Now, ironically, Diamond was at the crossroad. He felt the warmth stored up from the few days with Sarah drain out of his body, to be replaced by the special coldness of chess and Cernú. Without hesitating he told Dukess the details.

"Sounds pretty ingenious to me," Talmidge said.

"I'll take it up with the President," Buzz Martin said. "Meanwhile, so we don't lose time, why don't we let the Game Testing Center put it on the board and see if it plays, huh? After all, we'll still have all our options."

Outside the conference room, Dukess found himself alone with Diamond for a moment.

"This'll never get off the ground," Dukess said in a low, venomous growl. "Not if I have anything to say about it."

"I'm confident when you've had a chance to think about it, you'll see it's the only way," Diamond said evenly, his voice a parody of bureaucratic soft-sell.

"If you do run another operation, Leo, make sure you get written authorization this time."

"I wouldn't have it any other way, Harry."

17

THE MAN IDENTIFIED as Boris Avksentiev broke the ice.

"Frankly," he said, crinkling the facial muscles around his eyes as if he were straining for honesty, "I'm ambivalent." He spoke English with a faintly foreign accent—probably Slavic, though no one who heard him could ever quite identify it.

"Why ambivalent?" asked the only person in the room without a nameplate on his desk.

"Well, I'm ambitious of course—and a half-hearted opportunist."

"How do you mean half-hearted?"

"Ah, that is to say, I wouldn't go out of my way to kill my poor Polish peasant of a father to get ahead—but then I wouldn't go out of my way to save him if saving him would keep me from getting ahead." Laughter.

"We appreciate your candor," said the monitor. "Go on."

"Where was I?"

"You were explaining your ambivalence."

"Ah, yes, my ambivalence. You know that I became involved with economic reforms because it looked like a reasonably risk-free way to make some fairly rapid progress within the Party's inner circle. At first I proceeded cautiously, but as my reform program proved successful—higher production rates, higher profits, lower raw material wastage, et cetera—I allowed my name to become associated *in public* with the reforms. Nowadays, I'm generally identified by Western Sovietologists as one of those cautiously progressive pragmatists within the Soviet leadership, and I'm tipped for the premiership when the present incumbent tires of the job—if he ever tires of the job." More laughter.

"You still haven't explained the ambivalence."

"I'm coming to that." The speaker screwed up his facial muscles again. "As secretary of the Politburo committee that supervises my country's external security organs, I am, it goes without saying, smack in the middle of the Lewinter business. Now, I am one of those who takes a—how to phrase it— catholic view of Marxism-Leninism. I honestly believe that the course of history is preordained; thesis, antithesis, synthesis, thesis, antithesis, synthesis, ad infinitum. I wrote a monograph on the roots of the Hegelian dialectic when I attended the Party college in Moscow, but that's neither here nor there. The point is that individuals, as we know from the writings of Marx and Lenin, can't change the course of history, but they can speed it up if they take advantage of opportunities. And Lewinter smells like an opportunity—with a capital O. There you have it—the framework of my ambivalence; I'm wedded to economic reforms and loath to upset the economic applecart by reallocating resources and appropriations to missile defense, but I'm attracted by the idea that Lewinter can give us the means to achieve the upper hand over the capitalists."

"I see," the monitor said. "And which way will you eventually jump, do you think?"

"I'd be inclined, it seems to me, to support the necessary reallocation of resources for missile defense, if, as I suspect, the military people are moving in the same direction. I am aware that my military colleagues are wielding more influence these days. Supporting Lewinter may, in the end, present me with a faster and surer route to the top rank than economic reforms, which the military people support only grudgingly. Mind you, I wouldn't do any handstands, but with only the slightest encouragement, I'd be inclined to become reasonably enthusiastic about Lewinter."

"I see," said the monitor, and he wrote something on what looked like a score card. Then he turned to the man identified on his desk nameplate as General Aleksandr Sukhanov.

"My views are predictable," the general said. "I take the position that it is criminal to have such information and not turn it into a military advantage. I argue, forcefully and from conviction, that the Americans, for all their talk that they will never be the first to launch a preemptory first strike, are construdting a first-strike missile arsenal. Lewinter's information, I would tell my colleagues, may provide us with the means to survive such a first strike—"

"Can you be more specific about what you mean by survive?"

"Yes, of course. By survive, I mean hold the Americans to no more than a hundred and fifty one-megaton hits on urban targets. I expect that I would wind up saying that what we were discussing was not only the survival of the Soviet Union, but the survival of the socialist experiment begun by Lenin in our homeland. I would intimate that I and my colleagues in the military would consider it tantamount to treason if our political leaders were to put other principles ahead of the physical safety of the motherland."

Nikolai Khinchuk, speaking for the Soviet budget people, was next.

"I will argue that, under ordinary circumstances, a missile defense is much more costly than a missile offense, since it is generally agreed that we must have three antimissile missiles assigned to each incoming warhead to offer us a ninety per cent chance of stopping the warhead. Assuming that my colleagues in the Intelligence community are correct about Lewinter, this picture has now altered radically. As I understand it, using the signature trajectories, we can determine which of the incoming payloads are genuine warheads and concentrate on them, thus cutting our antimissile requirements by sixty-six and two-thirds per cent; cuffing them, in other words, to the point where the construction of an antimissile defense becomes economically feasible in relation to the cost of a missile offense."

"You would be inclined, then, to act on Lewinter's information?"

"From an economic point of view, yes, certainly."

"I see." Another mark on the scorecard. "Pogodin."

The man with Yefgeny Pogodin written on his nameplate spoke up. "I found him. It was largely on my say-so that my superiors in Moscow brought him back. My career is clearly tied up with him now. For better or for worse, I'll stick with him."

The monitor turned back to Avksentiev: "What influence will Pogodin's views have on you?"

"None whatsoever, I think. I'm aware that he *thinks* his career is intertwined with Lewinter—though it isn't really—and so I take his championing of Lewinter with a grain or two of salt."

The monitor called on Mikhail Rodzianko.

"Speaking for the scientific community, I'll argue that the problem is not quite as simple as the economic people make it out to be. It is not only a question of the cost of an antimissile defense. If the Americans observe us constructing an antimissile system, they will undoubtedly follow suit, which means that we will then have to augment our missile arsenal to account for the U.S. antimissile defenses. Thus we ought, from the start, to calculate the cost in terms of the proposed antimissile system plus the cost of augmenting our missile systems."

"But what position will you take on Lewinter's information?"

"I'll concede that, technically speaking, antimissile defense becomes for the first time a realistic possibility."

Another mark on the scorecard.

"That leaves you, Miliantovich, and the Chairman."

The man identified as Vyacheslav Miliantovich spoke. "I, of course, represent the U.S.A. Institute of the Academy of Sciences—in other words, Soviet Americanologists. My main contribution to the discussion will concern the long-term diplomatic implications of the Lewinter business. I'll contend that the Soviet Union has always done its best diplomatically when we talk from a position of strength, as for instance, in the years following the end of the Great Patriotic War when the Americans believed we had the capabilities of overrunning Western Europe. I'll conclude, then, that our diplomatic position vis-à-vis the capitalists will benefit immeasurably by the addition to our arsenal of an antimissile system."

"Will the Americans, then, have to know that we have deployed an antimissile system for the advantage to make itself felt?" the monitor asked.

"Not at all. They will simply notice that we approach the international bargaining market more confidently—with more spring in our step, as it were."

"And so you would favor making use of Lewinter's information?"

"From the point of view of international competition with the capitalists, from the point of view of the effect it will have on the Americans, yes."

"That leaves it up to you, Mr. Chairman."

The man with the word *Chairman* on his desk plate hesitated. "I tend to move more slowly," he said presently. "I like to see which way the wind is blowing. If mistakes are to be made, I want as many people as possible to share the responsibility for them. I'll tread water on this one for a while, I think. But when I see Avksentiev line up with the military people, I'll be tempted to move off in the same direction—ahead of them, it goes without saying. After all, I am their leader."

"What about Rodzianko's reservations?"

"As for that, Rodzianko's brother recently divorced my wife's sister after twelve years of marriage . . ." The Chairman shrugged. "I don't think I'll be swayed by the reservations of the scientific community."

A small group of observers listened attentively in the back of the auditorium—a doctoral candidate from the Brooking Institute doing research for his thesis on the Game Testing Center, two young Russian specialists from the State Department there to "game" some diplomatic gambits under consideration, a Yugoslavian defectee hired by the Testing Center to play Tito, and Leo Diamond.

Only Diamond failed to join in the general laughter that punctuated the dry dialogue. The "players" were having a good time—but he wasn't. Too much was riding on the seemingly off-the-cuff opinions.

Actually, the opinions were anything but off the cuff; each player was, in fact, a specialist on the Russian he purported to speak for. The person identified as the Chairman had been studying every aspect of his subject's private and public life for twelve years. The information that the Chairman was angry over the divorce of his wife's sister had been pieced together from cocktail-party chatter collected by Western intelligence agents in Moscow.

It was a strange Kafkaesque business, this Game Testing Center. It employed some 350 people on a full- or part-time basis. To become one of the center's "steadies," you had to have a "horse" (as the subject was called in Game Testing parlance) of some stature—and players with a good horse were assured of a lucrative career. The man who selected Avksentiev, for example, seemed certain of a secure future if, as it seemed, his horse rose to a position of prominence within the Soviet inner circle. Other players had not been so fortunate; one young behavioral psychologist had devoted three years of study to a dark horse who was subsequently exiled to Tashkent to run a water works. (The behavioral psychologist returned to private practice.) Then, too, there was always the hand of fate to be reckoned with; when a Politburo member died, it had become something of a tradition at the Game Testing Center to send flowers to the player who was now without a horse—or a job.

So far this morning, the players had addressed themselves

to what the monitor had described as the "warm-up" proposition: whether or not the subjects would tend to believe in the genuineness of Lewinter and act on the information he was presumed to have brought with him. That out of the way, they moved on to the second proposition. The monitor, who had been an Oxford don until lured to Washington in the exodus known as the brain drain, stated the problem. "Now, gentlemen, the signals with which we have been presented can be assumed to be on the board—the business about this fellow Chapin, the Boston purge, the MIRV conference, et cetera. The question, then, becomes: will the Soviets recognize them as signals, and if so, how will they react to them? I'll throw the floor open to anyone who cares to start in. Comrade Avksentiev."

His heart pounding, Diamond leaned forward to catch every word.

"This seems to me to be fairly easy." The man identified as Avksentiev finished stuffing tobacco into the bowl of his pipe. "Ah, excuse me," he said. He lit the pipe, puffed at it three or four times and looked up. "You ask about the signals, Monitor. The first thing to be said is that we will know immediately when these things happen. We will, as a matter of routine, be watching Chapin and the Boston people. I should think that there is a possibility that the first indication we receive will be taken at face value; that is to say, it will look as if the Americans are reacting to a genuine defection and thus tend to confirm our belief that Lewinter is the genuine article. But when we receive a second and a third indication—certainly by the time we learn that MIRV specialists have been summoned to Washington—we will get suspicious and instantly review the whole affair. By the time we learn of the assassination attempt, we will be convinced that we are receiving signals."

"And how will you interpret these signals?"

"We will conclude that the American Intelligence agencies, far from reacting to a genuine defection, are rather attempting to convince us that the defection is genuine, and so we will conclude that it is a fraud."

"I see." The monitor looked as if he was about to ask another question. He apparently thought better of it and turned to General Sukhanov.

"I myself and most of my senior colleagues in the military," said the general, "will remain wedded to the idea that Lewinter is genuine, but some of our younger sharpshooters will take their cue from Minister Avksentiev; they will conclude that the Americans are signaling us he is real and hence he must be false."

"What effect will the doubts of the sharpshooters have on you?"

"It will undermine our determination to push for action on the basis of Lewinter's information. I will continue to argue, but less forcefully—and I will begin to wonder, privately of course, if perhaps the others aren't correct."

"Nikolai Khinchuk," the monitor said, nodding at the next player.

"Once the seed is planted—"

"I'm sorry, but what seed is that?"

"The seed of doubt, Monitor. Once the seed of doubt is planted as to Lewinter's veracity, I will argue, on behalf of the budget bureau, that it is ridiculous to dislocate our current Five-Year Plan. Everything turns on whether Lewinter's information is genuine. If there is the slightest doubt about this, I will counsel caution. I will contend it is foolhardy to undertake construction of a missile defense which, as I explained before, from a cost-accounting point of view, is very much more expensive than a missile offense."

"And so, I take it, the original reservations you harbored will be reinforced?"

"Precisely."

"I see," the monitor said.

Pogodin was next.

"I still have a strong stake in Lewinter. I will suggest to my superiors that the Americans are not signaling us; on the contrary, from my knowledge of the country, it seems to me that they are simply going through the motions of reacting to a genuine defection. They have a saying for that in the United States—closing the barn door after the horse has fled."

Again the monitor asked Avksentiev what effect Pogodin's opinion would have on him.

"More than last time," Avksentiev said. He paused to collect his thoughts. "Pogodin is basically a first-class Intelligence agent. If it was only his career he was concerned about, he would have abandoned Lewinter as soon as the tide turned against him. But the fact that he sticks to his view will impress me—especially so since I am aware that he was raised and educated in the United States and has a feel for that country that many of our so-called experts lack. I think, in sum, I'd stick to my original view, but I'd be troubled by Pogodin's doubts. Yes, I'd definitely be troubled by them."

Vyacheslav Miliantovich, the Soviet Americanologist, spoke without waiting to be invited.

"I'd add to your troubles. Comrade Avksentiev. I'd agree with you that the Americans are probably signaling us—but to what purpose? Everything depends, in the end, on what the Americans *want* us to believe. If they want us to believe he is real, he must be a fake. If they want us to believe he is a fake, he must be real. Here is where it gets complicated. I will raise the possibility that the Americans are signaling us that Lewinter is real *in the expectation that we will discover they are signaling us that he is real and conclude he is a fraud.* Ergo, they want us to believe he is a fraud. Ergo, he must be real. Do you follow me?"

"Ah, the plot thickens," said Avksentiev.

"And what do you have to say to that?" asked the monitor. "I think it is characteristic of our professional Americanologists to look for profundity where there is only simplicity. I personally don't credit the Americans with that much subtlety. I think there are two possibilities—Pogodin's thesis, that the Americans are simply going through the motions of responding to a genuine defection; and my thesis, that they are trying, by means of signals, to convince us the defection is genuine, hence it must be false. And of the two possibilities, I still favor mine.

"You haven't given us your views yet, Rodzianko."

"My colleagues in the scientific community will eagerly support Comrade Avksentiev's thesis—that the Americans want us to believe the defection is genuine, hence it must be false. We are against entering a new round of the arms race, and will support any arguments that can be brought to bear to prevent this."

"I see. Well, that more or less leaves it, as always, up to the Chairman, doesn't it?"

"I'm uneasy," the Chairman said. "There are too many contradictory opinions floating around. No matter which way I turn, there will be people on the other side of the argument waiting to pounce and say I told you so."

"What are your inclinations?"

"I'm inclined to agree with Avksentiev and the Intelligence people—that is, I'm inclined to believe that the Americans are signaling us that Lewinter is real, and he therefore must be false."

The monitor thought for a moment. "Would you gentlemen feel more comfortable about it if two or three additional signals were put on the board?"

"Ah, decidedly," said Avksentiev. "With the addition of two or three indications, there could be no doubts that the Americans were signaling us that Lewinter is real. And hence, there could be no hesitation in concluding he is a fraud."

"The scientific community"—Rodzianko picked up the

nod of the man sitting next to him—"and the budget people would support that view too."

"With the addition of more signals, I would be inclined to come around also," Pogodin said.

"Even I would begin to have doubts that Lewinter is real," conceded General Sukhanov. "Anyhow, a bandwagon is something one climbs on."

"I am delighted to see the weight of opinion swinging to one side," the Chairman said. "I am delighted to find a consensus that coincides with my own inclinations. I would now make a decision—Lewinter is a fraud and is to be treated as such."

"Well, there you have it, gentlemen," the monitor said—and Diamond breathed an audible sigh of relief.

The session was almost over. The monitor collected his notes and said: "It's not exactly in our province, but as long as we're at it why don't we see if we can't come up with two or three additional signals." He looked around the room. "I'll take your thoughts."

Miliantovich, the Americanologist, raised his hand. "I and my colleagues, as I'm sure you're aware, keep a very close eye on the American press. Now, if an item were to appear, say, in the Periscope section of *Newsweek* . . ."

18

D EAD WEIGHT, the .45-caliber pistol pressed against
the life line in Diamond's palm. Feeling the clammy
metal against his skin, sensing its clumsiness intruding on his poise, he was transported back to the morning in
England when a British instructor had first introduced him to
the weapon. "This 'ere may turn out to be your best friend," he
had said, slamming it into Diamond's palm the way a nurse
gives a scalpel to a doctor. Diamond could hear the voice of the
instructor droning on, without inflection, without punctuation:

"Deep breath that's the ticket now expel 'all of it good
now wrap both 'ands 'round the grip there you go now bring the
sights up on an arc past the target then let 'er drop back of 'er
own weight that's it now when the front sight comes on target
shoot an' remember if you pull the trigger once you pull it twice
got that two times pros always shoot two times when I'm

through with you it'll be engraved on your soul in capital letters pros always shoot twice."

Suddenly the outline of a man—it was someone vaguely familiar!—appeared at a window forty feet in front and slightly to the left of Diamond. He dropped to one knee and thrust the .45 out in front of his face at arm's length, both hands wrapped around the grip. He took a full breath and expelled half of it and then let the sight rock up past the target. When the front sight drifted back on again, Diamond squeezed off a round—and the instinct engraved on his soul in capital letters made him squeeze off one more.

The explosions, dry thunder dampened by soundproof walls, filled the indoor shooting range.

"Two misses." The voice, impersonal, bored, came from the public-address system. With a touch of professional interest, it added: "You learned to shoot during the war, didn't you, Mr. Diamond?"

Diamond nodded toward the glass control booth.

"In England? At an M.I. five training camp in Sussex? Instructor name of Prichard?"

"Yeah," Diamond called. "How the hell d'ya know that?"

"Some guys can taste wine and tell you which field the grapes come from. I see a guy shoot and tell you where he learned. It's the way you hold the gun—that two-handed grip—and the two shots. Every once in a blue moon some old-timer comes in here and squeezes off two rounds at a time. You know Mr. Dukess over at the Agency? Same thing—*boom, boom.* It was this guy

Prichard's trademark. Everybody came through his course shoots off two rounds. Ha! You guys ought to form a club or something."

Diamond laughed along with the voice on the public-address system, but his laughter had a different quality. "I'd forgotten his name," he called, trying to keep up his end of the conversation. "That was it—Prichard. He used to say amateurs shot once but pros always shot twice."

"Like separating the men from the boys, I guess, huh?"

Diamond thought about the men and the boys, about the pros and the amateurs. He remembered, for no particular reason, the story about the teenagers in Mulhouse during the war. The Germans had forbidden the French to celebrate Independence Day, so the youngsters had painted a few thousand snails red, white, and blue and had turned them loose in the streets. The grand gesture! The local German commander had executed three teenagers—two of whom had had nothing to do with the snail prank. An amateur, Diamond thought, is someone who gets other people killed for things he does.

"You want to try some more, Mr. Diamond?" The voice had become impersonal again.

"Sure, why not," Diamond said.

This time a door sprang open revealing the silhouette of a man—still vaguely familiar!—holding a submachine gun. Again Diamond sank to one knee and went through the ritual he had learned amid the cut-grass of an English field so long before— the half-filled lungs; the sighting on the target; the two shots that, hit or miss, protected his professional rating with the instructor.

"Two misses. Correction. You nicked his left shoulder with the second shot."

The voice was still impersonal, but Diamond detected (he was becoming sensitive to such things) another note—contempt for the old pros who came out once a month with their old techniques and old reflexes and couldn't hit the side of a barn. Here, in the subbasement beneath the huge F.B.I. complex, it wasn't who you were or what you had achieved that counted; it was simply how well you could shoot.

And the truth of the matter was that Diamond couldn't shoot worth a damn—at least not at a faceless, nameless dummy on a target range. Something inside him always tightened up in anticipation of the instant when the powder would explode in the chamber and drill the business end of the bullet through the lands and grooves of the rifled bore. "Squeeze, don't jerk, the trigger," Prichard used to say over and over again. "That way you won't know when the shot is coming and freeze up."

Diamond had his own theory about why he tightened up at the last instant; He had never, in all his life, been much good at *practice.* Somehow he was only able to summon the adrenalin for the real thing—the competition. As a teenager, he had been a remarkably good basketball player, strong and fast, a hustler and a scorer. But only during a game. During practice sessions, he invariably lost his edge; smaller, slower players slapped the ball out of his hands or went up high to block his shots and make him look like a lead-footed idiot.

It was the same—or at least Diamond thought it was the

same—when it came to shooting. He had never fired a gun at a human being, but he had complete confidence that he could shoot accurately and quickly and coldly if he had to. The challenge of competition, Diamond knew, could turn him into an efficient marksman—and a cold-blooded killer. He remembered how he had waited in that barn in the Pyrenees during the war, the two British pilots cowering in a corner, hoping that the dogs *wouldn't* be fooled by the urine trick, hoping that the Vichy border guards *would* come through the door to find Diamond kneeling, his hands wrapped around a .45-caliber pistol extended at arm's length. He could almost feel their terror-filled eyes boring into him. He could almost hear the boom of the bullets—two for each man, of course. He could almost see the men being lifted off their feet by the impact and flung back, pieces of skin and bone spattering in every direction. Oh, how he had wished they would come through that door. It was, Diamond recalled, the part of the story he had not told to Sarah.

"Once more, Mr. Diamond," the voice from the loud speaker was saying.

This time the figure—slightly balding, pasty-faced—popped up from behind a crate and Diamond immediately recognized it. It looked remarkably like A. J. Lewinter. Diamond dropped to one knee and thrust out his hands and put two bullets between his eyes.

"You think you can kill him?" Steve Ferri asked in his vaguely flat Southern drawl. "The other signals sound reasonable enough, but an assassination—"

238

"I think we can make it look as if we tried to kill him—and that's all that counts," Diamond said.

"How?"

That, of course, was the sixty-four-dollar question. Diamond had still been wrestling with it when he stopped by Kunen's office before the 303 meeting to brief him on the Lewinter affair. "It's all well and good to propose assassinating Lewinter," Kunen had said. "But all you're doing is putting the ball in the Agency's court. They're the only ones equipped for this sort of thing and they'll snap it up—unless . . ." Kunen, a veteran Pentagon infighter, had begun to think out loud. How to set up the kill so that the operation would fall into the lap of the Pentagon's own Defense Intelligence Agency, that was the problem.

The solution came, almost by chance, from one of Kunen's whiz kids who barged in to drop off a medical report on a member of the Soviet Politburo. Kunen had put the problem to his staffer.

"Why don't you work through Zaitsev?" the whiz kid had suggested as if it were the most obvious thing in the world.

"Who's Zaitsev?" Kunen and Diamond had asked.

Zaitsev was Stoyan Alexandrovich Zaitsev, the whiz kid had explained, the famous Soviet chess Grand Master. It seems he had written a *samizdat*—a private essay intended, as the Russians say, for the desk drawer rather than for publication. Only this was no ordinary, irreverent *samizdat,* but the angry, eloquent *cri de coeur* of someone who had long since lost the last shred of self-respect. Ostensibly, Zaitsev's essay told the story of the Russian writer Andrei Axelrod: how he had boldly denounced censorship and neo-Stalinism at a Party Congress; how he had been sent to the Serbsky Institute of Psychiatric Diagnosis, an insane asylum outside of Leningrad; how (and this part was not known in the West) he had hanged himself in the latrine. Zaitsev's central preoccupation in the essay, however, was not Axelrod but Zaitsev; he excoriated himself for joining in the general condemnation of Axelrod that followed the Congress speech. "When it came to the test," he wrote, "I valued my apartment and my dacha and my car and my trips abroad more than I valued my humanity." In a final soul-searching passage, Zaitsev described his reaction to word of Axelrod's suicide and how, even then, he had been too much of a coward to attend the private funeral.

One day long after the funeral, Zaitsev had spilled his heart out to Timoshenko, the liberal editor of *Novi Mir,* and together the two of them had proceeded to drink themselves into a stupor. In the early hours of the morning, Zaitsev soaked his head in a basin of cold water and wrote out in longhand a *samizdat,* which he entitled a "Declaration of Conscience." When Timoshenko woke up, he found Zaitsev slumped over the essay, read it—and, assuming Zaitsev intended to circulate the manuscript, took it with him to show friends in the liberal community. Sometime around noon the Fat Cow finally managed to rouse Zaitsev, who realized what he had done and went tearing around Moscow in a desperate effort to destroy the document which was being passed from hand to hand as if it were a live bomb. Zaitsev finally caught up with the *samizdat* that evening, but not before one of Moscow's more enterprising liberal poets had photographed the document. After a circuitous journey and the exchange of a considerable amount of money, the negative arrived at the Pentagon's Defense Intelligence Agency.

"Our instinct was to use it for propaganda—forge a few dozen copies, feed them back into the Soviet Union through one of our conduits, and then leak the whole thing to the Western press," the whiz kid had explained. "Someone of Zaitsev's stature telling the story of Axelrod (you know, of course, they've since let on that he died of cancer) would be a block-buster." But then a clerk in Records, as a matter of routine, had checked the office file on Zaitsev and had discovered that he was a close friend of one Yefgeny Mikhailovich Pogodin, an up-and-coming Intelligence operative who was currently sta-tion chief in Tokyo—and this had opened up other possibilities.

"Pogodin!" Diamond was starting to put the gambit together. "He's the one who's been chaperoning Lewinter around."

"Exactly," the whiz kid had said.

"How close are Pogodin and Zaitsev?" Steve Ferri asked when Diamond finished telling how he learned about Zaitsev and the *samizdat*.

"Very—close enough for Pogodin to take Lewinter to Zaitsev's dacha for a party."

"And you obviously think that Zaitsev can get to see Lewinter again."

Diamond nodded. "We'll offer to trade his 'Declaration of Conscience' for a small favor."

"He won't bite—he won't commit murder for that," Ferri warned.

"He won't know he's committing murder."

"So all that remains is to get to Zaitsev and let him know you have the 'Declaration of Conscience,'" Ferri said. "You figured out how to do that yet without going through the Agency?"

"I think so," Diamond said.

The telephone rang for a long time. Just when Diamond was about to hang up, Sarah answered.

"Madame Defarge here," Diamond said.

"Leo, you bastard, where've you been?"

"Around."

For a moment the conversation balanced on the vagueness of "around."

"I want to talk to you, Leo. We sort of left things up in the air and I think we ought to talk it out."

"I thought we had."

Sarah lowered her voice to a whisper. "What's happening, Leo? Before you were a mystery and I liked you that way—I could keep discovering you, layers and layers of you. But now I think I know you too well and it scares me. Leo, are you there?"

"I'm here. You're romanticizing, Sarah. Everything's just as it was. We've reached a plateau, that's all—a place where we both pause for breath before going on."

Sarah said "Go on where?" but Diamond made believe he didn't hear her and continued. "When you come back from Russia, we'll sit down and talk this thing out calmly, O.K.?"

"I didn't know I was going to Russia!"

"Ah, that's what I called about, Sarah. I want you to do me a favor—" Diamond could feel the pulse beating in his forehead.

"In Russia?"

"Yes. There's no danger involved. None whatsoever. I promise you. I want you to look up someone in Moscow and give him a letter, that's all."

"Sounds like something I wouldn't want to miss." It was the old Sarah talking, enthralled at spy stories, excited at the prospect of playing a role in one. "Will I use my own name, or will you give me a new identity?"

"Don't get carried away, Sarah—you'll go as yourself, and all you have to do is chat with a guy for a few minutes and give him a letter and some hay-fever pills, that's all. I'll give you the details when I see you. And listen, there'll be some money in this for you—say three thousand dollars. How's that sound?"

"Sounds fine." But Sarah thought of a stumbling block. "Leo, I can't do it."

"What do you mean you can't do it? I thought you said it sounded exciting."

"It does—but I can't go. I've already told the fashion people I couldn't make the trip, and they booked another model in my place."

"That's all taken care of already," Diamond said matter of factly. "The other girl's been bought off and your name's been put back on the list."

"You're really pretty sure of me, aren't you, Leo? That's the second time you've put the cart before the horse."

"When was the first?"

"When you had them give me a security clearance so you could sleep with me. You were pretty sure you'd get me into bed, weren't you, Leo?"

"Sarah, I thought we've been all through that. I thought you understood about, well, about the kind of business I'm in. Listen, if you don't want to go to Russia, say so and we'll call the whole thing off."

Sarah hesitated, weighing the satisfaction it would give her to spoil Diamond's plans against the fun and excitement of making the trip. Finally she told him: "O.K., Leo, I'll go." There was a pause. "Tell me something, Leo, what would you have done if I said no?"

Diamond tried to save the conversation with an old line. "I would have taken you to bed," he said, "but I wouldn't have talked to you."

Sarah didn't laugh this time.

The next telephone call was easier.

"You don't know me," Diamond said politely. "My name's Carr with two R's. I'm with the State Department."

"Is it about Augustus?" asked Maureen Sinclair. Her

voice—tired, tentative—made it obvious that she had been through a lot.

"I know this must be very trying for you," Diamond said consolingly. "I want—"

"Mr. Carr, I'd like a straight answer to a straight question—can Augustus come back?"

"Come back?" For an instant Diamond wasn't sure what she meant. "What do you mean, come back?"

"Come back, come back," Maureen Sinclair said, as if repeating the phrase would clarify it.

Suddenly Diamond understood. "You mean can he come back without getting into trouble with us?"

"Yes, that's it exactly."

"As far as we're concerned, Miss Sinclair, Mr. Lewinter has not broken any laws simply because he has asked to be allowed to live in the Soviet Union. He has not, as far as I've heard, formally renounced his American citizenship yet, so he can turn around and come home any time he wants to. Of course, he may lose his job, and I very much doubt whether he'll ever get a security clearance again—"

"But he can come back?"

"Yes, I don't see any legal reason why he should be afraid to."

Maureen Sinclair appeared to draw some comfort from the reassurance.

"Actually," Diamond continued, "we're as anxious as you are for him to come home. Now don't quote me on this, of course, but it doesn't do our international image much good to have one of our bright, upstanding citizens decide he prefers it on the other side of the Iron Curtain, get my point?"

"If only I could talk to him—"

Diamond saw the opening he wanted. "You can't talk to him, Miss Sinclair, but you can write him a letter."

"A letter? I hadn't thought of a letter. How would I address it?"

"That's what I called about, actually. We're arranging to get a letter to Mr. Lewinter through private channels. That is, eh, without the knowledge of his hosts."

"You can do that?"

"I think we can, yes. You understand you are not to talk about this to a living soul?"

"Oh, absolutely, Mr. Carr. Absolutely. You have my word on that."

"Fine." Diamond saw that everything would go his way. "Now what I want you to do is sit down and write him a letter in your own handwriting. Keep it chatty—tell him what you're doing, talk about the weather, things like that. And sprinkle a few personal things through it so he'll know for sure that you wrote the letter, not us. Then around the second page, let the letter take a serious turn. I don't want to tell you what to say, except that it should be very spontaneous and very, well, emotional, if you get my point. Tell him how much you miss him, tell him you understand what prompted him to try and start a new life, but suggest to him that starting all over again in a strange country may be harder than he thought. Somewhere along the way you can tell him that you've checked with the

State Department and you have assurances that no charges will be lodged against him if he changes his mind and returns home. You get my drift, Miss Sinclair?"

"Yes, I understand perfectly. And of course I'll do it. I'll sit down and do it the instant you hang up, Mr. Carr."

"That's just fine, Miss Sinclair. I think you may be able to make him see the light if you put some thought into this. I'll have one of our people stop by later today and pick up the letter, O.K.?"

"Mr. Carr, I don't know how to thank you—"

"There's no need to thank me," Diamond said. "We're all on the same team. Oh, Miss Sinclair, there's one more thing. Did you see the transcript of the press conference—the part where Mr. Lewinter said he had lost his hay-fever pills?"

"Yes, I did. The poor dear, they were the only things that seemed to help him."

"I'm sure he'd appreciate it if you sent him some more. We'll get them to him along with the letter."

"But I don't have his prescription."

"I'll tell you what, Miss Sinclair, you leave that to me. All you have to do is mention, perhaps in a post script, that you're sending along a couple of hundred pills because you heard he misplaced the ones he had with him." And Diamond added encouragingly: "You know, it might be just the touch to make him realize how much he'd be giving up if he decides to stay there."

The Washington–New York shuttle was running late, and Diamond had trouble finding a cab at the La Guardia end.

Going into the city, the traffic wasn't heavy until he hit the Midtown Tunnel, but from there to 86th Street and Broadway took almost an hour. By the time Diamond got where he was going, it was almost high noon.

Diamond stood for a moment in front of a pharmacy studying his reflection in the window. Looking through his reflection, he saw that the store was empty except for one man. Moving quickly, Diamond pushed open the door—FLOWER PHARMACY was stenciled on it in gold letters—and flipped over the cardboard sign so that anyone coming after him would see the word *closed.*

"If this is a holdup, mister, I send the cash to the bank every two hours. I got nothing here except small change. You can come and see for yourself. I swear to God I only got small change." Seldon Flower had been held up thirty-six times in ten years; he had carved a notch in a broom handle for each robbery, so he had an exact count. He was terrified of blacks; store owners in the neighborhood said that the blacks often became angry and started breaking things if they didn't get any money, so Flower kept two tens under the counter for black hold-up men. But whites or Puerto Ricans, he just told them the truth: that he deposited the money in the bank down the block before it could accumulate in the cash register. Most of the hold-up men glanced in the register and backed out of the store without saying anything; one or two even took his word for it and left without looking for themselves.

"This isn't a holdup, Mr. Flower," Diamond said, advancing a step. "Don't you remember me?"

Flower shuffled out from behind the counter. He was near-sighted and didn't have his glasses on, so he leaned forward like an eagle on a perch and squinted, trying to bring the figure into focus.

"I know you," he said presently. "You're from the Agency—Leon Dunken"—Flower was gathering momentum—"Yes, yes, yes, Leon Dunken, I never forget a name."

"Diamond," Diamond corrected. "Leo Diamond."

"Yes, of course, Diamond. You came in right after the war, didn't you? Yes, yes, it's all coming back to me. You were a young hot shot in those days, a young hot shot. I remember you pulled off a coup in Rumania, or was it Czechoslovakia. It was the talk of the Agency. You must be one of their top bananas by now, I suppose, a young hot shot like you."

"I heard you left the Agency," Diamond said, trying to keep the conversation moving.

"Left in the early fifties—they ran out of work for someone with my skills."

"You have a nice thing going here," Diamond said, motioning toward the counters full of sunglasses and tooth-brushes and alarm clocks. Again, Diamond felt the pulse beating in his forehead. "Can you fill a prescription for me, Mr. Flower?"

Flower squinted at his visitor. It suddenly dawned on him that Diamond had not walked in off the street by chance. "Sure, I can fill a prescription—for a fee," Flower said, shuffling back behind the counter. "What do you have in mind?"

"You ever hear of Chlor-Trimeton hay-fever pills?" Diamond asked.

Later, hurrying to catch the 5 P.M. shuttle back to Washington, Diamond passed a bald man hawking newspapers at the entrance to the terminal. Speaking with a quiet madness, smiling at his own audacity, the man waded into the stream of people flowing toward the open door.

"The President has run off and they can't find him," he said, holding out folded newspapers. "The king's men have put Humpty-Dumpty together again. American troops have invaded China. Berlin has fallen to the Russians. Read it all in the late city edition. Buy now, pay later—if you're not satisfied with the news, you get your money back. The Kremlin denounces Lenin as a homosexual. The first man into space has changed into a woman . . ."

A prisoner of his own small field of vision, Diamond hurried by oblivious to what was happening in the world.

PART V

THE END GAME

19

THE BANQUET BEGAN with the *zakuska* (or "small bites") which included, among a sea of dishes, eight kinds of caviar, salted first-run herring in mustard sauce, a quivering mold of *kholodets,* highly seasoned meatballs called *bitki,* and *forshmak,* a dish in which herring, boiled potatoes, onions and apples are baked together in sour cream. All this was washed down, in a sort of counterpoint rhythm, with fifteen varieties of vodkas, including one flavored with truffles, another with lemon peel, and a third with stalks of buffalo grass. A mouthful of caviar, a shot of vodka. A bite of herring, a shot of vodka. A spoonful of *forshmak,* a shot of vodka. And of course there were the toasts.

"To our American friends," roared the managing director of the Moscow fashion house, "may they take home with them fond memories of our socialist homeland." Heads tilted back, angled for another shot of vodka.

"To our Russian ready-to-wear colleagues," called an American ready-to-wear manufacturer, his glass raised high over his head, "who know how to treat capitalists like kings." And the fifty-odd people in the banquet hail emptied their glasses again.

"My God," Sarah said to the man sitting on her right, "we'll all die."

Zaitsev studied Sarah through bloodshot eyes, smiled politely and shrugged. *"Ya ne panyemia Angliski."*

"Est-ce que vous parlez Français?" Sarah tried.

"Mais oui," Zaitsev shot back, delighted to have a language in common with the extraordinarily pretty American girl on his left.

"What I said before was, we'll all die," Sarah said in French.

Zaitsev flashed a smile that revealed his discolored teeth. "Inevitably," he replied.

Sarah realized he didn't understand her. "What I mean is, we'll all die of overeating," she explained, motioning to the long table filled, every square inch of it, with food.

"As for that, dear lady, there is an old Russian saying: 'What a way to go.' Zaitsev nudged Sarah with his elbow to encourage her laughter. "Do you follow? You said we would die of overeating. To which I replied: 'What a way to go.'" And he laughed again.

"We say the same thing," Sarah said pleasantly. "I suppose it's international." She tried a new subject. "Who are you?"

"What a coincidence you should ask," Zaitsev said. "I have more or less devoted my entire adult life to precisely that question. How to answer? I am a man, I am a Russian, I am a chess Grand Master, I am a Leninist—"

"Is that different from a Communist?"

Zaitsev was becoming more animated now. "I would say so, yes, quite different."

"And how would you define Leninism as opposed to Communism or, say, Marxism?" Sarah asked. She was starting to enjoy the conversation, even though she knew where it was leading.

"Why, dear lady, Marxism is reductivist; that is to say, it seeks to reduce everything—war, love, power, sex—to materialistic terms. Communism is old hat, sort of like last year's dance; at its core, it is a combination of two things that Europeans have kept for centuries in different compartments of their soul—religion and business. But Leninism. Ah, Leninism is the disease of idealism."

"That sounds very clever," Sarah said. "I would have thought that all three could be defined as the pursuit of power.

"My dear young American innocent," Zaitsev bellowed above the noise level at the banquet table. Heads turned, took in the two and turned away again. "When will you children of capitalism understand that the *Homo politicus* who pursues nothing but power is as unreal as the *Homo economicus* who pursues nothing but gain?"

"Homo politicus? Homo economicus? My God, but you're eclectic," Sarah said, impressed by his combination of arrogance and intellectualism. "Who are you?" she asked again.

"My name, dear lady, is Stoyan Zaitsev. Mere acquaintances call me Stoyan, but favored friends and mistresses call me Zaitsev. You may call me Zaitsev. As for being eclectic, your own Scott Fitzgerald supplied his epitaph—he said the well-rounded man was the most limited of all specialists, with the emphasis presumed to be on the word limited."

Sarah smiled sweetly. "It would be difficult, Zaitsev"—she felt uneasy with only the last name—"to think of you as limited."

"To Soviet-American cooperation in the field of fashion," called a tipsy Russian bureaucrat at the end of the table.

"To the couture superpowers," added an American reporter from *Women's Wear Daily.* Chilled white wine spilled from her raised glass.

"Try," said Zaitsev, and he turned back to the second course—a cold soup called *okroshka,* made of cucumbers, game and herbs in *kvas* and cream, served on ice cubes frozen into the shape of sickles.

Diamond had briefed Sarah on everything except the food. "You can't miss him," he had said. "They tell me he looks like a dirty old man."

"That could fit a lot of people," Sarah had said.

Diamond had bristled: "What does that mean?"

"My, but you're sensitive today," Sarah had chided him.

"Maybe it's because you're insensitive today."

"Enough is enough, Leo. All I meant is that a lot of people could fit the description of a dirty old man. Can't you be more specific? You don't want me giving the letter to the wrong dirty old man, do you?"

Diamond had stared at Sarah for a long moment. "It's not too late to back out of this, you know."

"I know," Sarah had said, returning the stare.

In the end, it was Diamond who turned away first. "Look," he said, "I appreciate what you're doing."

"I appreciate that you appreciate it," Sarah had said coldly. "Why don't you tell me what this Zaitsev looks like, O.K.?"

But Diamond had been unsure of himself. "Maybe we should talk this out first, Sarah. What's bugging you? Why are we at each other's throats all the time?"

Sarah backed off a bit. "I suppose we're both jumpy about the Russian thing," she said. The explanation was convenient— but inadequate.

"I suppose."

"You were describing Zaitsev," Sarah had prompted.

"Small eyes, large nostrils, discolored teeth, fortyish, flamboyant; he waves his arms a great deal when he talks. Drinks enormous amounts of liquor which he holds well. His full name is Stoyan Alexandrovich Zaitsev."

Sarah had repeated the name.

"Unless something goes wrong, he will be at the farewell banquet. Our cultural attaché has been instructed to request his presence, and there should be no problem about it; the Russians think of him as a cultural utility infielder and regularly trot him out for foreign visitors. With any luck, he should be sitting on your right. He speaks French, by the way."

"How do you know all this?" Sarah had asked.

"Let's just say I know and leave it at that, O.K.?"

"Why doesn't your cultural attaché pass the letter to Zaitsev himself?"

"The cultural attaché, like all the people in our embassy, is watched day and night. Zaitsev would not go near him, and if he did go near him, he would not accept a letter from him, and if he did take it he would immediately turn the letter over to the authorities because he would assume that the transaction had been observed."

Sarah had nodded. "What do I say to this Zaitsev character?"

"Start off slowly," Diamond had advised. "He'll be interested in you because you're pretty and he is always interested in pretty girls. Get his confidence. Talk about Moscow, talk about literature, talk about whatever comes up. At the end of the meal, try to get him alone. Ask him to drive you to the airport; he is one of the few people in Moscow with his own car. Tell him the limousines are a madhouse. When you have him alone, say to him . . ."

They were starting on the next course now: the *kulebiaka,* a flaky pastry crust wrapped around rich salmon and served with sour cream and Bulgarian white wine.

"What are your impressions of Moscow?" Zaitsev asked conversationally.

"I prefer Leningrad," Sarah said. "We were there for two days at the start of the tour, and I thought it was a truly beautiful city. Nevsky Prospekt. The Peter and Paul fortress. The tomb of Peter the Great. The Hermitage. Tell me, Zaitsev, why do they make you wear slippers over your shoes in Russian museums?"

"To preserve the floors, I would suspect."

"Some of the models on the tour joked that they wanted us to polish them."

"It is not impossible," Zaitsev conceded zestfully. "A minister buried in some bureaucratic backwater may have decided that as long as all these people were walking through our halls, they might as well perform some useful socialist labor. That, or a factory may have found itself with a surplus of slippers on its hands and traded it to the Ministry of Museums for God knows what. One never knows." Zaitsev gulped down another glass of wine. "You Americans," he went on, "are an odd race. I met another American recently. He said he was looking for spider webs."

"Spider webs? I don't understand."

"Neither do I, dear lady, neither do I. Perhaps he was trying to impress us with his sensitivity."

Sarah marveled at how much Zaitsev could drink and still appear sober. "Americans," she said, "are noted for their insensitivity, not their sensitivity."

"You think so?"

"I'll prove it," Sarah said. "You asked me my impressions of Moscow and I more or less changed the subject. The truth is that I hate this city. There is something cold and ugly and granite and grotesque about it. I'm depressed by the"—Sarah searched for a word—"sameness of life in Moscow. It seems as if everyone is conforming to some standard—and the standard is very drab. The stores all seem to sell the same things. The people all seem to dress alike. All your rooms, even those with chandeliers like this one, have the same plastic light switch at the entrance. Do they really make only one plastic light switch in all of Russia? And you're all so damn defensive about your imperfections. I discovered a louse in my bed last night. When I called the desk and complained, the clerk told me categorically that there were no lice in the Soviet Union and hung up on me."

Zaitsev was barely able to contain his exuberance. "Bravo, dear lady," he called, raising his glass in a private toast to Sarah. "I am delighted to hear someone discover flaws in the fabric of our socialist utopia. To listen to some of our own people speak, you would never know there are any. As for the louse you found, Lenin once decreed that the louse will defeat socialism or socialism will conquer the louse. This saying is well known in Russia. So we waged war on the louse. The few that survived, we simply ignore; thus we can claim that socialism has defeated the louse. That undoubtedly is why the clerk told you we had none in the Soviet Union. It is the same with racial discrimination, homosexuality, unemployment, and crime; they simply don't exist."

"What about conformity?" Despite herself, Sarah was getting to like Zaitsev.

"There, I think, you are mistaken, my dear American innocent abroad. They say the only people who really understand the Soviet Union are those who have been here less than three days or more than three years. You, unfortunately, fall in the middle. So you could not know that the late, and in some quarters great, Joseph Stalin has said that full conformity is possible only in a cemetery. He should have known; in his effort to make Russians conform, he sent a lot of them there. No, the conformity you see is superficial; you must look beneath the surface to observe the nuances of individuality. There is a Russian saying which I am about to invent; the sameness is in the eye of the beholder. All Japanese look alike, *n'est-ce pas*, until you sleep with one!"

They were up to the main course now: spring chickens stuffed with branches of herbs and roasted on spits, a saddle of lamb surrounded by pine nuts from the Caucasus, and a roast suckling pig prepared whole and served (with the traditional apple in its mouth) on a bed of kasha.

"Tell me, Zaitsev, what criticisms can *you* offer of your country?" Sarah asked. She was picking at a chicken leg; he was helping himself to generous portions of all three main courses.

"As for that, dear lady, I'm afraid we haven't the time. You must understand that I am intimate with the flaws—so much so that it sometimes seems as if I will drown in them. Life here, even for a Grand Master, is not without its frustrations."

"Why do you stay?"

"Because, dear woman, for all its faults my Russia is a beautiful country. It has an atmosphere, a spirit, a zest for life." Zaitsev threw up his hands. "I live here," he said quietly, "because it would be unthinkable to live anywhere else. As for the faults, we have an old saying: If you wish to have influence on a house, you must live within that house."

They ate for a time in silence. Then Zaitsev asked Sarah:

"I'm not sure I understand what it is exactly that you and these"—Zaitsev waved toward the guests at the banquet, half of whom were Americans—"people are doing in Moscow."

"We are part of a cultural exchange program. A year ago, Dom Modeli, which is your central fashion house, sent an exhibit of Russian couture to the United States. Now we are returning the compliment, showing American-designed clothes in Moscow and Leningrad."

"How extraordinarily uninteresting," Zaitsev said, and he and Sarah burst into laughter together.

When the dessert came, some of the Americans, Sarah included, let out sighs of pure pain. There was *gurev kasha,* a caramel glazed farina pudding studded with candied fruit and nuts, and *gozinakh,* small cakes shaped like diamonds and consisting of chopped nuts, honey and sugar. This was washed down, by the Russians at least, with an Armenian brandy that burned the throat. For anyone with strength to lift a cup, there was tea served from a huge golden samovar, and black coffee served from imported Pyrex pitchers.

"What a great pity, dear lady, that I meet you at the penultimate moment of your visit," Zaitsev said, munching some *gurev kasha*. "It would have been my pleasure to introduce you to some of the charms of Moscow, not the least of which are the occasional gatherings I hold in my apartment overlooking a bend in the Moscow River and the Kremlin walls." Zaitsev was one of the elite and he wanted her to know it.

"I'm sorry too," Sarah said. "Perhaps—"

"Perhaps what, dear lady?"

"No, I don't want to trouble you." Even as she said that, Sarah saw the irony in her choice of words. She was going to cause him a great deal of trouble.

"I do not concede that you could ever trouble me," Zaitsev said, and he pressed her to finish the sentence.

"I was wondering if you had a car?"

"As a matter of fact, I am the proud owner of a recent vintage black Moskva."

"And why did you select black?" Sarah asked.

"I did not choose the color; in the Soviet Union, one does not order a blue automobile or a red automobile or an orange automobile, one simply orders an automobile. If you are fortunate enough to obtain a position on the waiting list, a favor that comes upon payment of the full price of the automobile in advance, you take the first one that is offered you. When my turn came, the factory was apparently in a black mood. Why do you ask about my automobile?"

"Could I impose upon you to take me to the airport,

Zaitsev? The limousines are so mobbed, and there is such an unpleasant rush—"

"Say no more, dear lady. I'd be delighted to be of some small service to you."

Considering how much vodka, wine, and brandy he had consumed, Zaitsev drove extremely well. Diamond had been right about Zaitsev's ability to hold his liquor, Sarah thought. For a while, she watched Moscow street scenes through a window streaked with dried rain: a line of Russians waiting their turn at a kvass cart; two young soldiers admiring a parked foreign automobile; a man holding a small child so she could urinate into the gutter; two sturdy peasant women, their heads covered in babushkas, digging drainage ditches near a construction site. When she began to speak, Sarah discovered that she could barely get the words out because of her nervousness.

"You *are* Stoyan Alexandrovich Zaitsev?" she asked in a husky voice.

Zaitsev perked up. "How did you know my patronymic, dear lady?"

"I'm afraid I have to confess something—I knew who you were before I spoke to you at the banquet."

"Ah, that answers one question at least. I was wondering why I was invited to a fashion banquet. I was told only that some of the Americans expressly asked to meet me. It was you, wasn't it, dear lady, who instigated the invitation?"

Sarah nodded.

"You are no doubt a chess fan, eh? Have you seen a translation of my latest work in French?" Zaitsev asked. He pulled up behind a large open truck piled high with tomatoes to wait for a red light.

"I did see some of your work, yes," Sarah said, "but it wasn't in French."

"But you present me with a mystery—you don't read Russian, and I haven't been translated into English."

"But you have, Zaitsev," Sarah said.

"Then that comes as good news to me. I must look into getting the royalties. Tell me, what is it of mine you read in English?"

For the time it takes night vision to return after a bright light flares, Sarah panicked. It still wasn't too late to back out of the whole thing, she thought. But what could she tell Diamond? That she had been unable to get Zaitsev alone, that he didn't speak French well enough to understand her, that . . . Slowly Sarah felt herself being drawn into the experience of blackmail the way she was lured toward an unopened box for her I-don't-know collection. And so, speaking in a barely audible voice, she told Zaitsev what work of his she had read in English.

"It was your 'Declaration of Conscience.'"

Sarah watched Zaitsev closely. Except for a certain grimness to the set of his lips, his face betrayed no surprise, no apprehension. "And what did you think of it, my so-called 'Declaration of Conscience,' which, as you say, you read in an English translation you discovered in—"

"In Washington."

"Exactly. In Washington. What did you think of it?"

"I thought it was brave and brilliant," Sarah said. "And I'm sure the world will share that view when it is published."

"When it is published," Zaitsev repeated flatly.

"Will it hurt you to have it published in the West, Zaitsev?"

If Zaitsev was afraid, he hid it behind a mask of glibness. "Hurt me? Ah, dear lady, who can say how the bureaucrats who concern themselves with such things will react to the publication of my drunken ramblings. Actually, a touch of dissidence could do my reputation a world of good. If I play it carefully, I might pick up some international prize for my troubles. One never knows, does one?"

Sarah waited for Zaitsev to continue. "At this point, he'll ask you if there is anything he can do to prevent publication," Diamond had said. But Zaitsev seemed to have abandoned his part of the script.

"You know, Zaitsev, it hasn't been published yet, your Declaration," Sarah, said, trying to keep the conversation on the track. "I happen to know the man who is publishing it—perhaps something can be done to head him off."

"Are you suggesting, dear lady, that there is something *I* can do to head him off, or something *you* can do to head him off?"

"Something you can do." The words sounded hollow, as if they had come out of a long tube, as if they would be followed by an echo.

Zaitsev pulled the Moskva over to the side of the road near a crowded intersection and switched off the engine. He seemed all business now.

"How can I know that your friend has my 'Declaration of Conscience'?"

Without a word, Sarah reached into her pocketbook and took out a Polaroid photograph of herself mounted on cardboard. She peeled the photograph away from the cardboard and revealed a small photograph of a page from a handwritten manuscript. Zaitsev strained to read a few words on the manuscript, then handed the photograph back to Sarah, who replaced the Polaroid print.

"And what is it, dear lady, that your friend requires of me?"

"When he asks you what he can do," Diamond had instructed Sarah, "stress how harmless the favor is."

"It is a small, harmless thing, Zaitsev," Sarah said. And she explained that her friend in Washington simply wanted him to deliver a letter to the American defector Lewinter from his girl friend, a letter urging Lewinter to come home and telling him that he would not be prosecuted by the authorities if he decided to return. Oh, there was one more thing, Sarah said. The girl friend had sent along a few hundred of Lewinter's special hay-fever pills—he apparently lost the ones he had come with—because he suffers terribly in the summer months.

Zaitsev listened without a trace of emotion. "What if I tell you I do not enjoy access to Lewinter?"

"My friend says you can arrange to see him."

"Your friend seems to know quite a lot about me. And what is to prevent me from saying I'll give the letter and the pills to Lewinter and then quietly going back on my word?"

But Sarah had an answer for that too. "My friend says he'll know if you give them to Lewinter."

"That's all he says—that he'll know?"

"Yes. I'm afraid he's very confident. He says only that he'll know."

"Then I suppose I must believe him. It would be illogical if he had no way of checking up. And tell me this: what will prevent Lewinter from turning the letter—and me—over to the authorities out of his newly discovered sense of loyalty to Mother Russia?"

"He may."

"Only that—he may? Your friend has only that to say?" Sarah tried to fan herself with a folded newspaper. "He says that you'll have to take your chances. If you handle it well, Lewinter won't turn the letter in so as not to get you into trouble."

"I see," said Zaitsev, and he leaned back so that his face was only a few inches from the perforated plastic roof of the automobile. For a while he sat in the position, his eyes wide open, staring at the small holes. Finally, he pushed himself upright again and turned to Sarah.

"You must realize, of course, what you're doing, dear lady. Are you a professional or an amateur?"

"I'm"—Sarah hesitated—"I'm an amateur. I'm just doing a favor for a friend."

"Is he forcing you to do it?"

Sarah shook her head. "I don't think so, no."

"You are taking quite a risk for a friend, you know. I could turn you in to a militiaman, and then where would you be, eh? Caught trying to recruit me as an agent for the American Intelligence service. Don't you see that the friend who put you up to this is using you? That he is really no friend to you? Ah, dear lady, when I first looked into your face today, I didn't see naïveté, but I see it now."

"I was assured that—" Sarah was frightened now. She began again. "You have nothing to gain by turning me in to the authorities. I would deny everything."

"How would you deny the photograph of my manuscript?"

"It no longer exists—it was made so that it would fade without a trace five minutes after the photograph was peeled away from the cardboard."

"And the letter which is undoubtedly buried in your handbag? And the pills?"

"The pills are simple hay-fever pills made out in my name. And the letter is, after all, just a letter—surely it is not against Soviet law to send a letter." What Sarah didn't explain was that the letter was coated with potassium permanganate so that it would ignite if exposed to the slightest heat.

"In that case, dear lady, why don't you put some stamps on that letter of yours and post it?" Zaitsev was angry now—anger being the visible tip of his fear.

"Look, Zaitsev, let's both of us act calmly. If you're thinking of turning me in, I don't think the Soviet government will want to make a cause célèbre that could wreck the cultural exchange program over a simple thing like a letter. And think what it will mean to you. My friend will publish your Declaration and where will you be then?"

"Exactly," Zaitsev said with authority, though he wasn't sure what he meant by the word. "All they want me to do is give Lewinter a letter?"

"And the hay-fever pills."

"Ah, yes, dear lady, we must on no account forget the hay-fever pills."

Zaitsev started up the engine again and pulled back into traffic.

"Well?" said Sarah. "What are you going to do?"

"I will"—Sarah felt as if she were listening to a verdict at a murder trial in which she was the defendant—"reflect on this matter and let you know before we get to the airport." And Zaitsev reached up and wiped the perspiration off his forehead with the sleeve of his West German jacket.

Standing on the observation deck at Moscow International Airport, the American cultural attaché watched the silver Pan Am 707 roar down the runway and bank into the night sky. Then he walked over to a pay phone and dialed the embassy.

"Marston here—give me communications. Hi, Jean?

Listen, the tour got off O.K. I'm coming back for dinner. I'm famished."

The word *famished* was the tipoff, and Jean Shelton encoded and sent an urgent cable to Washington. It read:

INFORM KUNEN AT PENTAGON THAT MAILMAN DEPARTED ON SCHEDULE WITHOUT APPARENT COMPLICATIONS.

20

ZAITSEV TRIED to keep up a bold front. "For some-one with my experience," he quipped, *"facilis est descensus Averni."* And he translated the Latin into Russian for Pogodin: "The descent into hell is easy."

Pacing back and forth across the Persian carpet in Zaitsev's study, Pogodin ignored the glibness and went on with his questions.

"Are you positive she did not say who her so-called friend was?"

"Absolutely."

"Do you have a copy of your 'Declaration of Conscience'?"

"I destroyed it long ago."

"How was the original written?"

"What do you mean how?" Zaitsev leaned against the wall

next to the window, looking out over the French air-condition-ing unit toward the Kremlin.

"If it was typewritten"—Pogodin gestured toward the typewriter on the table—"and unsigned, you could denounce the whole thing as a forgery if they should publish it."

The musical voice of the Fat Cow drifted in from the liv-ing room: "Zaitsev, you darling, wherever in Moscow did you find—"

But Zaitsev cut her off with a yell. "Later, damn it, later." He turned back to Pogodin: "The Declaration was written out in longhand and signed. If I ever get out of this, I categorically vow never to sign my name again as long as I live."

"It was only a thought," Pogodin said glumly. "Where are the pills?"

Zaitsev patted his jacket pockets. "I must have left them in the other room."

"All right, I'll come back to that part later," Pogodin said. "Look, Zaitsev, old friend, the simple fact of—"

"Jesus, Yefgeny, will you stop prancing around like a caged lion?" Zaitsev snapped. "You'd think you were in hot water instead of me."

Pogodin sank into Zaitsev's desk chair and toyed with the keys on the typewriter. "The simple fact of the matter is that there is no easy way out of this."

But Zaitsev wasn't resigned to defeat yet. "If the letter is really harmless, would it hurt to give it to him?"

Pogodin waved the letter in the air. "Don't you have the

slightest understanding of what's going on?" he said angrily.

The strain was beginning to affect both Pogodin and Zaitsev. "No letter from someone in America to Lewinter is harmless," Pogodin continued. "This has to be studied dispassionately. For all we know the Americans may not have the slightest expectation of communicating with Lewinter. They may not even want to get a letter to him. They may simply want us to *think* they are trying to get a letter to him."

For the first time, Zaitsev's face betrayed the dread that he felt. "I am a professional chess player, but I don't understand this gamesmanship," he said softly. "All I know is that I am caught in the middle and about to be crushed for the sheer sport of it. I would not tell this to a living soul, Yefgeny Mikhailovich, but I am really quite frightened—I am frightened out of my skin by all this."

Both men waited for the fear to subside. Presently Zaitsev poured himself a stiff whiskey and drank it straight off. "Yefgeny, old friend of mine, perhaps I made a mistake bringing you in on this. Can you forget, for the sake of our long friendship, that you were here today?"

"And what would you do?"

"I'd do what the Americans want me to do—I'd give him the damn letter."

"Zaitsev, you innocent idiot, don't you see how naïve you are? Do you think the Americans will stop with this favor? If you deliver the letter, it will only give them more of a hold on you. Next time around, they'll threaten you with the Declaration *and* the delivery of their letter to Lewinter. They'll show you a Swiss bank book made out in your name with fifty thousand dollars in it and threaten to take it to the authorities. You'll be a fish wriggling on a hook. You'll be an American espionage agent. At first they'll only ask you to do small chores—delivering messages, picking up seemingly harmless scraps of information, passing on rumors about who is sleeping with whom. Then they'll make more demands on you—recruiting other agents, blackmailing party officials. Who can say where it will end? My poor Zaitsev, I know what I'm talking about; we do the same thing on their side. What do you think I did all those years in New York? Read the *New York Times?* Grow up, Zaitsev."

"You know what they'll do to me if that Declaration is published," Zaitsev said. "It will mean the end of my career."

"I know what they'll do to you if you become an American espionage agent. Believe me, Zaitsev, I love you like a brother, but I would tell my own brother the same—The moaning, low pitched and insistent like the feedback from a microphone, interrupted Pogodin. Suddenly it rose to a shriek of fears and then subsided into gasps. "Zait—Zait– Zait–"

Pogodin and Zaitsev burst into the other room. The Fat Cow lay on the floor sobbing and sucking in air. Then she stopped breathing and vomited and died.

"Facilis est descensus Averni," Zaitsev whispered—and he sank to his knees and stared in horror at the lifeless body of his mistress. Nearby, Chichikov, the cat, pawed playfully at the small blue-green pills scattered around the floor.

THE PASSED PAWN

21

SARAH TWISTED the button on her blouse and let it snap back again. "Do I have to stay on the couch?" she asked without looking up at the man she was talking to.

"No, not if you don't want to."

But Sarah made no move to get up.

"I remember I was buried up to my neck in volcanic ash," she said. "It looked like volcanic ash from the outside—fine and whitish, almost like talcum powder. But it felt like oatmeal underneath."

The doctor crossed his legs and adjusted the microphone on the tape recorder. "Being buried in this, eh, volcanic ash, did it protect you or threaten you?"

"Protect, I think." Sarah brushed a strand of hair out of

her eyes. Suddenly she shivered, as if she were trying to shake a weight from her shoulders. "What have you done to me?" she asked, almost in tears. Then, as if nothing had happened, she picked up where she had left off. "The reason I think it protected me is that I didn't attempt to get out. I had some difficulty breathing in the beginning, but I decided it was because I was very excited. It's difficult to breath when you're excited, you know. I remember there were some people struggling toward me. Each step they took made a great sucking sound."

"Who were they?"

"I don't remember."

"What were they doing as they struggled toward you?"

"They were scattering seeds, I think—only they weren't seeds but hay-fever pills."

"How do you know they were hay-fever pills?"

"I know," Sarah said belligerently.

The doctor ignored her belligerence. "These people who were struggling toward you, tell me, how did you feel about them?"

"I didn't know them, so how could I feel anything about them? They were just people who happened to be struggling toward me. I glanced from time to time to see if they were still coming."

"And were they?"

"I don't know how to answer that. They were picking up their feet in great sucking sounds and putting them back in again, and it looked as if they were walking toward me. But I knew they would never get there."

"How?"

"How what?"

"How did you know they would never reach you?"

"What makes you think they would never reach me?"

"You suggested it," the doctor said patiently. "You said you knew they would never get to you. How did you know that?"

Sarah thought about it for a few seconds. "I noticed that they didn't get any bigger, which meant that they were the same distance away."

Sarah twisted the button again and it came off in her fingers. "My button broke," she whined, and began weeping softly. The tears blurred her vision, and the blurred vision frightened her and she cried some more.

"Do you know why you are crying?"

"I'm crying because my god damn button came off," Sarah said. After a while Sarah stopped crying and asked: "Do I have to stay on the couch?"

"Not if you don't want to, no."

Again Sarah made no move to get up.

"Why don't we call it a morning," the doctor said presently. "You have a visitor at eleven, do you remember?"

Sarah said nothing.

"Do you want to see him?" the doctor asked, smiling his standard encouraging smile.

Sarah shrugged. "Why not," she said in the same tone of voice she would have used to describe the weather or the end of the world.

They sat for a long while in silence, Diamond on the cushionless wooden chair near the window, Sarah on the bed with the crisp hospital corners, thinking of things to say to each other that wouldn't hurt each other.

Finally Diamond asked, as naturally as he could: "Have they been treating you all right?"

But Sarah only tilted her head and smiled a vague, vacant half-smile.

"Eh, I see they brought you some things from your apartment," Diamond said.

His voice—husky and tense—betrayed his emotions.

"Poor Leo—this isn't easy for you, is it?" Sarah tucked her legs under her and leaned back against the wall. "I mean coming face to face with the corpus delicti." She pulled a strand of black hair across her eyes. "You didn't have to go through this kind of thing after Cernú did you? Poor Leo." And she smiled and sang "Poor Leo" over and over again as if it were the refrain from a children's song.

Diamond wiped his lips with the back of his hand. He slouched in his chair and the posture made him appear older and stouter than he really was. "Believe me, Sarah—" he started to say. He moistened his lips with his tongue and began again. "I swear to you by everything I hold holy—"

"And what's that, Leo?"

"What's what?"

"What is it you hold holy?" Sarah asked.

Diamond had not been prepared for this. He couldn't tell whether she was angry or bitter or joking or insane, and the uncertainty threw him off.

"I didn't want it to end like this, Sarah. Do you believe that?"

But Sarah didn't answer. "I had a dream last night," she said instead. "I thought I was buried up to my neck in volcanic ash. There were people struggling toward me. Each step they took made a great sucking sound." Something dawned on Sarah. *"You* were there, Leo. You were one of the people struggling toward me."

"I was—"

"But you never got any bigger."

"I don't understand—"

"Why did you publish Zaitsev's Declaration?" Sarah asked.

"It wasn't up to me, Sarah. There were others involved, and they had to publish the Declaration to back up their claim that the Russians were concocting the whole assassination business to discredit Zaitsev."

Sarah leaned forward so that her hair hung over her face like a curtain. Then she parted the curtain in the middle and peered out. "It was fine and powdery on the outside, like volcanic ash, but it was coarse and grainy like oatmeal underneath."

Diamond shrugged, unable to cope with the two sound tracks spliced into one tangled monologue. "Sarah, oh Sarah," he said gently, and she mimicked him, singing "Sarah oh Sarah oh Sarah oh Sarah" in a thin voice.

Suddenly she stopped singing and pushed her hair back over her ears so that her whole face was revealed. Her eyes, a luminescent green, seemed perfectly lucid. "What happened to Zaitsev, Leo?" she demanded. "Did they kill him too?"

"Zaitsev is fine, Sarah, I give you my word of honor he's fine. They packed him off to a mental asylum outside of Leningrad, that's all. I swear that's all. That's standard operating procedure with dissident intellectuals; they put them in an asylum when they step out of line."

"Zaitsev and Sarah," Sarah said sweetly. "Zaitsev in his asylum, Sarah in her clinic, all settled down for a long winter's nap." Rocking back and forth, Sarah began to cry softly. "And the girl I poisoned. They were telling the truth, weren't they, Leo? I did poison that girl, didn't I?"

"You didn't poison her, Sarah. It was an accident, a horrible, unavoidable accident—"

"But somebody would have taken those pills; if not the girl, then Lewinter."

"We calculated that the Soviet counterintelligence people would discover that the pills were poisoned. We wanted them to discover it. We wanted them to think we were attempting to assassinate Lewinter. That was one of our signals."

"My God, Leo, where did you come up with a scheme like

that?" Sarah asked. She had forgotten that she had given him the germ of the idea. "Zaitsev and Sarah, Sarah and Zaitsev," she chanted. Then she turned on him: "Do you know what they've done to me here, Leo?"

Diamond shook his head and said quietly: "You're not well, Sarah."

"I was well when I got here; *they* made me sick. They made me sick. They made me sick. They made . . ."

Diamond remembered the hurried meeting in room 303 that took place as Sarah's plane sped toward New York. "About the girl," Senator Talmidge had said, "we've got to make God Almighty sure she don't get the chance to queer the cover story." It was Dukess, sitting in for the C.I.A., who had offered to solve the problem.

"I think we can handle it," he had said.

"Mind, no fuss now," Talmidge had cautioned.

"There'll be no fuss, Senator, now or later," Dukess had said.

". . . me sick. *They made me sick.*" Sarah was sobbing now. "Stick out your arm—they made me all the time—I keep waiting for Leo—never let me wake up—fight to wake up and they gave me another injection." Sarah curled up in a ball on the bed and forced back the tears. Her eyes and cheeks looked swollen. "When they finally let me wake up I asked them—I begged them—not to tell me, but he said they would tell me everything—I tried not to listen—he told me I had killed the girl—showed me Zaitsev's Declaration in the newspaper—that

I had killed him too—stick out your arm—Aaaagh Leo, where were you?—You weren't out battling despair—were you, Leo?—you were adding to it."

The conversation lapsed into the silence that comes when you drop a pebble in an unexpectedly deep well and wait too long for the splash. Diamond thought of several things he could say, but they all seemed to end awkwardly—with him trying "We can start over again when you get out of here" and Sarah responding with some sing-song non sequitur.

Sarah's face—frighteningly pale—took on an expression that looked like a smile but conveyed no happiness. "Did you get the chief's job after all, Leo?" she asked.

"As a matter of fact," Diamond said, "I was transferred to the Defense Intelligence Agency on the strength of—"

"Go on," Sarah said. "You were transferred on the strength of the Lewinter operation; that's what you were going to say, wasn't it?"

"I'm the chief of operations," Diamond conceded.

"What does that mean, chief of operations?"

"I'm in charge of—"

Sarah finished the sentence for him. "Gambits."

The door of the room had been left ajar and the sharp odor of Lysol drifted in. "It's not very pleasant here, is it?" Diamond said.

"It's not unpleasant," Sarah said. "They brought me my I-don't-know things, see."

Diamond noticed that the small mahogany box with the

six brass bulbs and the steel thermometer had been thrown in the wastebasket. "Did you chuck that one out, Sarah?"

"Yes," she said absently. "One of the doctors recognized it. He said it's a Sacronometer—something that measures the alcohol content of wine—so I threw it out."

"You threw it out because it's a Sacronometer?"

"I threw it out because I knew what it was."

After a while Diamond straightened in his seat. "Well," he said, and he cleared his throat. He wanted very much to be somewhere else, anywhere else.

"Are you going now, Leo?"

"I've got to get back to Washington—"

Sarah slipped forward to the edge of the bed. "I don't want you to worry about me, Leo. It was just one of those things. It was just an operation that went wrong—"

But Diamond corrected her. "It went right, Sarah. You have to understand—it went right."

Sarah smiled—this time her expression had something in common with humor—and sang the refrain: "Right as rain, right as rain, right as rain."

22

THE MALE NURSE with the wild eye brought tea and a small tin of jam and posted himself at the door, his good eye fixed on the two men sitting across from each other at the far end of a long wooden table, his wild eye on the neon ceiling light enclosed in a rectangular plastic cover. The bottom of the cover was thick with moths; their shadows projected onto the plastic made them seem, in death, slightly larger than life. From time to time a few wings fluttered silently against the plastic cover in a grotesque pantomime of a prisoner pounding the walls of a cell.

"Imagine what goes on in that brain of his," Zaitsev said, inclining his head toward the male nurse. "One eye projects an image of us, the other an image of those moths up there. And the two images blend, giving him a"—Zaitsev hesitated—"giving him a headache!"

Pogodin couldn't bring himself to smile. He put a spoonful of jam in his tea and stirred it absently. He sat directly beneath an electric fan that hadn't worked in years. Except for a dozen long tables and a *trompe l'oeil* window with a scene of wheat fields receding to the horizon, the room itself was bare, and seemed to Pogodin like a theatrical set—a stage where footfalls sounded amplified and actors lurked behind shored-up walls straining for entrance cues.

Pogodin hadn't wanted to come at all; his instincts, in which he put great store, had warned him to steer clear. Oddly, it was Avksentiev who prompted him to change his mind. Immediately after the ceremony, Avksentiev had taken Pogodin aside. "You are dragging your friendship for Zaitsev around after you like a tail," he told him. "I've been through this myself, so I understand such things. The trick is to see him *once* more and free yourself."

"It's the last word in asylums," Zaitsev was saying. "They tell me it used to be the country home of a faggot Czarist minister who fled the Winter Palace in the same automobile as Kerensky. Good riddance, eh? Look there"—Zaitsev pointed to a corner where the plaster on the ceiling was falling away— "the whole place has gone to seed. Even the wire mesh on the windows is rusting; you can push it out with your hand, but nobody bothers. You saw the sign over the gate: SERBSKY INSTITUTE FOR PSYCHIATRIC DIAGNOSIS. Now if I were in charge here, I'd replace it with the wording that marked the entrance to Dante's hell: *'Lasciate ogni speranza, voi ch'entrate'*—'All hope abandon, ye who enter here.' More appropriate. But these people have no style."

Pogodin started to ask a question, thought better of it— and then came out with it anyway: "You're not going to do anything foolish, are you?"

"Don't concern yourself with morbid notions, Yefgeny; since Axelrod's day, they've substituted sponges for mops. Anyhow, like Tolstoi at eighty-two, I'm trying—how did he put it?—trying not to want to die. And succeeding, thanks to my ingrained cowardice. If I sound despairing, ah, well, it's because I was determined not to disappoint you."

"Disappoint me?"

"Exactly. Disappoint you. What would you have thought if you had come all this way and found me in a good mood as opposed to good form. My dear Yefgeny Mikhaiovich,

"Exactly. Disappoint you. What would you have thought if you had come all this way and found me in a good mood you would have thought me insane. Which of course, my surroundings notwithstanding, I am not."

"If you were insane, at least you'd be in an appropriate place," Pogodin quipped. That broke the ice, and the two of them laughed together for the first time in a long time.

Pogodin glanced at the male nurse near the door and at the moths striking sparks of life. "What do you do with yourself all the day long, Zaitsev?" he asked.

"As for that, they're fairly lenient here. The first thing every morning I clean out the latrine on my floor—two imported British urinals, a single Italian toilet, one made-in-Russia shower stall without a curtain. And I polish the curtain rail until it shines."

"But why?"

"That's where Axelrod hung himself from—it's a unique memorial, don't you think, a polished curtain rail."

"Extremely unique—I doubt anybody else could have thought of it. What about the rest of the day?"

"The rest of the day I seek asylum in boredom."

Pogodin looked shocked.

"And why the scowl, Yefgeny? It's a common enough refuge in our time. The American author Barth put it nicely:

'The fact,' he said, 'the fact that the situation is desperate doesn't make it any more interesting.' *Voila!*"—Zaitsev imitated a trumpet fanfare—"a one-sentence theme for our time; a brilliantly honest, brilliantly horrible summing up of what the spirit of man has shriveled into, eh?"

"It's too facile," Pogodin said. "And anyway, I don't believe you. Surely you read—"

"I have vowed not to read a sentence, a phrase, a word, a syllable until the literature I read is free of restraints."

"And when will that be?"

"Brecht said you'll be able to tell that the Soviet Union again has free literature when the first novel appears beginning 'Minsk is one of the most boring cities in the world.'"

"A good enough line—why don't you start a novel with it?"

Zaitsev lowered his voice to a mock whisper. "Actually, because it is not true. I've been to some chess tournaments in Minsk, and there's a plump little number there—"

Again the two men laced together their friendship, like two sides of a shoe, with laughter.

"So Brecht the Great doesn't know everything," Pogodin said.

"Which of us does," Zaitsev answered quietly. The mood had turned somber.

Pogodin sipped his tea. Zaitsev ate a spoonful of jam directly from the tin.

"Tell me, Zaitsev, are there any real patients here?"

"A few," Zaitsev said, running his fingers through his hair. For the first time Pogodin noticed that Zaitsev's hand trembled slightly. "There's one fellow, a Lithuanian, who eats at the same table I do. He writes down his dreams in the morning and submits them to the doctor immediately after lunch. Yesterday at lunch, the Lithuanian started screaming at his neighbor: 'Look out, you idiot, you're spilling salad dressing on my dreams.'" Waving his hand in disgust, Zaitsev repeated the line. "Salad dressing on his dreams!"

Zaitsev had jumped up to act out the vignette. Now he sank back onto the bench until it creaked under his weight. "There are a few crazy ones here. There's a Jew who claims he's Malechamovitz. That's the Yiddish name for 'the angel of death.' And there's another fellow who goes around all day collecting beautiful words. He puts them in long alphabetical lists.

Every time he gets a new word, he rewrites the entire list from beginning to end. I gave him *lagoon* and *damp* and *moisture*. I offered him *dewy* but he had it already. Except for these two or three, most of our residents have their wits about them. Remember the fellow you met at my dacha, the one who signed the petition about Axelrod published in the *New York Times?*"

"Antonov-Ovseenko."

"The very one; he's here." Zaitsev went on to name a well-known marine biologist, an astrophysicist, three poets, and a ballet impressario, all of whom were in the asylum. "The astrophysicist got here right after I did. They never even gave him the courtesy of sending someone to arrest him. They called him on the telephone and told him to bring a change of underwear and report to Lubyanka. The ultimate insult was their ultimate confidence. No midnight knock on the door like the good old days; just a phone call. And he went!"

"You're being unfair, Zaitsev; what else could he have done?"

"He could have run for it. I heard that there are people in the South who will get you across to Turkey for five thousand rubles."

"Then why didn't you try, if you're so brave?"

"I don't have the stamina for long treks," Zaitsev said. "And besides, I only heard it from a fellow I met in here."

The moths—fewer than before—fluttered their wings again, and both men watched until they quieted down.

Suddenly Pogodin slammed his spoon down on the table. "Why didn't you turn her in?" he asked.

"I suppose—" Zaitsev began, and paused to think of an answer. "I suppose because she was an amateur. Does that make sense to you? No, I can see it doesn't." Zaitsev turned on Pogodin: "Well, the hell with it. But you tell me something, Yefgeny Mikhailovich. What did the Americans hope to accomplish by killing Lewinter?"

Pogodin gestured with his head toward the male nurse at the door. "Can he overhear us?"

"It doesn't matter," Zaitsev said. "He's as thick as they come. He doesn't have three hundred words in his vocabulary."

"All right." Pogodin hunched forward, making his thin shoulders look more stooped than they were. "It's possible the Americans were reacting to a genuine defection—that they may have simply wanted to stop Lewinter from elaborating on any information he had already given us. They may also have wanted to make an example of him to deter future defectors. But it is also possible the Americans were trying to make it *appear* as if they were reacting to a genuine defection in order to convince us that Lewinter had valuable information. In which case, he would be a fraud. *Or* the Americans may have been trying to convince us he's real knowing we'd discover they were trying to convince us he's real and conclude instead he's a fraud. Which would mean they want us to think he's a fraud. Which would mean he's genuine.

"I see the affair hasn't lost any of its complexities," Zaitsev said dryly. "And which of these explanations is generally accepted nowadays?"

"Avksentiev is absolutely convinced the Americans are reacting to a genuine defection."

"On the basis of the assassination attempt?"

"On the basis of that and other signals."

"Which would make Lewinter's information genuine?"

"Which would make Lewinter's information genuine, yes."

Zaitsev ate another spoonful of jam. "But you don't share this view?"

"That's right. "I don't share this view."

"Why?"

"Because . . . because someone named Diamond is involved, and this man Diamond loves operations. He is quite capable of spending years planning an operation like this down to the last detail in order to make us swallow false information. Then too, there's the assassination—"

"Yes, there was the assassination *attempt.*"

By now Pogodin was talking for his own benefit. "It was so pointless—"

"So pointless," Zaitsev agreed.

"—they must have known that Lewinter would long since have been debriefed. No, that assassination wasn't a reaction to a defection, but a signal; they're trying to convince us they're reacting to a defection. They want us to accept Lewinter at face value."

"Which means he's a fraud."

"Yes, exactly. Lewinter is probably a fraud."

"Have you told this to Avksentiev—told him that you're convinced Lewinter's a fraud?"

Pogodin hesitated. "No," he said.

"Why not?"

"First of all, because I'm not sure myself—"

"Ah, come now, Yefgeny Mikhailovich, where is your old candor?"

"Frankly, I'm in a difficult situation," Pogodin said defensively. "I was the one who argued all along he was genuine. After the promotion, I can't just turn around and—"

"What promotion? Should I congratulate you, Yefgeny?"

"I was promoted to deputy chief of the Westwork Directorate; I'm attached to Avksentiev's staff now."

"What the devil is Westwork?"

"It's our name for espionage activities in the West."

"So you're a big fish now, eh? And that's why you can't—

"That's why. And yet"—Pogodin shook his head to sort out the options—"and yet, if I don't speak up, my country will wind up realigning its antiballistic system to cope with trajectories that may not exist."

"Do you want advice from someone living, when you come down to it, in an island of relative sanity? Well, you're going to get it anyhow." Zaitsev leaned toward Pogodin. "You had better begin playing the *real* game. And for those of you unfortunate to be in the madhouse outside, the real game is getting ahead."

Pogodin straightened on the bench. "You forget I am a Marxist, Zaitsev, and that implies a certain commitment to one's fellow citizens."

"I thought you were only one-quarter Marxist."

"There's no need to be sarcastic," Pogodin said.

"Listen, Comrade Pogodin—Communism is, at heart, an attempt to do away with the pecking order. But it has failed. We live in a country where the queue is king. And take it from me, people *don't* line up on a first come, first serve basis. So, if you have to get in line, you might as well go to the head of it."

The moths—there were only two that still had any life remaining—battered the bottom of the plastic cover again, and then sank back amid the shadowy bodies.

"That was my father's philosophy actually," Zaitsev went on. "He was a logger, my father, with big red knuckles and swollen fingers. And my mother, bless her Bolshevik soul, my mother was one of the first to join the Party in our neck of the woods. She joined because they used to have a picnic once a year, and she loved picnics. You know, Yefgeny, we've got to get back to the basics. My mother could take a sip of milk and tell which goat in the flock it came from. We lived in a wooden house with windows painted on the outside. Ha! I've come full circle. In my youth, the windows were painted on the outside; now they're painted on the inside." Zaitsev motioned toward the fading harvest scene painted on the wall. "Which dwelling, I put it to you, offers the real asylum from the world?"

But Pogodin had no ready answers for bitter-sweet questions.

Zaitsev went off on a tangent. "Did you ever notice . . ." he spoke excitedly, then seemed to lose heart for the conversation.

"Did I ever notice what, Stoyan Alexandrovich?" It was the first time Pogodin had ever called Zaitsev by his first name and patronymic.

Zaitsev was running out of steam. "Did you ever notice how innocent descriptions take on a meaning of their own, how they become euphemisms for the destructive power of men? Take, for instance, the German use of *concentration camp*. Or the American expression *free-fire zone*. Or our own *asylums.*" The word *asylum* led Zaitsev onto another track. "My whole life I've been afraid of this"—his hands shaking slightly, took in the surroundings—"but now that I'm here, it's a relief. I swear to you it's a relief. 'A person you've taken everything from is no longer in your power.' That's from Solzhenitsyn. Well, it's true. It's not nearly as bad here as I thought it would be." For an instant something of Zaitsev's old flame flashed in his eyes, and he said: "That, of course, says something about me, doesn't it?"

Zaitsev finished off the jam, rinsed the spoon in what was left of the tea, wiped it dry on his pants, and slipped it into his jacket pocket. Overhead, the last of the moths fluttered into life and died.

Zaitsev and Pogodin regarded each other across the table the way two men look at each other who have run out of things to say. Passengers on a train, they had arrived, silently and with contained regret, at the destination.

"You understand, Zaitsev, that it was out of my hands once there was a death involved." A bead of sweat glistened like a tear drop on Pogodin's high forehead. "It goes without saying: I'm sorry things ended this way." And then he choked with emotion. "Ah, dear Zaitsev, if only you had——"

Zaitsev seemed to sink into the bench under the weight of what might have been.

"Ifs," he told Pogodin. "Ifs, ifs, and more ifs, legions of ifs marching twenty abreast, stretched out as far as the eye can see—stretched across Russia, across Central Asia, across Siberia, all the way to Vladivostok."

Zaitsev beckoned with his open hand, as if summoning an endless file of men to pass in review.

"Stand to attention, Yefgeny Mikhailovich, stand to attention and salute my biographical ifs."

23

SAVINKOV WAS partially paralized, and so when he turned toward Pogodin his entire body pivoted as if it were in a cast. "I'm not sure I understand," he said cautiously. Daylight glancing off his steel-rimmed spectacles gave his eyes the appearance of sightless silver sockets. "Shredders, magnetic separators, centrifugal separators, one point two billion pounds of solid waste a day equals a ton of garbage per person per year. I had thought"—Savinkov lifted a page from the folder with both hands as if it were a tray—"I had thought we would be concerning ourselves with a question of national security."

Pogodin nodded toward the paper in Savinkov's hands. "That was merely his hobby; you'll find the matter we're dealing with on page eight."

"Just so," Savinkov said, and he, Dybenko, and Izvolsky thumbed through their folders to page eight and began reading.

Pogodin fidgeted in his chair. In recent days, he had gone out of his way to look totally Russian. The button-down shirt had been replaced by a white-on-white Polish import; the Harris tweed and slacks had given way to a dark business suit of Soviet manufacture. His hair had been trimmed so that it no longer bunched at the sides and back. If a quarter of Pogodin remained essentially humanist, it was obscured by the posturing of a bureaucrat: the expressionless face, the seemingly numb nerve endings, the insistent drumming of a pencil on the table.

Savinkov was the first to glance up. "This, of course, changes everything," he told Pogodin.

"What a windfall," said Dybenko, looking up in turn. He was a tall middle-aged Georgian with strands of hair pasted across his bald crown and cold, metallic features.

Izvolsky, at twenty-seven the youngest man in the room, whistled. "It's almost too good to believe," he said.

Pogodin spread his small green notebook—the jottings from that first interview with Lewinter were still in it—on the table. "You will need background information that is not in the folders," he began. "For a long while there was doubt in some circles"—Pogodin's tone made it clear that he had not shared this doubt—"as to what precisely we were dealing with. But the Americans soon made it unmistakably plain that we had on our hands a genuine defector who possessed critical information. The first indication of this came when they summarily fired the agent who had been assigned to watch Lewinter in Tokyo, a man by the name of Chapin. Soon after, they conducted a purge of Tokyo Control and the regional security office responsible for the New England area. And a number of specialists on MIRV were quietly summoned to Washington—for what purpose, we can only surmise. That same week a small item appeared in the Periscope section of the American magazine *Newsweek,* which has unusually good contacts inside the Pentagon. The item said simply that the defection of Lewinter was more serious than the authorities were publicly admitting. Then we discovered that a missile complex in Idaho scheduled to have MIRVs installed had been put back on operational duty with the *old* warheads still in place. About the same time a sub-committee under Senator Talmidge, who you will recall is a member of their Committee 303, launched a secret investigation into the defection. On top of all this there was the attempt to assassinate Lewinter."

Pogodin looked up. For a few fleeting seconds the grinding of gears from Dzershinski Street, four floors below, was the only sound in the room—that and Pogodin's pencil tapping on the table

For Pogodin, it was one of those special moments, not when things suddenly sort themselves out, but when you realize that things *have been* sorted out for some time. It was like waiting to capture the first instant of first light only to discover that you've been discerning objects for the last few minutes. As the sound of traffic rose and fell, Pogodin sensed that he had left his disabling ambiguities behind, that he was riding the crest of his ambition. And so when he began to speak again, his voice carried a new surge of self-confidence.

"Up to this moment," Pogodin said, "the Soviet Union has not devoted much time or effort or resources to the development of an antimissile system. Our scientists assured us that it was too difficult and we left it at that. It wasn't that we couldn't hit an incoming payload; the problem was that there would be too many incoming payloads to hit them all. Now, however, the situation has changed. We have got our hands on the signature trajectories, which gives us the possibility of knowing which of the incoming payloads are warheads. Once we know this, the problem of stopping them becomes relatively simple. In point of fact, our party leadership and our military leadership are in general agreement that we should now set about solving it."

Again Pogodin paused—to listen to the faint tramp of Zaitsev's ifs echoing through his mind. Before he could identify the sound, it faded and he went on:

"This brings us to the reason for the creation of this special working group. In order for the signature trajectories to be of any use to us, *we must first convince the Americans that we don't believe Lewinter.*"

"Quite obviously, to keep them from substituting new trajectories," Savinkov said matter of factly. He was an old hand at this game.

"Exactly that," Pogodin agreed. "If they believe we possess the trajectory signatures, they will of course change them.

So we must devise a series of signals designed to convince our counterparts in Washington that we do not trust Lewinter, that we suspect him of being a plant."

Once more the sound of traffic intruded into the room. Izvolsky began nibbling at his thumbnail. "Perhaps we could—" he said, and then shook his head. "No, no, they'd see through that easily."

Both Savinkov and Dybenko were already lost in thought. "I suppose," Pogodin said, tapping the point of the pencil on a piece of paper and watching the pattern of dots develop, "I suppose we could always begin by sending Lewinter back."